"Drolly humorous and gently paced . . .
an intriguing debut."

—*Publishers Weekly*

"Funny . . . A well-drawn narrator."

—*Chicago Tribune*

"If you have an allergic reaction to laughter,
do not—I repeat—do not buy this book."

—Tim Kazurinsky

"Dean Monti's hapless, neurotic narrator is a direct
descendant of Woody Allen's nebbishes and Bruce
Jay Friedman's lonely guys. Even as we laugh at his foibles,
we also feel the chilly undercurrents of his
distinctly modern malaise. Monti is a writer to watch."

—Carol Anshaw, author of *Aquamarine*

the sweep of the second hand

DEAN MONTI

Berkley Books, New York

𝕭

A Berkley Book
Published by The Berkley Publishing Group
A division of Penguin Putnam Inc.
375 Hudson Street
New York, New York 10014

PRINTING HISTORY
Academy Chicago hardcover edition published in 2001
Berkley trade paperback edition / December 2002

Visit our website at
www.penguinputnam.com

Library of Congress Cataloging-in-Publication Data

Monti, Dean.
The sweep of the second hand / Dean Monti.
p. cm.
ISBN 0-425-18625-3
1. Motion picture theater managers—Fiction. 2. Man-woman relationships—Fiction. 3. Fear of death—Fiction. 4. Insomnia—Fiction. I. Title.

PS3563.O54584 S8 2002
813'.54—dc21
2002023074

PRINTED IN THE UNITED STATES OF AMERICA

10 9 8 7 6 5 4 3 2 1

for CHEYENNE

acknowledgments

A special thanks to Carol Anshaw and members of her writer's workshop: Sydney Lewis, Adria Bernardi, Kelly Kleiman, Len Kraig, Kecia Lynn, Pam Sourelis and Brian Tolle. Also thanks to Carolyn Jenks, Jane Jordan-Browne, Danielle Egan-Miller, Tilo Eckhardt, M. Jennifer Huff, Sandy Prichard, Jordan and Anita Miller, Allison Liefer, Sarah Olson and all the good folks at Academy Chicago, my parents, family and friends.

Acknowledgments

the sweep of the second hand

chapter one

No doubt about it. A minute. Maybe more. But I was certainly losing at least a minute of sleep a night. I wasn't sure exactly when it had started. Sometime after my thirty-third birthday, I think, when I started taking the results of my annual life assessments a lot more seriously. The fact is, no matter how tired I was, no matter how strenuous or peaceful a day I'd had, no matter how late in the day I'd awakened, I couldn't fall asleep until after one in the morning.

I didn't see it as a problem at first. Just another mark of my much-anticipated maturity, I told myself. I was already noticing a few other innocuous signs. My speech, for instance, coming to a complete halt midway through a sentence while my brain anguished over an elusive word or name. A few persistent strands of gray in my temples and a few of those annoying little white hairs sprouting up in my ears. And losing things, of course, like my wristwatch. None of it worried me much. I figured I was entering a phase of my life when I'd require less sleep. I'd heard about such things happening. I seemed to recall it happening primarily to senior citizens, but why prolong the inevitable? Okay. Maybe I'd catch up on my reading. Finish that autobiography by Ingmar Bergman. Or finally finish all those foreign films I'd slipped into the VCR at eleven only to be awakened later by the sound of them rewinding.

No more bleary-eyed nights watching subtitles blur into non-sequiturs:

"Jacques . . . your luggage is cold . . . meet me on the cheese tray in fifteen minutes . . . not on this train, monsieur."

Maybe I'd use my new time to meditate. It had proved beneficial for someone I'd known in college. He'd been a literary snob and a boorish fellow, ranting all the time about social injustices and decaying values. Then he spent a summer with his nose in *The Seven Pillars of Zen* and started sitting with his legs crossed at parties. One day he must have reached satori because he cooled out. Began to enjoy sitcoms again. It was impressive.

So now that I could be assured I wasn't going to fall asleep, maybe I could put meditation on the late-night agenda. I had plenty of fodder for meditation. From the more general aspirations like: How could I achieve serenity in the world? and How could I attain harmony with my fellow man? to the more self-absorbed questions, like: If I wasn't managing my father's movie theater would I have any life at all? and Why was I still obsessing about Lena? Was it because I'd heard she was getting married soon? Why should that matter to me? And where was my wristwatch? Yes, I could easily turn this meditation thing into a full-time activity. I didn't want to spend all my time meditating, however. If I had extra time I wasn't sure I wanted to spend it with my legs crossed.

Anyway, I figured I could turn this thing to my advantage. Make this lack of sleep thing *work* for me. But as the weeks passed I somehow never got around to reading, watching films or meditating. I sat up in bed, mostly, losing sleep and getting increasingly irritable. I muttered to myself. I sent back food in restaurants when there was nothing wrong with it. I teased anything smaller than me. But above all, I yearned for sleep. I found myself staring at the clock more and more. And later and later.

It didn't occur to me that something might be seriously wrong until I noticed I wasn't nodding off until after one-thirty. I was dragging through my days, semi-fortified by huge mugs of black coffee and year-old boxes of Milk Duds that I'd rifled from the candy case at work. It was then I realized that it wasn't a matter of my requiring less sleep. No. I still needed the sleep, I just wasn't getting enough.

Fortunately, my job at the Arcadia Filmhaus was not too demanding. I showed nothing but foreign films and the turnout was invariably sparse, so I had very little to do with the general public. And that suited me just fine. I got to the theater around six, got everything up and running, threaded the film, turned down the house lights at seven and ran the film. When the film was over I turned up the house lights, rewound the film and shut everything down. Then I did it all over again for the nine o'clock show.

And if that wasn't easy enough, I'd hired a high school girl, Ginny, to work the concession stand. Since my apartment was only six blocks from the theater, I was usually home by eleven. This left me with approximately eighteen hours to call my own. Of these, I was being allowed six and a half for sleep.

By this time I was ready to admit I was suffering from insomnia. But I thought it was temporary and considered it more irritating than alarming. There were plenty of factors that could have contributed to insomnia. Worries about my future, or lack thereof. Confusion about my place in the world. My general lack of motivation and self-worth. And wondering where my wristwatch was. Basically, these were the same things I thought I could meditate on, but now they had a distinctly sleep-deprived, medical edge to them.

At first, insomnia didn't seem a valid enough reason to seek medical help. In my family you only went to the doctor if something burst, broke or ruptured. There was no history of insomnia in the Cicchio bloodline. My parents, Ernesto and Mary Lou Cicchio had, in their autumn years, achieved perfection in two areas of life: eating and sleeping. My mother cooked with a marked propensity for fat, flour and garlic. My father ate whatever my mother cooked, consuming most of it at dinner time and finishing off any leftovers just before bedtime.

The only real exercise my parents got was when my mother chased my father out of the room for failing to control his sphincter muscle after a typically gaseous repast. Their dog, Maggie, led a similar life to my parents, in that when she wasn't wolfing down leftovers, she was being chased out of the room for the same offense my father committed. My mother chased my father, and my mother and father chased the dog. All this eating, farting and chasing, I assumed, was tiring enough to allow them to sleep whenever they wanted.

I'd briefly considered discussing my sleep problem with my parents. My father, I knew, would personalize the problem.

"I worked two jobs when I was your age and when I went to bed I was plenty tired, you'd better believe it. Have a dish of lasagna and a couple of biscotti before bed."

My mother, on the other hand, would worry too much. My mother worried a lot. When she wasn't fretting about actual events involving her own family, she worried about the tattered lives of Tevin and Trish and other fictional characters who appeared on daytime television. My mother worried so much that I never told her anything because I worried about how worried she'd get. If she knew I wasn't sleeping she'd end up calling me at all hours to see if I was sleeping, thus robbing me of the precious minutes of sleep I could no longer afford to lose. So I decided, wisely I think, not to consult my parents.

But things got worse. Before long it was close to two in the morning before I was getting to sleep. I was still waking up at seven-thirty, with or without the alarm, and there was no getting back to sleep once I woke up. Then one day I discovered that if I got up an hour earlier, at six-thirty, my body allowed me a one-hour catnap in the afternoon. It appeared I was being granted a specific amount of sleep time within a twenty-four hour period. And this amount was being slowly denied me in small, progressive increments. It was this realization, that my body knew what it was doing to me, that began to make me really uneasy.

I tried an experiment. I stared at the digital clock at my bedside every night until I fell asleep. I could not, of course, pinpoint the exact time when I dozed off, but I diligently wrote down the last number I remembered when I woke up the next morning. The results were disturbing. Over the next ten days I compiled a log which read something like an auctioneer's litany: 1:47, 1:48, 1:48, 1:49, 1:50, 1:50, 1:51, 1:52, 1:52, 1:53. Certainly a pattern was developing.

I went to the library to see if a condition like mine had ever been documented. It hadn't. But in the course of my research I found a dusty old book written in the 1930s called *Dreaming,*

Dozing and Dementia, which seemed right up my alley. But skimming through the thick book I got the undeniable message that if I didn't get my required sleep I would suffer some ghastly afflictions. I might find myself barking at my reflection, like case number one hundred sixteen, or trying to pull my nose off, case number one hundred eighty-three. The prospects disturbed me to the point where I thumbed through the yellow pages and found the nearest physician. The receptionist must have sensed the tension in my voice because she allowed me to make one of those rare, life-threatening, same-day appointments.

Doctor Li looked into my ear with a cold, silver penlight. I sat dormant and allowed myself to be probed, staring off into the distance at a jar of tongue depressors.

"Any other symptoms? Headaches? Pains?"

"No," I said glumly. "A little trouble concentrating. And some trouble finishing sentences . . . sometimes."

Doctor Li instructed me to lie down and relax, though I found those two activities didn't mix particularly well.

"Are you relaxed?" she asked.

"Yes," I said, though I wasn't. My underwear was torn and the metal examining table was cold.

She pressed her fingers into my abdomen. "Does this hurt?"

"No," I said.

This cursory examination seemed to satisfy her. I don't know what she was looking for, a tumor maybe or a large gaping wound. Or maybe there was some adrenal gland in my abdomen that was supposed to come out when I was a child, but that they'd forgotten about, and which was now keeping me awake. I'd spend a night in the hospital, they'd cut out the gland

and I'd sleep like a baby again. But Doctor Li didn't mention anything about an abdominal adrenal gland.

"Have you been worried about anything?"

"I'm worried I'm not sleeping enough."

"How much coffee do you drink?"

"Not too much," I said, a bit too quickly. "Are you looking for an exact number?"

"Roughly."

"Roughly," I repeated. I gave it some thought. One cup before shower, one cup after shower. One cup mid-morning. One cup late afternoon before work. One cup upon arrival at work. One cup before the first and second screening of the film. "Three, I think. Roughly."

"Three?"

"Well, three good-sized mugs. I guess that works out to three or four."

"You might want to think about cutting down some."

"I will think about it," I promised, already wondering if there was a coffee machine in the lobby.

Doctor Li sat at her desk, pulled out a little pad of paper and began to write, saying, "I'm going to give you something to take at bedtime."

"How late should I be staying up?" I asked. It was a question I hadn't asked since I was five.

"The most important thing is to keep a regular schedule," she said. "The body doesn't like changes."

"Mine does," I said. "Look at these little hairs in my ears."

"The body does change," she said. "That's normal. But sleep is something that should be kept on a regular schedule."

"What happens if I lose my schedule?" I asked. "At what

point would I be looking at barking at myself or pulling off my nose?"

"Try not to worry so much," she said, smiling kindly.

I zipped up my trousers and buttoned my shirt. As Doctor Li leaned over her desk scribbling my prescription I stared at the curve of her neck. She looked to be about my age but didn't have any white hairs in her ears. Just a nice, smooth neck. I felt something stirring and was glad I had my pants back up. I wasn't sure whether I was aroused by the fact that she was an attractive woman or that someone I could have gone to high school with was already a doctor in private practice. She ripped the prescription off the pad and handed it to me. I stuffed it into my pocket, using the opportunity to rearrange some odds and ends in that area.

"Take this to help you sleep," Doctor Li said. She looked at me and frowned. "Did I take your temperature?"

"Yes," I said. "You said it was normal."

"You look flushed," she said.

I filled the prescription on the way home. A pharmacist with horn-rimmed glasses and a short-sleeved medical shirt scooped two dozen little white pills into a child-proof container and handed them over.

"You know you can't operate heavy machinery when you take these," he cautioned.

"I don't use heavy machinery," I said. "Unless you mean things like toasters, vacuum cleaners . . ."

"Heavy machinery," he said again.

"Heavy machinery," I repeated. "What about a projector? Do you think I'd be safe with a projector?"

"What kind of projector?"

"For films. A film projector."

"How heavy are they?"

"They're fairly heavy," I said.

"Fairly heavy. Well, see how you feel with it for a few days. I'll leave it up to you."

"Okay," I said.

I took my little white pharmacy bag with the little white pills in it and walked home. I don't know why I bothered to fill the prescription. I had no intention of taking the pills. When I was young my mother scared me off pill-taking. She told me you had to drink ten ounces of water, fast, for each pill you took. If you drank less than ten ounces of water, fast, according to my mother, you would, more than likely, choke and die.

"Remember Georgie Meyers on Second Avenue?" she'd say, as she pursed her lips and sadly shook her head.

Georgie Meyers was a childhood friend of mine who choked on one of those multi-colored, funny animal-shaped vitamins. It was a deer, I think, with legs and antlers and everything. You're supposed to chew the vitamins so you don't get a deer antler lodged in your throat. But Georgie swallowed his whole, so of course he choked. He didn't die but he coughed so long and so hard his face turned a bright crimson and his ears started twitching. It happened in my back yard, my mother saw it and added an extra rosary every time she prayed, specifically for boys choking on vitamins around the world. My mother had a number of specific fears like this. And most of my mother's fears were passed on, post-genetically, to me.

But I couldn't drink ten ounces of water, fast. I'd drown. And this fear of drowning usually caused me to spit out pills the moment I put them on my tongue. I ditched the pills in a trash can and headed home.

As I approached my apartment I saw my landlady, Missus Calabrone, watering her chrysanthemums. She was a squat woman in her late sixties and she always smelled of marinara sauce. I'd never been inside her apartment and a greasy steam made for a constant blur over her kitchen windows. Inside I imagined giant vats of red sauce being stirred with spoons the size of slave-ship oars. The aroma drifted up to my apartment daily and could be scratched and sniffed off the wallpaper in my living room.

Missus Calabrone had rented the second floor of her two-flat to me because I was willing to give her the first and last month's rent, but mainly, I think, because I had an Italian surname. It wasn't that she liked me, I don't think she did. I think I was just the first ethnically desirable person who showed up at her door.

She'd described the old apartment as "having character," which meant it was once beautiful, but was now falling apart. It had rounded doorways, arched ceilings and hardwood floors. I imagined it had been nice once, its occupant cranking up "Bye Bye Blackbird" on a Victrola and reclining on a divan. But those days were gone. Now it looked more like an attic you'd only go into once a year to bring down the Christmas tree. A handy person could have restored some of its former charm. But Missus Calabrone, recently widowed, was not about to undertake the task.

"Mister Calabrone used to do all that," she'd tell me whenever I mentioned to her that something might need fixing, so I understood from the start that I was my own maintenance man. I wasn't what you'd call a handy person, but I could plaster and paint and tighten and touch up. I also didn't complain much. I could live with peeling wallpaper and erratic water temperatures. The only thing that really bothered me were the yellow jackets living in my wall.

Their nest was somewhere in the hallway between my bedroom and bathroom. When my apartment was quiet, particularly at night, I could hear the hum, like a refrigerator engine that never shuts off. Once, I'd gotten up in the middle of the night to answer the call of nature and on the way back to bed I'd stopped and put my ear to the wall to locate the exact spot from which the sound was emanating. Not as loud here. Louder here. And then the horrible moment. A thick, snarling concentration of buzzes. Representing hundreds of yellow jackets living in the wall. Yellow jackets circling and pushing and shoving for space. Yellow jackets making more yellow jackets.

Yellow jackets don't sleep. They don't even relax. No Stratarloungers or hot tubs for these industrious little pests. Just a few simple goals: work, protect the hive and be prepared to give up your life by stinging. With that kind of work ethic, I didn't imagine it was a very happy life. But why should they be happy? It was summer and they lived on the top floor of an apartment without air conditioning.

I'd accepted a non-air-conditioned apartment on the second floor because Missus Calabrone had convinced me about the wonders of a cross-breeze. I never experienced it. I think you need some sort of wind to get it going. But if this stuffy, stifling hovel made me irritable, the yellow jackets had no one but themselves to blame for their situation. By chewing a hole in the rotted siding just outside my landing, they'd chosen to join me in the heat, attracted, I guess, by a home that was rent-free and low maintenance. Their hole did not quite reach through into my apartment. My greatest fear was that the only thing keeping them out was a thin piece of floral wallpaper. I pictured them, just the other side of the marigold pattern, munching away at the last of the dried wallpaper paste. An appetizer before the main course.

Some got in anyway. How they got in was a moot point. There were enough cracks in the floorboards and windowsills to keep me justifiably paranoid. My saving grace, I suppose, was that they never converged on me as a group. A solitary drone usually descended on me while I was having my morning coffee. They never darted at me so much as drifted, lazily, like those little helicopter seed buds. These strays were easy to kill. One swipe of the morning newspaper usually did it. Not even a swipe, really. Nothing you'd have to scrape off your paper. Just a tap on the head and they'd plummet like Japanese Zeroes. It was the heat. They were weighted down, their wings saturated with yellow jacket sweat.

Many of them died off naturally. Again, it was probably the choking, humid air that did it. Every day I'd find at least half a dozen of their dried, curled-up corpses in corners and window ledges. I put the ones that died off by themselves in one jar and the ones I'd killed myself in another jar. There was no real point to this dubious scientific experiment, I just liked seeing a lot of them dead and didn't want to take credit for the ones I hadn't slain myself. But the odds were against me in the game. Even with a hundred dead, there would always be a hundred more. Meanwhile, there was only one of me. At the end of the summer I pictured myself dried up, curled up, sitting alone in the bottom of a jar. A big jar.

I tried spraying their hole once, when I still believed I had a fighting chance. They market sprays to exterminate everything from black widows to boll weevils. For yellow jackets, wasps and hornets, there's a spray with a tube you can aim directly into the entry hole of their nest. No matter how long the tube was, it wouldn't be long enough, but you're supplied with a modest eight inches. Just enough to spray and run like hell. I tried it late one night. It took enormous courage and a shot of Jack Daniels to put my hand eight inches from their front door. I screwed up my nerve, inserted the tube, grimaced and jammed my thumb down hard on the sprayer. Then I ran like hell, swatting madly at phantom sensations of my flesh crawling with yellow jackets.

The next morning I put my ear to the wall. I wasn't expecting miracles. I never hoped to kill them all. I'd hoped, at best, that they would sound sluggish. Apathetic. But to my horror I heard a sound more intense than before. A buzz with intention. What if, instead of killing them, I'd only gotten their dander up? And worse, what if all that spraying had moistened, softened and broken down that thin tissue of wallpaper that separated me from them? If yellow jackets could organize and plan revenge, I was a dead man. The thought of an incensed swarm of yellow jackets retaliating en masse did not, I imagine, help my sleep problem any. Increasingly, I sought opportunities to get out of my apartment.

chapter two

There was a yellow notice stuck to the glass front door of the Arcadia Filmhaus. UPS had made a delivery and left it next door at the bakery. I went in, jingling the baker's little overhead doorbells. A round old man, white with flour, stopped kneading a large roll of dough to acknowledge me with a nod. The Pillsbury Doughboy in his autumn years.

"Package for Mister Malcolm Cicchio," he announced. He nodded a powdered nose in the direction of a box leaning against the cruller case. It was a familiar brown-wrapped package from Film-o-rama Film Distributors.

"Thanks." I hefted the package and put it under my arm. The baker knew my name from the label on the package, but damned if I knew his. It wasn't a reciprocal relationship. The Doughboy always arrived at his job in the morning, before I did, so he always collected my UPS packages.

"What's that, another one of them films?" he asked.

"Yes."

"What kind of film is it?"

"It's a foreign film. From Japan," I said.

He gave me a view of his upper teeth. It was the kind of smile that made you want to get a sandblaster and go to work.

"Oh. From Japan. I get you. I get you."

I don't know what kind of films he imagined were in those packages he accepted. He seemed afraid to ask, for fear it was some sort of large-cast, Asian porno extravaganza.

"When are you going to get some Betty Grable in there?" he said, still smiling.

"I don't really do those films," I said.

"Hey look, I'm not telling you how to run your business. I know you want to be different, show films that no one else is showing. That's fine. But you're gonna get a few more people in there if you show some of those all-time favorites. *Million Dollar Legs. Moon Over Miami.* People stop in here after your movies to get a bear claw and their chins are on the ground. Think about it."

"I'll think about it," I said.

I returned to the Arcadia Filmhaus and locked myself up inside. I went into my office, made some coffee and tore at the brown wrapper of the package. There were three shiny silver cans inside. I checked the labels: Kurosawa: *High & Low Pt. 1*, Kurosawa: *High & Low Pt. 2*, and Kurosawa: *High & Low Pt. 3*.

I always checked the labels. Once, I'd segued from Cocteau's *Orpheus* to *The Shakiest Gun in the West* with Don Knotts. Never again. *High and Low* isn't what you typically think of from Kurosawa. No samurai, no swords. It has Toshiro Mifune, but in this film he plays a wealthy shoe company executive whose chauffeur's son is kidnapped. The kidnapper means to kidnap the executive's son, but he botches it and grabs the wrong kid by mistake. The kidnapper demands ransom from Mifune anyway and Mifune has to pay it, just because it's the right thing to do. They save the kid, but Mifune loses his business and a lot of money. It's a good thriller with a kind of bleak ending. I didn't think many people would come to see it. I didn't care. I wanted to see it.

I took the film upstairs to the projection booth, threaded it into the Bell & Howell and checked it for breaks. There were none. I went back downstairs, sat at my desk, drank coffee and did the daily crossword in the paper. Since I was sitting at a desk, it almost felt like a real job.

Around mid-afternoon I heard a tapping sound on the front door glass. I peered out of the office warily, on the lookout for anyone with an oversized suitcase, which meant a salesman with samples. But this time it was an attractive woman with an armful of posters. I couldn't tell what kind of posters they were. I was bored enough to find out.

I pushed my hair out of my face and went to the front door. When she saw me she smiled—the kind of sweet, caring smile that makes you want to go to confession even when you haven't done anything wrong. She had coal-black hair, shiny like a freshly-tarred highway, and it ran long and straight down her back. And yes, there were curves at the end of the road. I let her in.

"Hi," she said, brightly. "Would it be okay if I put up a poster in your theater?"

"A poster? Is the circus in town?"

"It's not for the circus. I'm from Dialogue."

"Dialogue? What's that?" It seemed like I'd asked myself the same question before.

She pulled a poster out of the giant deck under her arm and dealt it to me. I held it at arm's length and gave it a onceover. The poster was simple. A black telephone and a powerful-looking hand above it reaching for the receiver. Just below the picture were the words:

WHEN YOU NEED US, WE'RE THERE. D-I-A-L-O-G-U-E

"We're trying to get a hotline going in this area. We work out of the Lotus Flower Temple on the corner of Maple and Elwood."

"Maple and Elwood? You mean the Buddhist temple about three blocks from here?"

"That's the one."

"So this is what, some sort of hotline for despondent Buddhists?"

She smiled. "No, it's for everyone. The temple just lets us use the space."

I shrugged. "Oh. Well, sure. I'll put up the poster." I looked it over once more to make sure there were no subliminal messages, no hidden suggestive shapes in the folds of the hand or the curves of the telephone receiver. "There's no phone number here. How do people get in touch with you?"

"They just dial the letters. The word, 'Dialogue.'"

"I see. But that's eight letters, isn't it?"

"Yes. But they get us after they dial seven letters. The connection completes on the U."

"So they just push that extra E for nothing, is that it?"

"Yes."

"I see."

I stood there for a moment, nodding and studying the poster. I was stalling. I wanted to talk to her.

"And this hotline is open twenty-four hours?" I finally asked.

"No," she said. "Not enough staff for that. Eight until midnight. Seven days a week."

"Eight until midnight?" I frowned. "What happens if someone gets depressed at two in the morning?"

"There's an answering machine, explaining when we're open and it refers them to an emergency number."

"So the poster's a little misleading, isn't it?"

"I'm sorry?"

"Well, it's not exactly, 'when you need us, we're there' is it? More like 'try to need us between eight and midnight.' I mean, if someone called after midnight, they'd be out of luck." I was thinking, in particular, of my own case. The time from midnight until one-thirty was when I was at my worst.

"It's a very friendly voice on the answering machine," she countered.

"Most people hate to get machines, don't they? And then if they're unhappy already and then they get the machine . . ."

"If you'd rather not put up the poster . . ."

I suddenly realized how petulant I must have sounded. She was trying to do something decent for the community and I was grilling her like a bad detective. And I wasn't exactly enhancing my desire to make conversational inroads with a member of the opposite sex.

"No," I said. "I'm sorry. I'd be happy to put up the poster." I shook my head. "You'll have to excuse me. I haven't been getting enough sleep lately. And I have yellow jackets living in my wall."

"Oh," she said. "I'm very sorry to hear that."

"I plan to get it under control," I said.

I held the poster up to the wall in the lobby next to a film poster from Fassbinder's *Despair*.

"What do you think?"

She nodded. "Nice juxtaposition."

"You think a lot of depressed people are going to be wandering through my lobby? I thought people went to the movies to escape all that."

"I get the feeling your customers are into angst," she said, looking first at the *Despair* poster, and then further down the wall at the posters of Kurosawa's *The Bad Sleep Well* and Bergman's *Cries and Whispers*.

She was probably right. I hadn't shown a film here in the last year without a cynical, if not downright depressing, ending. I was the king of angst and this was my kingdom. Abandon hope all ye who enter. Sad souls whose only indulgence is extra butter on their popcorn.

"You don't like foreign films?"

"I do, actually," she said.

"I've never seen you in here."

"I wasn't sure if this was a real theater," she said. "I never see any lines outside this place."

"I don't have lines," I said.

"I'm sorry," she said.

"Don't be," I said. "It doesn't bother me. So, what do you do at Dialogue? Are you a psychologist, a psychotherapist? Are you a psycho-something?"

"No. It's just volunteer work. They trained me how to answer the phone, handle calls. How to be empathetic and a good listener. I'm actually a dental assistant."

No wonder her smile was so arresting. I wondered if people who called the hotline and poured out their problems knew they were doing so with a person who made a living out of draining saliva with a sucking question mark. Still, there was something genuine about her. Something that was putting fer-romagnetic wind in my sails. I imagined for a moment her lift-ing the dark cloud from my shoulders. And removing the plaque from my molars. Fantasy. I didn't even know her name.

"If I called this hotline, who would I ask for?"

"Oh, all the volunteers are fully trained. Anyone could help you."

"But I mean if I . . . if someone . . . wanted to talk specifically to *you*. . . ."

"Me? I work Tuesdays and Thursdays."

"So if someone wanted to speak to you specifically, they'd ask for . . ?"

". . . they could speak to me specifically, yes."

I wanted to ask, After I finish pulling these teeth are you going to clean and floss them?

"Anne," she finally uttered, out of the blue. "But you some-times have to ask for 'Kristen Anne' because we already have an Anne working there. Anne is actually my middle name, but I go by Anne. With my friends, I mean. Except at the hotline if I'm working with the other Anne, then I have to be Kristen Anne. But normally, I'm just Anne."

"Anne," I repeated, trying to remember this root name to the exclusion of all of its derivations. Anne. It was a pretty name and I wasn't going to spoil it by pressing for a last name that might disappoint, like "Felch" or "Suggs." Just plain Anne was good enough.

"You can call me Anne," she said. "Unless you call the hotline, of course. Then it's Kristen Anne."

Anne or Kristen Anne Something gathered up the remaining posters in her arms and turned to leave. I didn't want her to go.

But I couldn't think of anything else to make her stay. Maybe if I offered to show an up-tempo film at my theater. Something with Betty Grable?

"Are you one of those people that like old Betty Grable films?"

"Betty Grable?"

"*Moon Over Miami. Million Dollar Legs.* She was very big during World War II. Great morale-booster for the troops."

"I wasn't kidding when I said I liked foreign films," Anne said. "What are you showing this week?"

"*High and Low.*"

"I don't know that one."

"It's Kurosawa. But not one of his more well-known films."

"I'm not a big fan of samurai movies."

"Oh no, this isn't a samurai movie. It's got Toshiro Mifune, but he plays a shoe company executive. It's a crime story, actually. About a kidnapping. Lots of moral issues. Very compelling."

"A happy ending?"

"Well . . . no. I mean, it's very . . . thought-provoking."

"I'm just teasing. It sounds very interesting."

"You should come and see it."

"I don't know. I'm on my feet all day, cleaning and flossing teeth, and then I work at the hotline. I don't have a lot of free time."

"Why aren't you flossing someone today?"

"It's my day off."

"Do you want to see the film now? Come on in and I'll thread it up."

"I have to distribute these posters."

"I can show it whenever you want. Or if there's another film you'd rather see, you know, just name it. I can get it. I can get it and then I can show it whenever you're free."

"Why should I pay four dollars here when I can rent it for three?" Anne said, smiling.

"I could get you in for free," I said. "Besides, it's much better in the theater. It's dark, there's no distractions. I could arrange a private screening."

"A private screening. Uh huh." She laughed doubtfully. Maybe a little shyly. "You can't do that."

"I can do whatever I want," I said. "I run the theater." It was probably the first time I'd proclaimed this fact so proudly.

She laughed. "Oh, it's that easy, is it?"

"Sure," I said. "You like Bergman?"

"Ingmar or Ingrid?"

"Take your pick. I can get either one."

"What's the film with the old man, there's that dream sequence in the beginning with the coffin . . ."

"*Wild Strawberries*?"

"That's the one."

"Good choice." I was impressed. "Would you come if I showed it?"

She laughed again. It was consistent with her last laugh. No snorting or machine guns. Just a good healthy laugh. I liked it.

"I'm sorry, I'm embarrassing you."

"No, that's all right," she said.

"Does that mean you'd come?"

"I'll think about it," she said. We both let that remark hang in the air for a bit. "Thanks for letting me put the poster up."

She pushed through the glass door and was gone.

"It's Malcolm," I said, when she was already out of sight. "My name's Malcolm."

I had nothing better to do, so I hid in the ticket booth facing the street and waited for her inevitable return back down Maple Street. About thirty minutes later Anne glided by, looking lighter now that she'd unloaded her posters. Maybe I'll call her, I thought. Her number was easy to remember.

Around six that evening I heard keys in the front door. The odor of a carry-out bag from Taco Don's filled the theater. Ginny, my assistant and concession stand person, had arrived. I was in awe of the metabolism of this fifteen-year-old high school junior. Her regular diet of a double Mexi-burger, a sombrero order of fries and a south-of-the-border strawberry shake had enough fat and calories to scare the needle off a bathroom scale but she still looked anorexia-bound. I heard her call my name.

"Mister Cicchio? Are you here?"

"In the office," I called out.

I heard her approach my office and pause just outside my door.

"Ginny?"

"Yes?"

"What are you doing?"

I heard her sigh deeply, then she stuck her head, just her head, inside my office.

"I'm going to eat dinner," she said. "Then I'll make the popcorn."

She never looked at me directly. Her eyes darted all over the room, looking for, but never finding, a place to land.

"That's fine, Ginny," I said. "Take your time."

She ducked her head shyly back out of the office. I heard her heels clack clack over to the candy counter. Ginny and I didn't spend much time together and she never came in my office or the projection booth. This was my fault. Once, during a screening of *Seven Samurai,* she walked into the booth and caught me in a rather private, self-absorbed act. I wanted to tell her that the deed had not been inspired by the film. Although I appreciated their bravado, there was no place in my bed for a single samurai, let alone seven. At the sight of me, Ginny had stopped in her tracks, dropped her armful of popcorn, Mars Bars and diet cola on the cement floor with a splat and opened her eyes wider than a girl her age was ever meant to. Her eyes jumped quickly in and out of my lap, recording a mental estimate by which all future sexual encounters would be measured, probably to my detriment. Then her legs mechanically backed her out of the projection booth.

When I was finished, and this meant zipping up because I certainly couldn't continue, I wanted to hunt her down and try to explain things, but I was too embarrassed. I imaged a siege of parents, teachers and the entire town showing up at the door to the projection room with a battering ram. The school principal leading them with a torch.

"Inside is the beast who satisfies his desires with subtitles!"

"Kill the beast! Kill the beast!"

But that didn't happen. I don't think she ever told anyone. What did happen was that Ginny became too frightened ever to meet my gaze again. She looked at the floor when I spoke to her and nodded nervously when I asked her to do something. The rest of the time she avoided me. Or I avoided her.

What I'd wanted to tell Ginny was that I hadn't even been

watching the film that night. I'd been doing what I usually did when I was alone in the dark. I was thinking of Lena. Years ago on a Friday night it would have been Lena's hands, not mine, wandering through the field. Her hands knew the terrain better than mine did. So much better, in fact, that when the relationship ended, my body spurned early solo attempts to recreate the satisfaction. Donor rejected as unsuitable. My body missed the soft, lotioned hands, the manicured fingers. My hands were too rough, too hard. Too much like me.

Lena was an X-ray technician's assistant and the day we met was the day I slipped on a December sidewalk and landed on the index finger of my right hand. Lena x-rayed it in a dark room of a local hospital. She put her delicate hand on my fractured finger and I felt it healing at her touch. She put a lead apron on me and I felt protected as never before. Women before Lena had been nice, but none of them had ever sheathed me in lead. There was something distinctly non-clinical about the way she positioned my finger to be photographed. A soft, lingering touch, perhaps.

"Don't move," she said.

I didn't. In fact I didn't move from the lobby of the hospital the rest of the day. I waited until she got off work and then I asked her if she wanted to have dinner.

We found areas of compatibility. It seemed there were some meaningful conversations to be had between a person who looks at film negatives and a person who looks at negative films. That night I wrote down her number on the dinner check stub. I called her and told her how my fractured finger was progressing. By the time I could wiggle it again, we were a couple.

In the years that followed we indulged in great sex and fine dining, which slowly segued into fine dining and arguments and a lot less great sex. We began to argue frequently, she cheated on me twice, alienated the few friends I had, filled me with self-doubt and never let me drive her Mustang.

By the time I broke up with Lena, however, most of those transgressions were long past. I'd just never exactly gotten around to forgiving her. And in an attempt to assert myself, just once, to be the person who drops rather than the dropped one, I let her go. It felt like a mistake immediately afterwards. It reminded me of being in a restaurant and changing my order at the last minute. The sudden shift from the chicken marsala to the brook trout and then the realization I'd have been happier with the chicken. So life served me up a bland, flavorless trout and I ate it because I'd asked for it and thought it was what I'd wanted.

Lena had recently become engaged to a cardiologist. It seemed an odd choice for her, but I guess she felt sure that she would suffer no broken heart in the arms of a trained cardiologist. I'd read about the engagement in the local papers. Doctor Andrew Buntrock. Soon to be Doctor and Missus Andrew Buntrock. I hadn't spoken to Lena since our breakup. I'd dialed the number a few times and hung up. I'd seen her mother once at Sears.

"He's a cardiologist," she'd said.

"I know, I read about it in the papers. When's the wedding?"

"They haven't set a date yet. How are you doing, Malcolm?"

"I have yellow jackets in my wall and I'm not getting enough sleep."

"Well, it was nice to see you again."

"You too."

I had a feeling the wedding would be soon. When I thought

about her being married, I longed for her to come back to me one last time. Not so that I could drop her again, but so that she could drop me. I needed the pain of rejection, not the pain of knowing I'd let her go. I studied the papers daily for the announcement of the exact time and place of the wedding. It was never my intention to stop it, but I had to know when it was happening and prepare for it. Like setting my watch for another time zone.

That night I screened *High and Low*. God knows what Ginny thought upon discovering it was another Kurosawa film. I imagined her imagining me in the dark of the projection booth, laying out towels and heating up some petroleum jelly. Eighteen people came to see the movie. Not a bad turnout. You had to consider that on a summer night in July people could be sitting at quaint little sidewalk cafes, spooning frozen vanilla yogurt into their mouths and sipping their lattés. Instead, they chose to sit in a dark, badly ventilated movie theater and chew over the moral implications raised by a two-and-a-half-hour Kurosawa film. Who were these eighteen people? I never knew. I avoided associating with the patrons. I never went into the lobby while they were buying popcorn and Jujubes, and I barricaded myself inside the projection booth until the last person left. Some people came back more than once to see the same film. I recognized them and even felt some vague kinship with them, but I never spoke to them. I wondered if I forced myself to do something more socially engaging, have something like a film discussion night for instance, maybe I'd draw people more like Anne. Maybe I'd even draw Anne. It was something to think about, anyway.

Knowing that I had a film for an entire week allowed me the

luxury of not having to pay attention to the film every night. I always figured I'd have plenty of opportunities to see whatever part of the film I wanted whenever I desired. Besides, it's different up there in the projection booth. It's not the same as being down in one of the velvet seats, in the dark. The steady cranking of the celluloid in the sprockets can become increasingly hypnotic. Many evenings I caught myself mesmerized by the projector itself, watching it glow and flicker like a firefly as the images flashed by, twenty-four frames per second. Sometimes I simply watched the take-up reel as it slowly, imperceptibly grew fatter, feeding on a rich stock of thirty-five millimeter film.

I never actually planned for a life in the cinema. When I was in high school I'd worked in the audio-visual department. If it was audio or visual, I probably operated, loaded or monkeyed around with it at one time or another. Mister Agnew, the audio-visual instructor, kept a long list of equipment and as I became knowledgeable in the operation of each piece, he'd put my initials next to it. Movie projectors, slide projectors, overhead projectors, opaque projectors, splicing and editing machines, cameras, microphones and tape recorders, I knew them all, tip to stern, reel-to-reel.

When there was nothing to do, I'd grab a film out of the film library. Chaplin, Keaton, Harold Lloyd, Ben Turpin, Laurel and Hardy. We had dozens of Blackhawk comedy shorts in the archives. They didn't have sound, so I could run them through the splicing machine, pretending to be checking for breaks in the film. Mister Agnew never caught on. In fact, he came to regard me as a responsible, conscientious student.

Mister Agnew had big, sweaty hands, which seemed like an awful liability for someone whose business it is to touch electrical equipment all day. He'd pat my back with his moist palms, saying "Good, Mister Cicchio, very good." He probably had some high hopes for me to become a film editor or a sound technician or something. Something audio or visual. But I wasn't really interested too much in the technical end of things. I just wanted to watch the films.

They let me do just that in college. I took whatever the community college had to offer in the film department. We studied Buster Keaton's *The General* and since I'd already watched it seven or eight times on the sly in my audio-visual class in high school, I was able to talk intelligently about it and write the kinds of papers teachers want you to write. I was subjected to a lot of films in college and I was particularly interested in most of the foreign films I saw. I guess it isn't really that much of a stretch from Buster Keaton to Ingmar Bergman— it's all about angst. So I immersed myself in foreign cinema. Books about foreign films started popping up on my shelves. A lot of them were dry, uninteresting volumes written by pompous cineastes and university professors, but I read them anyway. Heady, psychological babble, sure, but I also learned a lot about directors like Bergman, Fassbinder, Wenders, Kurosawa, Fellini. I copied down filmographies and tracked down the films. My film professors loved me. They probably had high hopes for me too, I guess, expecting me to become a director or film critic. But I wasn't interested in any of that, either. I still just wanted to watch the films.

My father bought and sold real estate for a living and one day he acquired an old movie palace in the suburbs, about twenty minutes outside the city. I wasn't working and he asked me if I wanted to run it. He needed a failing, unprofitable business to show Sheldon, his tax man, I'm not sure why exactly. Since I hadn't found a career objective in college, I guess my father figured I knew something about failure and unprofitability. Anyway, I was happy to accommodate him, since I was only interested in screening films I liked, mostly foreign films, and those didn't make any money in the city, much less in the suburbs.

It was supposed to be a temporary thing, until I latched onto a serious career objective, but it was dangerously comfortable. I could order any film I wanted and watch it whenever I pleased, without having to worry about Mister Agnew's sweaty hands or the lofty expectations of stuffy film professors.

The only people who expected anything of me were those eighteen people in the dark down there, whose only hope was that I remain ever-vigilant for the evil nemeses of film-goers: frame flutters and breaks. But if I continued to lose a minute of sleep each night, I could kiss my vigilance good-bye. If I couldn't run my projector, I'd have to find a real job, or worse, I'd have to spend more time at home with the yellow jackets.

With paper, pen and pocket calculator, I'd recently worked out my sleep loss exponentially to a very dire conclusion. One lost minute of sleep a night meant about thirty minutes lost a month. Every two months I would lose one hour. In four months, two hours. In eight months, four hours. In sixteen months, eight hours. I was already down to about seven hours, so I could expect to be getting no sleep at all in sixteen months. How long could a person survive without sleep?

I called Doctor Li and asked. She didn't give me a direct answer. I told Doctor Li that the pills weren't working. She recommended more pills or a larger variety of the same pill. Since I had never taken the first pills in the first place, I was worried that the increased dosage might put me in a coma. I asked if there was another alternative. There was.

chapter three

The Becker Sleep Clinic was on the first floor of a large university hospital in the city. It took more than an hour to drive into the city, and find a parking space in the ten-story parking garage that was not reserved for doctors or the handicapped. I found something on level nine, the blue level, section F-6. I repeated the information like a mantra (nine-blue level, F-6) all the way down the elevator to the first floor, then across the street to the hospital, then down long, busy corridors that covered at least five city blocks.

"Where can I find Doctor Jean-Paul Villard?" I asked a woman at the front desk, thinking nine, blue level, F-6 and trying not to be distracted by her thick, cerulean eye shadow.

"You go left down this hallway," she said, pointing with a similarly distracting index finger that had a long, curved fingernail with a similarly cerulean blue tint. "Then a right past the gift shop, another right at Urology, then down to room twenty-two."

I moved down the hallway quickly, my short-term memory drowning in a pool of cerulean blue. On the front burner of my brain was left, gift shop right, Urology right and room twenty-two. Meanwhile, nine, blue, F-6 still simmering at a reduced heat on the rear burner of my brain.

Perhaps, I thought, the idea is to totally short out the system. Sort of like finding satori after the nothingness of Zen, or having a lobotomy. Once my body was exhausted and my brain was fried, perhaps I'd relax back down into a state where I could sleep normally.

I found room twenty-two and settled in for the obligatory wait. I flipped through several magazines while waiting to see Doctor Villard. I avoided *Time*, the irony not lost on me, and chose instead from plentiful stacks of women's magazines. I wondered if the magazines were predominantly female based on some poll of neurological problems that favored women. Or maybe men didn't read magazines when they waited. Or maybe ladies' magazines were cheaper. It seemed every ladies' magazine had a story about how to please a man and a real-life chronicle of a terminal illness. I was too busy trying to retain my parking space location (nine-blue-F-6) to make any kind of meaningful connection.

After my next obligatory wait, inside the doctor's office, I finally met Doctor Jean-Paul Villard. I liked that he was French. He looked a little like Yves Montand and even though I was not a smoker, I would not have been at all disappointed if he'd opened a silver cigarette case and lit up a Gauloise during our conversation.

"What is this thing that is happening to you?" he asked.

He was looking at my file as he spoke, and since I was a referral I knew that my problem had probably been noted in the file by Doctor Li. It made me nervous, as though I was going to be tested on my previous testimony. Was the first determination of how you would be treated based on the consistency of your answers?

"You are losing a minute of sleep a night?"

"If that's what it says," I said, indicating the file. Then I answered more affirmatively. "Yes."

He smiled.

"This is not the worst problem," he said.

"No?"

"Oh, no," he said shaking his head. "We have had people in here who wake up strangling their loved ones. I had a fellow who came to me because he'd woken up screaming and crashed through a plate glass door."

"My God."

Doctor Villard kept smiling through these horror stories as if it were all in a day's work. I guess he thought it was comforting telling me about people who didn't have the same problems I had. Yet.

"Our rooms have no windows. And they're soundproofed. Nothing gets out and nothing gets in."

"A little air, I hope." I chuckled nervously.

"Not to worry. And it's not by accident that we've situated the sleep clinic on the first floor."

"Oh?"

"We don't want anyone flinging themselves off any buildings. Every precaution is taken."

"I know you're not intentionally trying to scare me," I said. "But I live on the second floor of a two-flat. Should I move to a first-floor apartment?"

"I don't think you should change your routine at the moment."

"Strange. I thought the idea of coming here had something to do with changing my routine. You know, correcting it. By seeing a doctor. If I didn't want to change my routine I could have just stayed home."

"I'm sure you misunderstand," said Doctor Villard. "Besides, these are not the problems you are having. Just a little insomnia, no?"

"I'm not sure. I figured I'm losing something like a minute of sleep a night. In about sixteen months I could stop sleeping altogether. I worked it out on a calculator."

"A person who does not sleep does not live." He turned his palm up in an "oh well" gesture.

"Maybe you *are* intentionally trying to scare me."

"I think you need to stop worrying. We are going to study you for two nights. Observe your sleep. I'm sure it is something manageable."

"Okay. I guess. But I can tell you anything you want to know. I've been observing myself and watching the clock and I can tell you, I'm losing a minute a night."

"Well, we'll just watch and we'll see."

Stripped down to my torn underwear again, this time on a hospital bed, I patiently abided a woman named Doris as she spent the better part of an hour wiring me up for a good night's sleep study. She attached several electrodes to my head, at least four on each hemisphere, one right at the top of my forehead at the hairline, and maybe a couple more to the area just below my ear. It was meticulous work. First she wiped an area with alcohol, then dried it with a small blow dryer (something that looked like a dental tool, but whose motor made a hell of a loud noise). Then a drop or so of glue was injected through a syringe and into a tube so that it went exactly to where Doris wanted. It seemed a difficult, tedious process.

In addition to my skull, there were also electrodes attached to my temples, to measure rapid eye movement (REM). She attached another wire and electrode to my chin to find out if I was grinding my teeth in my sleep. The myriad of wires from these plugs were inserted into a large pegboard and from there into an electroencephalogram. I asked Doris when she was going to put the lid locks on my eyes, then realized from her bewildered expression that she hadn't seen *A Clockwork Orange*. I wised up quickly: a person being covered with electrodes should refrain from making cracks or confusing remarks. One crossed wire and I might end up looking like I'd been left on the stove too long.

Two more electrodes were attached to the lower part of each of my legs (to determine if I was having leg spasms). Everything was taped down with white tape. "You've got hairy legs," Doris said. "That's going to hurt in the morning."

She placed an irritating tube under my nostrils that checked the breathing from my nose (this was one of the more uncomfortable ones). Another electrode was attached to my chest, around the area of my left clavicle. Then another one, a plastic cap over the ring finger of my right hand, something like one of those machines you can check your pulse with. More white tape. Then there was a band placed around my chest and one around my stomach to check my respiration. Each time another wire was glued on, taped over and plugged in, I'd kind of chuckle, nervously. Part of my nervousness had to do with the fact that for the first time I was beginning to really feel that I was *in the hospital*, undergoing something that would only happen in a hospital. I'd never been in the hospital before and now I felt like I was being *worked on*.

Once I was completely hooked up, I was a prisoner of my

hospital bed. In this modern age of remote control, I would have thought much of this could have been done without so many wires. There were no red, blue, green or black wires from my bed to the ceiling-mounted Magnavox television. Just a little box with a lot of buttons. But there was tri-colored spaghetti emanating from every square inch of my body. I began to suspect the wires were there to keep you tethered to the bed. So you don't go flinging yourself around, hurting yourself, hurting the doctors and nurses.

"Just sleep like you normally would," Doris told me while she was hooking me up. There I was, flat on my back, haphazardly wired like the sound board at Woodstock and yet the advice was given sincerely. "You can sleep on your side, or your stomach, whatever is most comfortable for you."

What would have been most comfortable would have been if Doris and Doctor Villard could have come back to my place and watched me on my convertible sofa. But science works empirically, not logically. I felt absurd, very vulnerable and wide awake.

Doris told me I'd be surprised how well I'd be able to sleep. Then she told me that she had to "check on her other bodies" and that if I needed anything I should wave at the camera (mounted on the wall to the left of the television) and eventually she'd see me and come running. She would be watching me and two other guinea pigs all night, she said. Apparently there was a room down the hall with monitors and she was going to play night watchman until dawn.

Before she left me alone, Doris told me how to work the remote control for the television.

"Don't hit this button," she said, indicating a red button on the dial, "or the nurses will come running in here with electric paddles."

I wasn't sure what that meant, whether it was a joke or not, and I decided not to ask. Doris turned out the lights and left the room. There was a spotlight over my head shining a low bronze light over my body so she could still see me, it. I'd hoped to get drowsy watching television, but I was so uncomfortable that I couldn't even begin to concentrate on the late show.

Doris had lowered my body from the comfortable position you see in those info-mercials with people who have bought those orthopedic hospital beds, to a flat slab like you see in morgues. The pillow was cardboard thin, and it would have taken six of them to make up for the two fluffy ones I was used to at my apartment. I don't know what I expected, it was a hospital after all, not a hotel. But I thought perhaps because it was a *sleep* clinic they'd do everything they could to help me *sleep* there. Unless the plan was to make me so uncomfortable that I'd never complain about sleeping again.

My immediate problem was my bladder. The moment Doris left the room, I had to go. She'd given me a plastic container, like a sports bottle, to urinate into. But no helpful tips to execute any urinary plans. And since there was a camera on me at all times, I didn't know for sure if Doris was watching me. In fact, I couldn't be sure if there wasn't a roomful of first year residents laughing, eating pizza and watching.

I shyly stuck the bottle under the covers. I held the sheet with my teeth, the bottle with my right hand and my shrunken-under-the circumstances penis with my left hand. Even with everything in place, it was extraordinarily difficult to urinate. I don't imagine this is too unusual— after early years of being trained not to urinate carelessly, suddenly you're asked to throw all those ideas away and pee into a sports bottle.

I thought of everything, I thought of nothing. I tried to relax but I found it difficult enough to relax when I was in an average men's room. What I needed was the right combination of relaxation and concentration. Too much of either was no good. There's a perfect balance and a man must hit it just right in order to urinate. And relaxation was hampered by the underlying knowledge that if you can't urinate, *they have ways*. Finally, luckily, I caught the right combination of detachment and desire, and did what I had to. I surreptitiously put the bottle on the floor next to the bed.

I tried to buy into the fantasy of sleeping as I normally would. The first thing I did was to turn on my side, my preferred position. And as soon as I did, two plugs came off my legs.

I began to wave at the camera. I waved and waved and waved and no one responded and I thought maybe it's too dark and they can't see me waving, but if I got up and turned on the light, all my plugs would come out and I knew Doris wouldn't like that. So I just kept waving and waving and thought, maybe this is part of it. Maybe the waving is supposed to make me tired enough to nod off so that they can get on with observing me sleep. Then I realized Doris was probably checking her other "bodies" and was not monitoring me at the moment. I was forced to just keep waving, helplessly, for about fifteen minutes.

Doris finally came back into the room.

"I was waving," I said. I said it helplessly rather than in an accusatory tone. After all, most of me was hooked up to electrical equipment and for all I knew Doris could "accidentally" plug me into the main generator of the hospital if she got pissed at me.

Doris wasn't put out. Apparently this happened all the time. She plugged me back in.

"I had some other patients to attend to, but when I got to the room I saw you waving."

Good, I thought. Maybe she didn't see my acrobatic urination act.

I don't know how long it took me to finally fall asleep but somewhere along the line, I slept. I had a soft-core sex dream, the details of which immediately eluded me. I hoped it wasn't anything that could be seen graphically in my body language or encoded onto my EEG.

I was awakened at five-thirty by Doris's voice and the flash of rude, fluorescent lights.

"Good morning, " I said, automatically.

"Good morning," Doris echoed cheerfully.

"Did I do anything interesting in my sleep?"

"You tossed a bit during REM sleep. And you twitch a lot before you go into that stage."

"What does that mean?" I wondered if it had anything to do with the soft-core sex dream.

"Doctor Villard will look at the tapes and he'll talk to you."

"What time did I go out?"

"One fifty-three."

"That's another minute gone," I said.

Then the electrodes came off, a perfect yin/yang of pain and pleasure. On the one hand, I felt like a dolphin being cut loose after getting accidentally caught up in a tuna net. But Doris ripped the white tape from my body with no regard for the sensitivity of my epidermis. And yes, I learned the hard way that the more hairless you are, the better off you are. The glue was removed from my skull with some kind of solvent, roughly applied with a paper towel. Since it was the first thing in the morning, I reacted like a cringing two-year-old who doesn't want to have his face washed.

I felt ragged. I looked at my face in the bathroom mirror and I saw a sticky white residue on my temples and chin and deep crevices in my cheeks from the tape pressure. I didn't shower. I didn't want to be there any longer than I had to.

I dressed and prepared to leave.

As I exited my room and walked down the hall, I saw the monitoring room. It was smaller than I imagined and didn't have the kind of HAL super computer I'd expected would be processing all the information my body had revealed during the night. On the left wall was a bank of black-and-white TV monitors with VCRs under them, about five in all. On the first screen I could see my now-empty bed. I tried to imagine what I would have looked like. Not a pretty sight, certainly. I was no prize in my underwear *without* wires. The extra electrical equipment couldn't have added anything positive to my appearance.

There were EEG graphs crowding the monitoring room and a desk with a couple of chairs. Paper plates from some middle-of-the-night dinner were in the garbage can and I pictured Doris in there all night, watching people sleep. I wondered how much they paid her.

By now I'd forgotten the exact location of my car. All I remembered was blue level. But once I got to the blue level it wasn't difficult to spot a VW Camper at six in the morning in a nearly deserted parking garage. I drove home and crashed on my couch. I didn't sleep much, but I slept unfettered.

The following week I had another meeting with Doctor Villard.

"We can't really find anything wrong with you."

"That's not good," I said.

That's never good, I thought. When a specialist can't find anything wrong with you and you know something's wrong, it's time to do some heavy duty worrying.

"You fell asleep at approximately one fifty-three . . ." he said, looking at some notes and reiterating the same information I already knew.

"Yes, I know. That's another minute gone," I said. "I've been afraid to even watch the clock anymore."

"There doesn't seem to be anything clinically wrong with you. Your respiration is fine. Your heart rate increased a bit when you became anxious just before dreaming, but it's nothing to be concerned about. If you were older, it might be a problem."

"But I will get older, won't I? I mean, the sleep study didn't indicate I'm in some arrested stage of aging, did it?"

"No."

"So eventually my heart could get weaker, not be able to take the strain." I suddenly saw myself as an inverted Glen Manning, the Amazing Colossal Man. His heart couldn't keep up with his rapid growth rate. My heart wouldn't be able to keep up with my decreasing sleep rate. In the movie, Manning's heart was expected to explode, it was a time bomb waiting to go off. I felt the same ticking in my chest.

"You tossed a bit in your REM sleep," he said, as if he were looking for some other symptom that would take my mind off heart explosions.

"Yes. I understand I also twitched a bit."

"Before dreaming. Yes. Are you troubled about anything?"

"You mean apart from losing sleep? And these new fears about my heart?" I thought for a moment. "I've got some yellow jackets living in my wall. And I've got an old girlfriend who's getting married. It shouldn't bother me. I don't know why it does. There's a wristwatch I can't find."

He nodded.

"Those are the things that spring to mind," I said. "I could probably come up with more."

"Have you talked to anyone about this?"

"No. I mean, just a few people." I flashed on Glen Manning again. Did he want me to keep this a secret? Did they intend to put me in a circus tent and observe my slow deterioration? "My father knows because he handles the health insurance. My mother doesn't know because if she did, she'd be here now. She doesn't believe in doctors and hospitals but she likes to visit people when they're in them."

"I was thinking more along the lines of a therapist."

"A therapist?"

"Someone to talk things over with."

I thought about Kristen Anne, the poster girl from Dialogue. I wondered if Doctor Villard would be willing to write it down, like a prescription, so that I could show up on Kristen Anne's doorstep with a doctor's authorization.

"You think that would help me?"

"Like I said, I can't find anything clinically wrong with you. If you want to take medication, you can, but it's not a permanent solution. It won't cure you of whatever it is that's troubling you."

"You think I'm troubled?"

He raised his eyebrows about as judgmentally high as eyebrows can go on a forehead.

"Okay," I said. "Okay."

chapter four

High and Low was purring contentedly through the projector without any problems. Occasionally I leaned out of my perch in the projection booth, peered down with slitted eyes, and counted heads. No one had vacated their seats, but one woman had settled comfortably into her boyfriend's shoulder for a nap.

I wanted to get a long stick, something like the ones those Zen masters used during meditation, so that I could discreetly whack cinema sleepers back to attention. Maybe I was just jealous. But what was I jealous of? The effortless way some people drifted off to sleep? Maybe I was jealous because I wanted a woman nuzzling into my shoulder.

I started thinking about Anne, the Dialogue poster girl. It was a little after nine o'clock. Dialogue had been comforting the downtrodden for over an hour. I wondered if depression had its peak hours, its prime time. Were there more calls on a bad television night? Desperate people brandishing a razor blade in one hand and thumbing the channel changer with the other. I didn't use blades. I shaved with cartridges. The worst I could do to myself was make my wrists smoother.

Regardless of how dire my straits were, Doctor Villard had given me a legitimate excuse to call the hot line. He'd never directly suggested that dating a telephone therapist would help cure my sleep problem, nor did he say that a dental hygienist who answered a hotline qualified as the type of therapist I required, but it was, I felt, a step in the right direction. In my opinion, the therapy was secondary. What I needed was a good date. If I got some therapy out of it, it was a bonus. And who knows, maybe I'd get my sleep back on an even keel in the process.

But just calling Anne for a date seemed too direct. I needed the subterfuge of a few manageable psychological problems to get a foot in the door.

Anyway, I didn't feel my problems were all that dire. Not sleeping and not feeling motivated, that wasn't so bad, was it? Obsessing about an ex-girlfriend, that happens. I certainly didn't want to present myself to Anne as a person with too many problems. I wanted to create a nice balance of psychosis and self-confidence.

I figured it this way. If I called, laid a couple of my lesser anxieties on her, went through the motions of feeling better, Anne would feel good because she'd helped me and then she'd see me as a person headed towards self-actualization, the kind of person you might want to have pie and coffee with some evening.

I'd also been mulling over my plan to get Anne back into my movie theater. I was desperate to bring things back to my turf, where I felt a bit more confident. I thought maybe I could impress her by having a special film festival. It wouldn't actually be a festival, it would only be a night or two, but I could call it a festival. My idea was that I would screen *Wild Strawberries* and present a guest lecturer at the Arcadia Filmhaus. Not Bergman, certainly, but perhaps some out-of-work ex-Bergman actor who could talk about his days with the old master. I thought maybe if I showed the film, served a little schnapps with cheese and crackers, and led a discussion with an actor, maybe the Arcadia would seem more like a real movie house. It would mean dealing with more people and making a few phone calls, but it seemed worth it if I could get Anne to see me in a new light.

Whatever I was going to do, I had to do it soon. Before long *High and Low* would let out, my moviegoers would go home, get depressed and then they'd be calling Anne instead of me. There was no telephone in the projection booth. I needed Ginny to watch the film for a bit while I made the call from my office.

This wouldn't be easy. Ginny never watched the films. She was supposed to be watching, studying and taking notes on the films so she could receive three credits worth of high school English and wouldn't have to go to summer school. This was, I'd discovered, why she'd taken the job in the first place. But instead she parked herself behind the rarely-visited candy counter all night and composed honey-glazed love letters to her boyfriend. I often found poorly-written early drafts when I emptied the garbage. I wondered what kind of final paper she would turn in to her school at the end of the summer:

> Foreign films are called that because they come
> from foreign countries. Some foreign films come
> from Germany, Japan, England, France and Spain.
> Foreign films are "subtitled" so you can read the
> film if you don't want to watch it.

I dreaded the day Ginny's teacher would call me, demanding to know if she was actually studying anything and I would have

to lie, lest she tattle to anyone about my projection room indis-
cretion. If Ginny kept quiet, I would too. But in return, and at
six bucks an hour, I figured I ought to be able to enlist her help
to watch the film for a few minutes. I gave the projector one
last hopeful glance, then emerged from the booth and descended
the stairs to the lobby.

As I approached the candy counter, I spied Ginny pushing a
couple of boxes of empty Raisinettes into the trash can. Maybe
her guilt would make her a bit more gracious, I thought. I led
with an uncharacteristic smile.

"Hi. I'm sorry, but would you do me a big favor?"

Her eyes began to dart around the room.

"I need to make a phone call and I have to leave the projector alone for a few minutes."

"I don't know how to run it," Ginny said, very matter-of-
factly. Her tone implied: This is not part of my job description
and it never will be.

"You don't have to run it," I said. "Just let me know if the
film breaks or burns up."

She twisted her hair and her eyes glazed over.

"What if it does that jumpy thing?"

"Jumpy thing? You mean if the film goes out of frame? There's
a little knob on the side of the projector that says 'frame'. You
can't miss it. Just turn it until the film is back on track. It's very
simple."

"I don't know . . . I don't know what you're talking about."

"Why don't you come upstairs and I'll show you."

Her confused look was replaced by one of absolute terror.
So this was my real motive, she probably thought. Get her up
there with all those straps and chains dangling from the ceiling

of the projection room. How would she explain the bruises to her boyfriend?

"It's just the frame," I said more sharply. "It says 'frame' on the side of the projector."

"But it's dark up there."

"All right," I said. "Never mind. Just do this. Sit in the back of the theater and watch the film. If it breaks, burns or does anything strange, anything at all, come and get me."

"And you'll be in your office?"

No, I'll be in the row behind you, wearing an overcoat and a goat's head mask, my little flower.

"Yes. I'll be in my office."

"And you want me to knock?"

"Yes."

"Knock and go away?"

"Yes. Knock and go away. That'd be swell." Don't push me, I thought. I haven't had enough sleep and I've got yellow jackets in my wall.

I watched her pick up her large diet cola and shuffle reluctantly into the theater. I went into my office and closed the door. I picked up the phone and dialed the letters

D-I-A-L-O-G-U. I harbored a strong desire to complete the word and my finger hovered for a moment over the silent "E" but I resisted. It rang once.

"Hello, this is Dialogue. How may I help you?"

It was a sweet, feminine voice, filled with professionally-trained empathy. But was it my Anne or the other Anne? I remained silent as I tried to decide.

"Hello?" the voice said again.

Most people would have hung up by this time. Dialogue volunteers, I imagined, were trained to stay on the phone until the line was dead. Or the caller.

"Hello," said the voice a third time, this time with a hint of irritation. Even hotline workers get impatient, I noted.

"I'm sorry," I finally said. "I was thinking."

"That's all right." The practiced ring of concern returned to her voice. "My name's Mary. How can I help you?"

Mary? It wasn't Anne or Kristen Anne. It was Mary. I wasn't prepared for a Mary.

"Mary?"

"Yes. What's your name?"

The gear working my mouth seized up again.

"You don't have to give me your real name," she said, carefully. "You can make up a name if you like."

"It's Malcolm," I said. I figured if any name sounded made-up it was my own.

"How can I help you tonight, Malcolm?"

It sounded odd when she said my name. I suppose some people find it comforting to hear their own names but whenever I heard mine I saw home movies of my third birthday and heard my mother's voice. "Isn't Malcolm cute. He thinks he's talking on a real telephone." I suddenly wished my name was "Phillip" or "Trevor." The phone felt thick and useless in my hand. I sighed and her trained ear detected it.

"Take your time," she said.

While I was taking my time, deciding whether to ask for Kristen Anne or hang up, I heard her voice. Anne was in the room with Mary, on the phone with another caller. It was that same lyrical voice I'd heard that afternoon. No mistaking it. If the hotline held a contest for the most concerned, sincere-sounding voice, Mary might win the bronze, but Anne would certainly take home the gold.

Even using such trite expressions such as "What do *you* think you should do?" and "Listen to your inner self," Anne managed to tug at my heart strings. Her voice was just so comforting, like eiderdown pillows and cool lake breezes. My spirits lifted even though Anne was currently lifting someone else's spirits. She was lifting two spirits at once. What a gal.

"Who else is there?" I asked abruptly.

The question took Mary by surprise.

"That's . . . another volunteer," she said.

"I think I'd prefer to talk to her, if you don't mind."

"You'd like to speak to Anne?"

"Would that be Kristen Anne?"

"Yes, Kristen Anne is Anne," she said. "But here she's Kristen Anne."

"Then I'd like to speak to Anne, please."

"Kristen Anne?"

"Yes."

"Oh," Mary said, sounding crestfallen. I think I'd unintentionally bruised Mary's ego. She sounded a little older. Perhaps she had more experience and resented callers who wanted the younger women. The Annes and the Kristen Annes. I wanted to tell Mary that it wasn't personal and maybe emphasize that business about how I genuinely believed her voice would bronze in some concerned voice contest. But I didn't say any of that. Instead, I lied.

"Actually, I'm having some . . . problems. I told Anne a bit about it last time. She already knows quite a bit about it and I didn't want to start all over again from the beginning if I didn't have to."

"Oh, dear," Mary said, forgetting her pride and remembering her place. "I'm so sorry. Of course you can speak with her. Please stay on the line."

She didn't put me on hold. I could still hear Anne's end of the conversation. She made a pact with the caller. Apparently the caller agreed to contact a social worker, call back in a few days if needed and refrain from sitting in the car when the garage door was closed. When she was finished, Anne picked up the line I was on.

"Hello? How may I help you?"

"Hello," I said. "This is Malcolm."

"Malcolm?"

"I spoke to you this afternoon. I work at the Arcadia Filmhaus."

"Oh, yes. Hello."

"I just called to say hello."

"Hello," she said.

"The poster's up in the lobby," I said. "It looks good." It sounded like the first page of a Berlitz book of useful phrases. It looks good. How much is that hat? Where is the train station? My name is Malcolm. Where are Phillip and Trevor?

"That's nice," she said cordially. She seemed a bit preoccupied. Probably still thinking about the last caller. It must be difficult, I thought, for her to switch from passionate consolation to inane banter.

"I was hoping we could get together; I'd like to talk to you." I was pleased with myself—already I was forming compound sentences.

"We can talk now," Anne said.

There were about a hundred ways to interpret a response like that and I went through about forty of them in the next moment. Did Anne mean we *shouldn't* talk in person? Wouldn't? Mustn't? Was she saying that I would never get any closer to her than a voice at the other end of the line, would be left to have my spirits lifted over the phone? Did Anne mean that the only time I would see her would be professionally, when I, as an art house theater manager, let her, as Dialogue volunteer, into the theater to replace the poster when it became dog-eared every three years or so?

Or was she saying that we could certainly get together at some later time but that the time for talking was right now? Not later tonight or tomorrow, but now, because the bird of time has but a little time to fly and the bird is on the wing.

Or was she being ironic? Was she saying, sure, we can talk now but if you were a real man you'd close down your theater, march up to the front door of the Buddhist temple, push aside the bodhisattva, using utmost compassion of course, fly up the stairs, take me in your arms and whisk me off to Denny's for blueberry pie and decaf?

"You mean we can't get together?" I finally asked, my internal ramblings momentarily depleted.

"We don't need to," she said. "That's the advantage of Dialogue."

"Oh," I said. There it was in a nutshell. A fine romance, I thought. No wine and roses. No exchange of double entendre greeting cards. No moonlit walks on the pier. No bagel and cream cheese Sunday brunches, fighting over who gets the funnies first.

"So tell me what's troubling you," she said.

I made a quick mental list of my problems. The short list, not the one including the fear my heart might explode in sixteen months.

"Well, as I've told you, there are yellow jackets in my wall. And I'm not getting all the sleep I should be getting."

"You've seen a doctor?"

"Yes. A French doctor. A specialist. He says there's nothing clinically wrong with me. But I'm still losing a minute of sleep a night."

"And this is causing you a lot of stress," she said.

"A bit, " I said. "You know. Some."

"Have you talked to anyone about this?"

"Not really," I said, wondering why everyone wanted to know if I'd talked to someone else. "I thought maybe I could talk to you."

"I'm assuming if you called the hotline that you don't have a significant other to talk to."

"You mean a girlfriend? No, it's true. I don't have a girlfriend. I had a girlfriend for many years, but she's marrying a cardiologist this summer."

"How does that make you feel?"

"I kind of wanted to be invited."

"You're feeling left out?"

"I guess so."

"Do you want to talk about your relationships with women?"

"Gee, I don't know," I said.

It wasn't exactly the direction I wanted the phone call to take. It didn't seem a good tactic to begin a relationship by categorizing the shortcomings of earlier relationships. By the same token, I had Anne on the phone now, and she sounded interested.

"How much would you like to know?" I asked.

I ended up playing into her hands more than I intended to. Once you start talking about yourself, it's hard not to talk about yourself a lot. I talked about some things in my childhood, trying to put off talking about Lena as long as possible. I told Anne how awful I felt when Ginger, my Springer Spaniel, was put to sleep when I was eleven. Did my parents ever stop to think that if they acquired a puppy when I was an infant that they'd end up with an impressionable eleven-year-old boy and a dead dog?

I talked about Carlotta, my first high school love. Carlotta had flirted with me in Biology class so that I'd ask her to the Junior homecoming dance. But then she dropped me the day after the dance, after I'd been up all night composing a poem dedicated to our night of passion. It wasn't really passion, however, it was more like mutually tentative groping and petting that favored the stomach, because the area above or below the stomach was far too exhausting to consider at that age. And the whole thing was interrupted so regularly by a flashlight-wielding policeman that I often mistook the location of my memory as a lighthouse, rather than the parking pool of the driver's education class just outside our high school. I didn't go into the details with Anne, of course. I just told Anne that Carlotta had broken my heart when I was seventeen and that I'd written the poem. I thought it might make me sound serious and sensitive.

Gradually I moved into more recent history and we came around to Lena, whom I'd met shortly after high school and dated for almost ten years. I didn't know why I'd dated her as long as I had, I only knew that whenever I wanted to break up with her it was too close to Christmas or Sweetest Day or her birthday or some major holiday and I couldn't bear to do it. I tried not to talk too much about Lena because I didn't want Anne to think I was on the rebound. And I didn't want Anne to think I was the kind of guy who broke it off with someone for no compelling reason, although that may have been the case at the time. All I knew for sure was that I had a problem letting go of things, be they pets or relationships. Ginger still visited me in my dreams, begging for table scraps.

Healing seemed to take longer for me. My problem was that by the time I was prepared to come to terms with some of the major issues in my life, I'd forgotten what most of them were. And when I tallied it all up, it never seemed to amount to anything much, nothing that would explain the nonspecific disenchantment I was currently suffering from.

So, when I thought I'd adequately expressed my remorse at the loss of one Springer Spaniel and two women, I sighed, exhausted, and climbed out of the driver's seat. Let Anne drive for a while, I thought. Let her do whatever it is she does when people reduce their sad lives to fifteen minutes.

I think Anne may have said some good things. Unfortunately, I wasn't really concentrating on what she was saying. I just let the cool mountain stream of her voice trickle down over the rocks in my head. Anne talked for about ten minutes, all of it delivered in a seductively soothing half-whisper. When I sensed she was wrapping it up, I tried to sound like I'd been paying attention.

"Yes," I said. "Yes. I hadn't thought of that. That makes a lot of sense."

There, I thought. Cured. Praise be. Now let's move on to the next phase of this relationship. The dating game part.

"There are some good books out there," Anne said.

"Books?"

"Books that I think could help you."

"You think . . . you think I still need help?" The more I stammered, the more I sounded like someone who did indeed need help.

"I think you'd find them of real value to you." As she began to rattle off the names of some books, I fumbled in my desk for a pencil. I wrote down some of the titles. *Living, Loving, Giving, Sharing, and Seeing What Happens. Looking In on Your Outlook. Move Over, I'm Motivated.* Then I had to make a pact with her, similar to the one she'd made with the last caller, in which I promised I'd call her back. I hated the way it was all turning out, with me as her patient or something, though I relished the idea of a built-in guarantee that I'd have to call her again.

"Call me when you've taken a look at some of those books," she said.

"But you *do* want me to call."

"Yes. When you've taken a look at the books."

"All the books?"

"No. Just get yourself started. Go to a bookstore and see what's out there."

"Is there anything else we could do?" I wanted to make it sound somewhat suggestive, rekindle the idea of going out somewhere together, but I guess it sounded pathetic, like I needed all the help I could get.

"Mister Takahashi would say 'try a little meditation.'"

"Mister Takahashi?"

"He's the priest who runs the Zen temple here. He also does all the gardening. You've probably seen him edging?"

"No."

I told Anne I'd already considered meditation. But when you're raised a Catholic boy you get used to the swift expediency of absolution. Meditation takes time and patience. Confession takes only a few uncomfortable minutes, in and out and you're clean again, like a car wash.

"I'll try the books," I said. "Thanks."

"Good," she said enthusiastically. I prided myself on my ability to sound sincere when I needed to. She confirmed again that I'd call back. This time it didn't feel so much comforting as it did precautionary. I knew it was standard procedure, but it made me feel as if I was on the ledge of a tall building waiting for the nets to arrive. I needed to sound more assertive. It was time for Plan B.

"One other thing," I said. "You were telling me you liked Bergman films. You said you might come if I showed *Wild Strawberries*."

"Yes."

"Well, I'm putting together a film night. A film festival. I'm planning to screen *Wild Strawberries* and have Q and A with one of the actors from the film. And maybe some cheese. And schnapps. I don't have all the details worked out yet. But it's coming together."

"That sounds lovely," she said. "It sounds like a good way to get yourself motivated."

"Yes, that's a good thing, I'm sure. Motivation couldn't hurt me, I'm sure. But I'm also wondering about your motivation. Would you be motivated? I mean, would that motivate you to come if I had a night like that?"

"It sounds like a wonderful evening."

"I'm sorry, I just want to be sure, is that something like 'yes'? You know, like if I asked you if I should floss, you'd just say 'yes', unequivocally. I was looking for more of a direct answer like that."

"Malcolm," she said, "we're not supposed to date people we talk to on the phone."

"Let's get off the phone then," I said. "I don't like the phone much anyway."

She laughed. "I don't know about this. You seem like a very nice person. But this is kind of awkward, you calling here with your problems."

"I don't want to call with my problems. I just want to talk to you."

"But if you have problems, you should be able to call here. That's what we're here for."

"So . . . you don't want me to call anymore?"

"No . . . I would like you to call back."

"To talk about self-help books?"

"Yes. But also, if you have this film night, let me know."

When I hung up the phone I sat very still for a few minutes. I felt as if I'd just had a big meal and needed to digest it.

Outside the office door I heard an upsurge in the music on the soundtrack, suggesting the movie might be coming to an end. I came out of my office and went into the theater. Ginny saw the light stream in when I opened the door and got up quickly. She appeared to be very glad to be relieved of her as-signment. I imagined it must have felt quite oppressive for her. Absorbing a foreign film could be arduous enough. Sitting down and watching the last part of it without a clue to the plot must have been sheer torture. I felt like I had to make it up to her. Do something nice. But it had to be something that couldn't be misinterpreted as a sexual advance. Money. All teenagers understood money. I fished into my trouser pocket and pulled out a wad of bills. I peeled a five off the top and handed it to her.

"What's this for?"

"It's for watching the film."

She held the bill furtively between her thumb and forefinger. Like it was dirty and by taking it she might be condoning something awful I'd done in my office.

"I had to make a phone call," I said.

It sounded lame but she nodded and kept the five.

chapter five

That night, during another abbreviated session of sleep, I dreamed of a winged yellow army. More specifically, of an all-out mass-mobilization and assault by the yellow jackets, orchestrated by one particularly mean-spirited, highly organized, dictatorial leader, with three armbands on the left flank of his legs.

I'd fallen asleep on my arm, and, thinking that the fuzzy sensation was a formation of hungry insects, I'd smacked my limb repeatedly against the wall next to my sleeper sofa, yelling my fool head off. A couple of angry thumps from Missus Calabrone's broom handle on her ceiling (my floor) set me right again. Once I woke up, the heat in my apartment kept me from falling asleep again. It remained hot as a chicken rotisserie all night and there was no logical reason to believe it would cool off when the sun came up. A cold shower and several mugs of black coffee the next morning failed to slap me awake.

I'd decided to take Anne's advice and see if I could find a self-help book that would address my problem. But what was my problem? Sleep deprivation? Lack of motivation? Perhaps lack of motivation caused by sleep deprivation. Perhaps sleep deprivation caused by yellow jackets and the heat. Clearly, I needed a wide range of self-help books, so my best bet was one of those super-sized, mega-bookstores like Bandini's Book-a-Rama.

By the time I'd dragged myself to Bandini's that afternoon in the hot July sun, it seemed a journey akin to T.E. Lawrence's trek across the Arabian desert. And he had a hood. The bookstore loomed over me, three stories tall, a great mirage of amber bricks. When I entered, I was momentarily refreshed by a blast of cold air from the air conditioning system, then I felt my body dragging again, anticipating the task of hunting down self-help books. Bandini's had more aisles than the average library and the books were crammed into overstuffed, sagging shelves and spilled out onto display tables. Some books were even stacked on tables outside the doorway. Ostensibly reduced in price, the real message seemed to be: We have too many books. Just take some.

I wasn't a frequent customer at Bandini's because I didn't read much popular fiction. I suffered from reader's amnesia. I leafed through the text at a rapid pace, my finger registering every syllable as I made a beeline for the bottom of the page. A moment later I couldn't tell you what I'd read. I had dozens of books at home on my shelves that I'm fairly certain I enjoyed, but whose contents remained a complete mystery to me. Mostly I bought film quarterlies and magazines. They required a lower level of attention and the text was broken up with pictures.

I'd never purchased a self-help book. I didn't know whether they were subheaded under psychology or whether they were located near the Martha Stewart type that told you how to turn doors into coffee tables. As ironic as it seemed, I'd have to *ask* for self-help.

I approached the man at the front counter. He was thin, wore silver wire-rimmed glasses and had long hair in a ponytail. He smelled like a library and had his nose buried in a copy of *Being and Nothingness.*

"Where can I find self-help?" I said, still very aware of the contradictory nature of the question.

The man at the counter cast his eyes upward and his ponytail whipped to the left, towards the stairs.

"Second floor?"

He rolled his eyes up further into his head.

"Third floor?"

He nodded.

A captivatingly rude way of communicating, I thought. Eyes at ground level meant stay on the ground floor, slightly raised eyebrows meant the second floor and eyes heavenward meant the third floor. If his eyes disappeared entirely, I guess it meant head for the roof.

The old building that housed Bandini's Books had originally been Frank's Finer Fish Warehouse. The water-weathered oak floors were badly stained and buckled and they creaked loudly when you stepped on them, far more than I thought should be acceptable in the quiet, studious confines of a book shop. I self-consciously creaked my way across the store to the stairwell. I saw a long flight of narrow stairs and I multiplied what I saw by three. We can do this, I told my tired body. We won't be able to do anything else afterward, but we can do this. When I was done, they'd have to airlift my body to a local hospital. The paramedics would speak to the ponytailed gentleman at the front desk and he would roll his eyes up into his head so the helicopter would know where to land.

I put one foot in front of the other and trudged up to the third floor. Mine was not the first flag on the bookstore's summit, however. Others had come before me. Around the time I was plodding up the landing to the second floor, I'd begun to hear the laughter and hushed whisper of children. I imagined the way they would have bounded up the stairs, taking them two at a time, and I hated them for it. They sounded like an orderly group of children. They laughed in unison. Then I heard an adult voice in the midst of it all and realized that the third floor also housed the children's book section and I'd arrived during story time.

Not wanting to interrupt, I avoided the far aisle of the store where the gathering was taking place and ducked into the aisle next to it. I looked around and sighed. I was surrounded by a mind-boggling array of books from Doctor A to Doctor Z and there were no apparent guidelines explaining how the books had been arranged on the shelves. Maybe they hadn't been arranged at all; just stuffed in wherever possible as they arrived at the store.

I decided to enlist the help of someone who looked like he needed more self-help than I did. A man was sitting on a wooden bench in the middle of the aisle, oblivious to me and everything around him, pulling thoughtfully on his lip, tapping staccato-like with his foot and reading a paperback whose title was buried in his lap.

"Is this the entire self-help section?" I asked.

His head popped out of his book.

"Yes," he said curtly. Suddenly aware of himself, he immediately stopped pulling on his lip and tapping his foot. He hid the title of the book from me, re-shelved it when my back was turned and was gone a moment later. I'd probably set back whatever self-help he was helping himself with, by several years. I sighed and took up his space on the bench. It was still warm, which made me a little uncomfortable, but I stayed seated. I scanned the titles on the rows of books before me but nothing jumped out at me. There were just too many books. What a cruel trick, I thought, to put so many selections in the path of people who had enough trouble making decisions in life.

To escape the overwhelming array before me, I began to tune out of the self-help section and tune in to the story being told in the children's aisle next door. The reader was a woman with a pleasant, measured voice and she was reading a book from the *Tucker the Tuckered-Out Bear* series. When I was a child, my mother had read me *Tucker the Tuckered-Out Bear Finds His Nightcap*, and *Tucker the Tuckered-Out Bear Makes Tuckered-Out Friends*.

Tucker was a pint-sized black bear from North Dakota who wore a porkpie hat, red sneakers and spectacles. He'd earned his name by being one of the few bears who failed to understand and adhere to the rules of hibernation. He'd simply stayed up throughout the winter months, fearing he'd miss out on all manner of amazing adventures if he went to sleep. As a result he spent most of the winter without his bear friends and family, walking around in a semi-stupor. Thus, most of Tucker's amazing adventures were amazing in that one never knew if Tucker might, at any moment, no matter how dangerous, tucker out and suddenly nod off. And it was the threat of these unpredictable attacks of narcolepsy that made the books so entertaining. And a nightly rendering by a parent could usually convince a child of the importance of bedtime.

In the installment being read aloud at the bookstore, one I was unfamiliar with, Tucker was crossing a narrow log bridge over a deep ravine. The task would have been a cakewalk for any normal bear, but Tucker, well, he might just choose this moment to tucker out. And sure enough, as the torrent of water below went whoosh whoosh whoosh and the log began to go creak creak creak, Tucker felt his eyelids becoming oh so heavy. And about the same time Tucker nodded off, I guess I must have, too.

When I woke up, the sound of children was gone. Story time was over. My arms felt sore and I rubbed them. Then I noticed a woman standing in the aisle browsing the alcohol/recovery section. She noticed me rousing myself, shaking out my limbs like, well, like a bear.

"I fell asleep," I said.

"That's cool," she said, and returned to her browsing.

As the fog in my head lifted and I could see her more clearly, I noticed she was sort of attractive in an odd, eclectic kind of way. She had a pale, yet clear, complexion. Her smear of ruby lipstick and dark crescents under her eyes jumped out of her face and demanded attention. She was on the chunky side, but the extras were all in places I didn't mind so much—hips, buttocks and breasts. Her hair was black and stringy, curling down around her face in an unstylish manner, but it was also kind of exotic-looking. Like an untamed woman from some jungle who hasn't been brought into the twentieth century by civilization or hair stylists. I wrestled for a few moments with these contradictory feelings of revulsion and lust. Then I got up.

"My arms are sore, " I said, still rubbing them.

"I'd imagine so," she said. "You were hugging that bench like your life depended on it."

I remembered Tucker and wondered if he'd managed to complete his journey over the bridge unscathed. No doubt he had, but I made a mental note to discreetly visit the children's section some time and find out for sure.

"I don't usually fall asleep in public," I said.

"You sleep when you gotta," she said. She didn't turn around. Then she pulled a book off the shelf and waved it in my direction.

"Read this one?"

She flashed it by my face pretty fast, but I was fairly certain I hadn't read it. It was *I Think You've Had Enough* or something.

"No," I said. Suddenly I realized I must have appeared like some Bowery bum who'd found a temporary resting place before scrounging up his paper bag of red wine. "I don't have a drinking problem," I said.

"Whatever," she said.

"Actually," I said, clearing my throat, "actually, I'm not getting all the sleep I should." I didn't mention the yellow jackets. I didn't know her well enough. And I was afraid she might interpret it as some sort of *Lost Weekend*-delusional-seeing-insects-everywhere-I-go kind of thing.

"Your circadian rhythms are probably screwed up," she said.

"I'm sorry," I said. "My what?"

"Circadian rhythms. Your patterns of day and night. You know, your twenty-four hour cycles."

"Oh," I said. I wasn't sure I really understood, but this was the first person I'd talked to about my lack of sleep who actually had some sort of complex theory about it, so instead of walking away, as I normally would have in this situation, I decided to continue to talk to her.

"Are you a student?" I asked. Based on her appearance I'd worked my way down the career ladder of possibilities from biologist to science major to the person who reads *Science Digest* in the dentist's office. I gave her the benefit of the doubt and moved her up a notch.

"No," she said. "I'm in a band. So I know about rhythms getting screwed up."

"Really? In a band? What do you play?"

"I play a little guitar, I know a few chords. But I'm mainly a singer. I do post-punk ballads and dirges."

"Okay," I said. "I'm not sure exactly what that would sound like, but . . ."

"You should check it out, then."

She turned around and opened a bag that I guessed was her purse, but looked more like a feed bag for some farm animal. Inside I saw a sheaf of papers about two inches thick. She plucked one sheet from the middle of the pile and handed it to me. I held the paper up to my face and blinked at it. It was a black-and-white mimeo sheet, crudely designed with a black ink drawing depicting the silhouette of a man who appeared to be biting into a microphone. Beneath this disturbing picture were splashy black letters which said:

> 3-D CLUB
> DRINK/DANCE/DEBAUCHERY
> THREE DOLLAR DONATION

and below that, in letters no less bold:

> DREAM RESEARCH
> SOILED SHEETS
> CIRCADIAN RHYTHM SECTION

I assumed it was a roster of musical groups. I pointed to the last name on the list.

"Is this you? Your group, I mean. 'Circadian Rhythm Section'?"

"Yep. That's us. We're on right after Soiled Sheets."

I knew enough about music to know that the headliner was usually saved for last but I wasn't sure what kind of distinction it was to follow a group named Soiled Sheets, and I voiced my concern.

"Is that good? Coming on after Soiled Sheets?"

She shrugged. "I guess so. Anyway, that's how I know about circadian rhythms. Kevin says ours are all screwed up because of the weird hours we keep playing these gigs."

"Kevin?"

"Our drummer. He started the group after he broke off from Raw Dogs. Do you know Raw Dogs? They had an indie album out a few years back. Got major college airplay. Anyway, he's pretty brilliant. Classically trained."

"Classically? Meaning . . . ?"

"Classical. You know Bach. Mozart, Beethoven. He plays all that shit."

"On drums?"

"No. On piano. I can sing classical. Sometimes Kevin plays for me when I sing classical."

"I see."

I pretended to study the sheet again while she continued to pull books off the shelves. She'd browse them in a cursory fashion and put them back on the shelf.

"It's a lot of books, isn't it?" I said.

She nodded, continued her search for a book that fit her discerning criteria of how an alcoholic should recover, and finally decided on *I Think You've Had Enough*. She waved it at me again.

"I'm getting this for Mister P.C., our bass player."

"Oh. I thought maybe you . . ."

"Me? No, I don't touch the hard stuff. Maybe a beer now and then. I try to stay away from that stuff. I'm pretty much a vegetarian. Except some nights all you can find open is a burger joint and you're starving, you know?"

"Yes," I said. "Life throws us a lot of curves. I guess you've got to roll with the punches." I hoped she wouldn't notice that I'd mixed a few sports metaphors.

"No, Mister P.C. is the one with the problem," she continued. "He's falling behind the beat."

"I'm sorry to hear that. What do you do when that happens?"

"Our music is not really beat driven, so it's not a huge problem. With dirges and ballads, though, you have to be able to keep time. He keeps hitting his chin on the cowbell when he nods off."

"I'm sorry," I said again. I'd thought life couldn't be worse, but maybe I was wrong.

"You don't look like you have a problem with drinking," she said. "You just look like you have a problem with sleeping."

"You got that right." I pushed my hair out of my face. "I look pretty bad, I know."

"No, you don't look bad. You're kind of a nice-looking tired guy." She gave the book she was holding another once-over. "This looks like a good book for Mister P.C. It's got large print."

She opened her feed bag purse again and slipped the book snugly next to her flyers. She didn't make any attempt to cover up her actions, executing the theft with the calm of a person spreading marmalade on a scone. She looked at me directly for the first time.

"So are you going to come see me?"

My mind was on other things. Her arrest, arraignment and imprisonment. I looked over her shoulder to see if I could spot a book on compulsive behavior. In retrospect, however, I think I probably needed it more than she did, because I suddenly found myself saying:

"Sure. I'd like to see you. What time do you go on?"

"It varies," she said. "If the Sheets do an encore then we usually don't go on until after midnight. I don't get out of there some nights until two or three in the morning. Sometimes later."

Now here's a gal who knows how to stay up late, I thought. While the rest of the people in the world were rubbing their knuckles into their bloodshot eyes and turning over on their sides to go to sleep, these doughnut shop Draculas were just getting revved up. If my body was being banished to the grave-yard shift, then maybe I needed to make new friends that fit my nocturnal schedule. Perhaps I should let go of my old acquaintances—the milkman, the newspaper boy and the mailman. My new friends would be night owls—musicians, insomniacs and convenience store managers.

"I'll try to make it," I said. I didn't know if I meant it, but I said it.

"Good," she said, and she sounded as though she meant it. It wasn't like a date, but it was a member of the opposite sex inviting me to something. Could I really afford to be picky about who she was or what it was she wanted me to attend? There was a serpentine smile on her face and a glint in her eyes that said: I am mischief, come play with me. I wasn't sure if I was ready to play with mischief. I wasn't even sure if I could afford to associate with mischief.

I thought about Anne again for a moment. Anne was great and all. Nice personality. Great voice. But I was probably kidding myself with Anne. And Anne's hours were from eight until midnight. This singer would be around at two or three in the morning when I really needed someone. And this woman knew something about circadian rhythms. Anne was a trained hot line volunteer and she never mentioned circadian rhythms. If the hot line knew a thing or two about circadian rhythms, they'd know enough to be open after midnight just in case someone's rhythms got screwed up.

She turned away and I watched her disappear from the third floor, creaking down the stairs with the stolen book in her bag. I creaked after her in stealthful pursuit, peering around corners, skulking around shelves. As I reached the first floor landing I stopped and crouched down by the stair railing. I gripped the bars and stared through them balefully, like a gorilla whose mate has been removed from his cage.

I was still hunched in this position when she spotted me and waved before going out the front door, attracting the attention of shoppers who stopped and pointed at the man crouching in the stairwell.

Feeling too foolish to remain in the store, I straightened up and made for the door with a slow purposeful stride. At least I could attempt an exit with a bit of class. I ignored the stares and pushed my way through the double glass doors with a flourish. My stylish exit had cost me precious time, however. The singer from the Circadian Rhythm Section was gone. I wandered up and down the block for a few minutes, hoping she was still shoplifting in the immediate area. But the late afternoon sun was burning a brain-numbing hole in my head. I looked at the digital display above the downtown bank. Ninety-two degrees. Four minutes after five o'clock. The afternoon had escaped me in a most unproductive way. I hadn't acquired any self-help books and I'd been caught napping on a public bench. People who snoozed on public benches weren't exactly the kind of people I wanted to emulate. I folded up the flyer from the 3-D Club, stuffed it in my front pocket and headed for the Arcadia Filmhaus. Maybe I'll go, I thought. If I'm awake.

chapter six

Whenever I felt myself nearing a precipice, needing a little push off the edge, I called my friend, Bix. I did most things alone, assuming I was too eclectic or self-conscious to sustain a friendship with anyone. But every so often, mostly when I needed someone to share in and validate a negative experience, like going to a wake, or renewing my driver's license, I called Bix.

I'd met Bix in college. He was majoring in Acting and I was majoring in Film with a minor in Unmotivated. Bix sat behind me in a film appreciation course. His full name was Artie Beiderbecke. I mentioned to him one day that his last name was the same as someone I'd long admired, the legendary 1920s jazz trumpeter, Leon "Bix" Beiderbecke. I inquired if perhaps there was any relation, any shared blood line. Artie had never heard of Bix Beiderbecke, didn't listen to music from the 1920s and didn't think he was in any way related. But he liked the nickname "Bix," much more than the name "Artie." Our friendship developed then, mostly because he enjoyed the new moniker I'd given him. It wasn't the strongest basis for a friendship, but somehow it survived.

Once I'd made this obscure connection with him, Bix made it a point to talk to me in class. Each time the lights came up after a film, Bix would invariably tap me on the shoulder and ask, "Well Mal, what'd you think of it?"

Whenever I expressed something vague like, "I felt very tense when Dennis Hopper was pointing at that one guy," he'd fire back "Do you know *why* you felt that way?" And before I could answer he'd proceed to tell me exactly how the actor had elicited the response from me.

"The reason you felt tense is because Hopper's pointing at the guy with his index *and* middle finger. Not just his index finger. Both fingers. Like the double barrel of a shotgun." And here Bix would demonstrate, aiming his sawed-off fingers right between my eyes. "Bang!" and his fingers would jerk up like the aftershock of a powerful discharge.

Bix tried to convince me that I might enjoy acting, because I was interested in film. Since I had no clear idea about my future, I tended to become docile and accept other people's simplistic conclusions about the direction of my life. So when the drama department posted a notice indicating they were looking for actors to perform in a couple of one-act plays, I went with Bix to an audition.

Bix was very good, while I gave a sheepish, mumbling audition. Much to my surprise, I was cast in a prominent role in one of the plays, while Bix was cast prominently in the other. My role was that of a sheepish, mumbling hotel clerk and I became so assured of my proficiency that I was convinced I was about to become the new Brando of my generation. They would dedicate a wing of the college to me. New Brando Wing.

Nine weeks later the curtain went up on the two plays, mine first, followed by Bix's. The next day the plays were reviewed, in chronological order, by the college paper, where they were described as ". . . a night of one-acts—from wooden to won-derful." The critic was particularly vexed by the sheepish mum-bling I was doing, which I had come to regard as my forte. I posted my wooden self back into the safe soil of cinema and Bix pursued his acting career.

Years later, when Bix found out I was running a movie the-ater, he started showing up at the Arcadia Filmhaus. He wasn't crazy about films with subtitles. He claimed they detracted from the furrowed brows, wry smiles and nose twitches, which he believed were loaded with heavy, method-actor meaning. But I let him watch films for nothing, so he came in on a semi-regu-lar basis, when he wasn't auditioning or doing a show.

Bix was the kind of actor who believed that all life experi-ences provided grist for the actor's mill. There was no event that was too trivial or absurd. Everything could be filed away for future use. This gave him the green light to engage in all manner of spontaneous and indulgent behavior. It could all be chalked up, in Bix's philosophy, to artistic growth.

Once, after a binge in a local micro brewery, Bix had drunk-enly confided to me: "You never know when a casting director will ask you to portray a man who's had eleven beers."

But Bix was also intelligent and sensible. He hungered for experience, but once he'd experienced something unpleasant he wasn't prone to repeating it. This is where Bix could be my ally. Whenever I was about to do something I thought I might regret, I'd drag Bix along. He'd accompany me, we'd have a terrible time and when I felt the urge to do it again I'd call Bix and he'd remind me of how terrible a time I'd had and then I wouldn't do it again. The only danger was that there was no experience that could be recognized beforehand as undesirable.

With Bix you had to burn your fingers before you knew not to play with fire. But it was Bix I called when I decided to go see the post-punk dirge singer at the 3-D Club that weekend.

I'd made up my mind that evening at the Arcadia Filmhaus after my return from the bookstore. When I arrived, Ginny was already there, parked behind the candy counter squeezing an Italian beef sandwich between her sculptured nails. I was still unhappy about the unproductive experience I'd had at the bookstore and thought perhaps I could salvage a bit of the day by making some headway in bridging the gulf between Ginny and myself. I wasn't really that much older than she and I figured there must be some way for us to work together without fear of eye contact. I'd already tried to bribe her with money, so I went down a notch on the totem pole of adolescent idolatry and came up with the next most sacred thing in the life of a teenager. Music. Maybe she'd be impressed that I'd met and had a conversation with a real live post-punk dirge singer.

As I approached the candy counter Ginny saw me and started rattling.

"I just got here a few minutes ago and I didn't start making the popcorn because you said never make it before six-thirty . . ."

"I know. That's fine," I said. She'd tossed my thoughts into the spin cycle, so I took a moment to regroup, then reached into my pocket and pulled out the flyer from the 3-D Club.

"Ever heard of this group?" I handed her the flyer and pointed to the third name on the bill. Since I'd heard the word "circadian" for only the first time that afternoon, I began to pronounce it for her, but she beat me to the punch.

"Circadian Rhythm Section."

"You've heard of them?"

"They play post-punk ballads and dirges." She offered the information so readily I imagined her up the night before preparing for my question with post-punk flash cards.

"So you're familiar with their music?"

"Not really. They're from around here. They were on 'Wake Up, It's Morning' a few weeks ago. I think their music is kind of creepy."

"Ever gone to see them perform?"

She wrinkled her nose and made a face as though she'd just bitten into something sour.

"No. They're strictly twenty-one and over."

"Oh. I didn't know that."

Suddenly I wished I was sixteen again. Being young had its restrictions, but it also kept you out of places you probably didn't want to be anyway.

Ginny had been fielding my questions like someone in a line-up and looked as if she wanted to be somewhere else. I wasn't gaining any ground with her and telling her I'd met the lead singer of the Circadian Rhythm Section wasn't going to get me in any tighter. I took the flyer back.

"Someone handed this to me in a bookstore," I said.

"And you took it?" she asked, incredulously.

I was amazed how guilty a sixteen-year-old girl could make me feel. I'd taken that creepy flyer from that creepy person who played creepy music. What was my problem?

But later that night, while the film was rolling, I pulled out the flyer and studied it again. Maybe I need someone to talk me out of this, I thought. And a short while later I was again requesting Ginny to watch the film while I made a phone call. She expelled a lot of air in a great juvenile sigh, but she did as I asked.

I went into my office with the idea that I was going to call Bix. But when I started dialing, I dialed D-I-A-L-O-G-U.

"Dialogue, this is Anne, how may I help you?"

As usual, just her voice was a comfort, like a gentle hand had begun to massage my temples. I felt like I wanted to purr and roll over and have her scratch my belly. But instead I reverted to my standard tentative patter.

"Hello . . . it's Malcolm."

"Malcolm?"

A mantra began in my head as the seconds ticked by. Malcolm. Malcolm. Malcolm.

"Malcolm . . . yes! Hello. I didn't expect to hear from you so soon."

"I didn't expect to call so soon. But I was in the bookstore today. I spent all afternoon there."

"That's wonderful!" she said. "Which books did you get?"

"I didn't get any books, actually, " I said. "Mostly I slept. I slept on a bench."

"In the bookstore?"

"Yes."

"That's probably not a good thing."

"I slept okay. A little fitfully. I dreamed I was falling off a log."

"Dreams can tell you a lot about yourself, Malcolm."

"I know not to walk on logs," I said.

"There are some wonderful books about dreams out there. *Dream It and You Are It, Slumbernetics. . . .*"

"I can't go back to the bookstore for a while," I said. "It takes too much out of me. I was hoping we could forget about sleep and problems and all that and maybe have a nice normal chat. Maybe get some coffee. Or pie. Pie and coffee, I guess, is what I'm suggesting. What do you think? You think maybe we could swing that?"

"I thought we talked about this," she said. "This is a hotline. You can't call here for dates." She wasn't mean about it. It was a slap on the wrist, and a very light one at that.

"I know. I know that. But I don't have your home phone number. Otherwise I would have called you there. Wherever *there* is. That's why I called here."

"I thought you had some things you wanted to work out. I thought that's why you called the hotline."

"I know. And I don't want to discount the work we've done. But actually I know I'd feel a whole lot better if you'd have some coffee with me. Or pie. Pie or coffee, pie and coffee, it makes no difference to me."

She hesitated. That could be good and it could be bad, I thought.

"I told you, Malcolm, we really aren't supposed to do anything like that," she said. "With callers, I mean." It was bad. Unless she followed with a "but." A "but" would open up a world of possibilities. I waited a moment. The "but" didn't come.

"I understand," I said. "Look, why don't we pretend I didn't call. Not this time, I mean the first time. After all, my problems aren't so bad, are they? Failed relationships, insomnia. Yellow jackets in the wall. I'm sure you've heard worse. My problems are probably about a five. On a scale of one to ten, I'm saying. Ten being the worst, of course. Ten being people who have lost all hope. That's not me. I'd say I'm a good five steps away from losing hope. I think, as problems go, I have just the right amount.

Medium. Medium depression. Medium problems, I'd say. Medium across the board."

I rattled on like this, trying to sound like I needed her, but not desperately or psychotically so. It was a difficult balance.

"I don't know," Anne said.

"The thing is, you'd really be helping me out, because if we don't get together I'm probably going to do something I'll regret."

"My God," she said.

"Oh no, nothing desperate," I said. "Just something that might become unpleasant." I wasn't about to talk to Anne specifically about the post-punk dirge singer and my inexplicable desire to see her, so I dodged into a bunker of half-truths.

"There's a club in the city," I said. "The 3-D Club. A friend of mine wants me to go with him to see some girl singer. Normally I wouldn't go to a place like the 3-D Club, but this guy is a friend of mine and he wants me to go, so I'm thinking maybe I should."

People in the helping professions treat the word "should" like the plague because they detest the guilt feelings that usually accompany it. Instead they use soft, happy phrases like "be good to yourself" and "treat yourself better." All of which mean, *you should*, you idiot. Anne used the word "should" as an opening to jump back into her role as telephone therapist.

"Don't do something because you think you should. Do it because you want to do it. Do you want to go to this club?"

"I'm not sure," I said. "I've never been there. It might be a bad thing."

"Experiencing a bad thing doesn't make you a bad person," she said. Then she shoveled on top of that some other buffered phrases like "finding out for yourself can be rewarding" and "you'll never know unless you try." It was this last phrase that made me think of Bix. I wondered if Bix and Anne had cards at the same in-crowd library somewhere. Anyway, Anne wasn't going to give me the kind of lecturing, motherly advice I wanted; something along the lines of, "You can't go into the city at night. It's dark and dangerous and dirty and there's major streets you have to cross."

So while Anne was giving me some more obligatory, supportive pearls, I started rummaging through my wallet for Bix's phone number.

"Anything else on your mind tonight, Malcolm?"

"Yes," I said. "Ever heard of circadian rhythms?"

"You mean the twenty-four hour cycles of night and day?"

It was beginning to sink in. It was me. I was the one from another planet. I'd fallen from space and been dropped on my head on a part of the earth where post-punk ballads and circadian rhythms are common topics around the dinner table. I'd go to the 3-D Club and there would be my mother, belting out post-punk dirges while my father accompanied her on the electric concertina. The usual. The norm.

"Thanks for your help," I said. "I'll talk to you later, I guess."

"Wait a minute," Anne said. "Have you thought any more about your film festival?"

"As a matter of fact, I have," I said. "Would you still be interested?"

"When is it?"

"When is it? When would you like it to be?"

Anne sighed in mock scorn. "I hope you're not planning this around me. I'd have to discourage behavior like that." It was that light slap on the wrist again. I was starting to enjoy it.

"I'm not planning it around you, exactly, I'm just conducting an informal poll. I'm polling people who might be interested."

"How many people have you talked to?"

"How many? Well . . . just you. So far."

"Not much of a poll, is it, Malcolm?"

"Well, it's an informal poll. The size is what makes it informal."

"Call back again," Anne said. It sounded sincere, but I couldn't tell if the sincerity was some encouragement to continue to try and woo her or some standard Dialogue lip service. She never actually told me she wouldn't have pie and coffee with me, but it seemed clear she was still steering me towards an off-ramp. It didn't feel good, but it sort of gave me a little more closure with Anne. She'd never go for me. Post-punk dirge singers. That's the direction I was going.

I put the phone down on the receiver, tapped it a few times with my finger then picked it up again and called Bix. Pinning Bix down to spend an evening together was a whole other kettle of fish. Bix was a long-standing member of the call-you-back-in-ten-minutes school of phone etiquette. During this time he claimed the need to find and check his appointment book to avoid any overlaps in his schedule. I'd never seen Bix's appointment book. I sometimes looked around his apartment trying to see if it actually existed. I kind of doubted it. It was never at hand when I called, leading me to believe he actually used the ten-minute reprieve to consider whether the event was worth his while, or more interesting, at least, than his current plans.

This presented a challenge to me, but I had the feeling the 3-D Club was just the kind of thing Bix would be interested in.

Before I could enter the realm of Bix's alleged appointment book, however, I had to get past his answering machine. Bix never picked up his phone until he knew who was calling and why. If Bix didn't pick up, there was always the possibility that he wasn't there, since he did lead an active social life. But I also had to accept that I might be suffering a personal rejection as he listened in. I chose my words carefully.

"Bix? It's Malcolm. Listen, Bix, there's something pretty strange going on in the city at a place called the 3-D Club. Mayhem with a touch of dance music, I think. I'm going to check it out and I thought maybe you'd want to come along."

I heard his machine click off as he picked up the phone. "Mal? What's up, Mal?"

Bix sounded enthusiastic. I'd stroked those frantic nerve ends of his experience-hungry brain.

"I was at Bandini's Bookshop today and I was handed this really bizarre flyer from the 3-D Club."

"So what kind of place is this? Is it really nuts, or what?"

"I don't know. I imagine it's a pretty wild scene. People screaming. People jumping around. Post-punk ballads and dirges."

"Oh yeah. I saw something about that on 'Wake Up, It's Morning.'"

I made a mental note to try to catch this trendy morning show so that I could carry on some trendy conversations in the future.

"So I'm going to check it out," I said, trying to make it sound like a happening.

"When?"

I paused. "Tomorrow night?"

"Thursday?" He paused. "I'll tell you what, Mal. Let me call you back in ten minutes."

I hung up and waited. I didn't leave my office. When Bix said ten minutes, he meant it. And if I wasn't there to take the return call, all bets were off. Bix called back ten minutes later and told me he was attending a "body spinning seminar" at the Holiday Inn on Thursday night. I wondered how something like that could have slipped his mind, but he talked about it with an enthusiasm that sounded genuine.

"It should be very exciting," he said. "Apparently you spin until you feel like you're going to pass out. Then when your resources are down, you tune into a deeper level of yourself. You spin, you fall down and tune in."

"Are you going to do this?" I asked.

"No, no," he said. "I can't even tie my shoes without some lower back pain. But at least I can study them. It's invaluable for an actor. Watch their faces. See what makes people tick. See what kind of expression a person has when he's been spinning."

I was prepared with a back-up plan. If Bix was semi-interested in going to the 3-D Club, and I suspected he was, I could suggest an alternate night. Backed into a corner with his alleged appointment book in hand, Bix sometimes caved in.

"What about Friday?" I said.

"Friday?" He paused again. A bit longer this time. I could almost hear him weighing the possibilities in his mind. *Friday? Wasn't that the opening night of the midget mime fest? Can't make it. Invaluable for an actor.* But Bix drew a blank for Friday and relented.

"Okay, Mal. Friday night. What time?"

"Late. Come by here after the theater closes. Around eleven-thirty."

"See you Friday, Mal."

I hung up the phone before he had a chance to change his mind. I was a little disappointed that I'd been held up a day because of the contortionist convention. I wanted to get this business with the 3-D Club and the post-punk dirge singer out of my system. Pronto.

chapter seven

Friday arrived none too soon. Around eleven-fifteen *High and Low* flickered its last and I turned on the house lights. I watched eight people silently file out. When they were all gone I locked the doors and swept up the stray popcorn, Milk Duds and Raisinettes that had escaped from boxes and scurried like ferrets down towards the front of the theater.

Cleaning up was normally part of Ginny's job, but I let her go early, still trying to curry favor with her. I'd also become concerned about her contact with the patrons. I'd received a few pointed complaints about her attitude from the theatergoers who filled out the little three-by-five comment cards I left in the lobby. I'd put the cards out to solicit ideas for future films, most of which I ignored, but instead I was receiving comments that indicated Ginny was giving people the third degree at the candy counter.

"Why would you see a movie like this?" she was alleged to have demanded of one of the patrons. Or she'd recognize a return customer and shake her head in disbelief. "You're going to see it again?" she was reported to have asked as she pumped butter on his popcorn, clucking her tongue in a "tsk" that carries so much more weight from a teenager.

So when the last reel was rolling on Friday night I told Ginny she could go home. Then I added, in the friendliest tone I could muster: "Is everything going okay down here? Are you getting along with the customers?"

"Tsk," she said, dropping me over the falls without a barrel. Then she grabbed her book bag and diet cola and beat it out the front door.

Normally, I didn't mind sweeping up. Manual labor made me feel like I was working at a real job. On hot summer nights like these, however, chocolate and caramel held fast to the concrete floor and green velvet seats like sticky sloths and had to be scraped off with whatever was at hand. In my current state of perpetual drowsiness, I felt like someone should be scraping *me* off the floor.

After this messy task was completed, I brewed a pot of coffee and waited for Bix. The smell of coffee perked me up a little, but only slightly. As I lost more and more sleep each night I grew increasingly anxious about the inevitable day when my heart would explode. I pictured the agonizing moment when I would clutch my chest, keel over and fall off my stool in the projection booth. I stole a cup of coffee out of the pot before it had finished dripping through and drank deeply. I was anxious to feel the caffeine massage my heart, get it going, make it pump. Remind me that it was still throbbing in my chest.

I'd made some headway in the last couple of days in connection with my ill-conceived film festival idea. I was beginning to doubt I would actually impress Anne with any of this business, but it kept my mind occupied during my down time, which I seemed to have more than most people.

I'd done some research in the library on potential lecture candidates for the film festival. Anne's foreign film of choice,

Wild Strawberries, was my jumping-off point. I was able to track down the addresses and phone numbers of most of the living and dead Swedish film personalities on my A-list. In short order, I was shot down by Bergman's people, who were a bit rude, telling me they'd never heard of my film festival even after I explained that this was the first annual festival.

So Bergman was out. Victor Sjöström was very dead. Naima Wifstrand, the actress who had played Sjöström's mother, was even more dead. Gunnar Bjornstrand, dead. Bibi Andersson, unavailable. Ingrid Thulin, unavailable and uninterested. Max Von Sydow had played a bit part as a gas station attendant and probably would have happily come to America to lecture in 1957, but these days he was starring in filmed adaptations of Stephen King novels and that put his budget way out of the question. All other actors from the film were missing, unaccounted for, or unavailable.

In what I can only describe as a quick downward spiral, I went through my A-list, then just as quickly through my B-list. I didn't have a C-list. As I went along, I tried to make the event sound more appealing. It went from film night to film festival, to first annual Arcadia Filmhaus Film Festival, but nothing drew them in. Not even the prospect of free schnapps.

I was soon reduced to asking if anyone knew *anyone* who might be connected to Bergman, even remotely. I would have been ready to settle for a real gas station attendant who'd perhaps cleaned the windshield of Bergman's Volvo in 1957 and could offer some *bon mot* surrounding the incident. I would even hype it appropriately, tabloid style. MAN WHO GAVE INGMAR BERGMAN CLEAR VISION TO LECTURE AT ARCADIA FILMHAUS FILM FESTIVAL. It was a cheap, dishonest ploy, but I was ready to go that route.

Finally, just as I was about to give it all up, one agent gave me the number of another agent who gave me the number of someone who might be available. I was racking up quite a Euro-telephone bill and was hesitant to call another dead end, but I dialed the international exchange one last time. I got an old man who spoke English but definitely had a Swedish accent.

Soren Sonderby was not in *Wild Strawberries*. But he claimed to have worked with Ingmar Bergman in the fifties. Apparently, he'd portrayed one of the villagers with the plague in *The Seventh Seal*. "The one with the cudgel," is what he told me. I made a mental note to see if I could find a videotape of the film and locate any scenes with cudgels. I imagined he played one of the scared villagers who tormented Jof at the inn or one of the scared villagers who feared the plague or one of the scared villagers who helped take the girl who had carnal knowledge with the devil and burn her at the stake.

Sonderby was quick to tell me that he was not one of the self-flagellating monks, as if to imply that having the plague was not in the same class as having the plague and beating yourself up over it. I remembered the film well, but I did not recall that the self-flagellating monks looked any worse than people who just had the plague. Maybe it was a status thing. Higher or lower billing in the credits based on how comparatively tragic you were or how much of the plague covered your body.

I had several books about Bergman and looked through them all but nowhere in any of his filmographies could I find the name Soren Sonderby. By his own admission, however, he was a small kipper in a big pond. He had no lines in the film and had done no other work with Bergman. Apart from this small uncredited role, there was nothing to distinguish him. But he was cheap, he was willing and he was Swedish. And he liked the idea of free schnapps. So I made arrangements for him to fly in for the festival.

I gave him the dates and specific directions from the airport to the theater. He was more concerned about where he would be housed during the festival. I told him it would be all right if he stayed at my place, but then I thought about Missus Calabrone and the heat and the yellow jackets in my wall. I tried to explain this to him as simply as I could, but I don't think he understood. I'm not even sure they have yellow jackets in Sweden. And even if they did, they probably aren't living in the walls of the homes there. Anyway, I think he expected to stay in a hotel.

I got out my phone book. It occurred to me that this whole thing was going to cost me more money than it would make me. If I could impress Anne it might be worth it, but there was certainly no guarantee of that. Still, I kept him on the line while I checked the rates of some very cheap motels in the area. I found one called Best Rooms for forty-four dollars a night and Quality Nook for forty-two dollars a night. I wasn't sure what other costs I'd end up incurring, like taxis or rental cars, so I went with the cheaper of the two. I felt like a skinflint, but to someone who's never been to America, and didn't speak much English, the name of the motel probably didn't sound so cheap.

"You're staying at a . . . 'Qvality Nook,'" I said, in a very poor accent. "Not far from the theater." He sounded excited.

Around eleven-thirty Bix showed up, tapping his car keys on the front door glass. I let him in and he followed me back to my office. After I'd poured out two large mugs of coffee we sat back and updated each other on our lives.

Bix had just been cast in a small theater production of a play set during the Spanish Civil War. His official role in the play was listed as "Rifle Carrier Number Two." There was only one other rifle carrier, "Rifle Carrier Number One" and Bix was quick to point out that the numbering had been arbitrary and had nothing to do with the status of the roles. Rifle Carrier Number One had no lines and had to spend most of his time standing at attention. Rifle Carrier Number Two, Bix explained to me, got to utter the word "halt" and also got to do "some good action" which consisted of throwing an adversary down a flight of stairs.

"You'd be amazed how many different ways you can interpret a simple word like 'halt,'" Bix said, and he tried out a few on me. He experimented with inflection, tone, made it a question rather than a demand. I had to admit, Bix got a lot of mileage out of one syllable. When he'd exhausted all the interpretive possibilities, he asked for my input. What did I think worked best?

"Does the person halt?" I asked.

"No. That's why I have to throw him down the stairs."

I nodded. "I don't know. They all sound pretty good to me."

Gradually the conversation turned to me. I didn't have much to tell. I told Bix about the yellow jackets in my wall. My ever-increasing lack of sleep.

"I think I'm turning into a night person," I said. "I'm certainly not getting much out of my days."

"Nothing wrong with that." He blew at the steam on his second cup of coffee. "I got into that groove for a while when I worked as a security guard. Spent a lot of time making up word games. Permutations on four-letter words. Like "band." Nab, ban, dab, bad. Time passes. You get used to it. And you get to sleep when everyone else is at work."

"Yes, but I'm not sleeping during the day, either. I'm tired all the time." I was even too tired to talk about it, but the coffee was pushing my words forward like a squirrel in a cage.

"Well, if that's the case," Bix said, leaning back in his chair and thoughtfully thumbing his chin, "technically, you're not a night person."

"What am I then?"

He gave it some serious thought for a moment. "Damned if I know, Mal."

Well, enough about me, I thought. I turned our attention to the evening's agenda. I pulled the flyer from the 3-D Club out of my pocket and handed it to Bix to whet his appetite.

"Drinks . . . dance . . . debauchery . . ." Bix reeled off the words in his best W.C. Fields imitation. If there was a sucker born every minute, I had the feeling Bix and I were about to become the latest casualties. I leaned over his shoulder and pointed at the word "circadian."

"Ever heard of this?"

"No."

Well, at least I'm not the only one, I thought.

"It has to do with the twenty-four hour cycles of sleeping and waking," I explained.

"I know that," Bix said. "I read about it in *Be Healthy* magazine. Your cycles get messed up and you don't know what you're doing anymore."

"Then you have heard of it."

"Circadian? Sure. But this group? No. Unless they were the ones I saw on 'Wake Up, It's Morning.'"

"Yes, that's probably them."

I was curious to know whether Bix had seen the post-punk dirge singer who'd tweaked the tendrils of my libido. And what had he thought of her? But I didn't mention her to Bix. I knew Bix might feel uncomfortable if he knew I was going there to meet a woman.

Meet a woman? Is that, in fact, what I was doing? All she had done was hand me a flyer in the bookstore and encourage me to come see her sing. And she'd only really become interesting to me after Anne had treated me more like a patient than a possibility. And what did I intend to do when I met up again with the post-punk dirge singer? I hadn't a clue. Anyway, I kept mute about my interest in her. If Bix recognized her in the club I'd deal with it then.

"Do you have any idea where this place is?" I asked.

Bix looked at the address on the flyer.

"It's in the city. Not the best neighborhood to be walking around in at night. Kinda rough. But there's a few coffee shops and some theaters. I auditioned down there at the Sui Generis Theater. It seats about twenty people. They did a production of *Hamlet, Prince of the Rink.*"

"Prince of the Rink?"

"New interpretation," Bix said. "Roller Tragedy."

I wondered how a man could get a really good stride going on roller skates in a place that only had twenty seats. It seemed potentially tragic for actor and audience alike.

"I didn't get cast," said Bix. "Got my face in there, though."

This was paramount in Bix's struggling actor life. Getting

his face in there. If he got his face in there enough someone, hopefully someone important, might remember it, and someday cry, "Get me that face!"

Bix's face had been reproduced on a hundred or so eight-by-ten glossy photographs—"head shots" he called them. The photos accompanied Bix everywhere. He handed them out to anyone who would take them—directors, producers, other actors. He'd even provided me with a stack of photos to distribute to "anyone who looked like they might be involved in theater." The unretouched photos remained in my office, collecting dust. No one wanted to retouch them.

Bix pointed to the stack. "Are you moving any of those photos?"

"I think some have moved," I said.

The city was about a twenty-minute trip, straight highway all the way. Bix pushed his blue Plymouth Duster along at an even sixty-five miles per hour while I fiddled with the radio dial. Bix's Duster had dents on all four sides from minor traffic accidents, none of which, he claimed, were his fault. His left rear tail light was out and his black rally stripe was peeling off the passenger side of the vehicle. It whipped steadily against the car, like a shoestring in a blender.

"It's not pretty, but it gets me where I'm going," Bix would say, stroking the dashboard as if it was a piece of fine porcelain. "And I never have to worry about it getting banged up."

If the car got us in and out of the city without breaking down in a bad neighborhood, it was fine with me. I watched the rally stripe beating the car, urging it on.

"I'm having a film festival," I said. "Well, actually just a couple of nights where I'll be showing the same film. *Wild Straw-berries*."

"How does that differ from business as usual, Mal?"

"I'm going to have cheese. And, maybe some schnapps."

"Schnapps!" Bix came alive. "Outstanding. During the movie?"

"After the movie," I clarified. "I can't have people drinking inside the theater. I probably can't have them drinking any-where inside the building, but it's just schnapps. It won't be like I'll have a full bar. And I've got a guest speaker coming in to lecture."

"No kidding? Some professor coming in with a film class?"

"No, actually this is an actor."

"An actor?" I suddenly had Bix's full attention. As he turned to me, he failed to properly negotiate a curve in the highway. The right front tire bounced against the median. "Geez, Mal. Why didn't you say so? Who'd you get? Don't tell me you got Max Von Fucking Sydow. He's worked with absolutely every-body."

"No, I didn't get Max Von Sydow," I said, anxious to re-store his name to its proper number of syllables. "But this actor was in *The Seventh Seal* and Max Von Sydow was in that. So I guess you could say he's worked with someone who's worked with absolutely everyone. His name is Soren Sonderby."

"Who?"

"Soren Sonderby. He was one of the village people."

"You mean like 'YMCA'? Those village people?"

"No, one of the villagers with the plague in *The Seventh Seal*."

"He played someone with the plague?"

"Yes."

"That's fantastic. I bet there's a lot of strong emotion that goes along with that."

"I would imagine."

"So this guy is brooming into town for your film festival?"

"Yes, he's brooming in," I said, wondering if Sonderby might be taking time off from actually pushing a broom profession- ally to come to my film festival.

"This is very cool," Bix said. "I get to meet him, don't I?"

"Of course," I said. "You come to the festival, you'll meet him."

"I bet he's got lots of stories."

"I hope so."

Bix grinned and pushed the gas pedal hard, as if to urge the event forward, but I felt myself pulling back, sinking into the car seat.

When we hit the city, Bix made a series of turns down ever- darkening streets until he said we were on the one where the 3- D Club was located. It didn't look like a real happening neigh- borhood. Depressing amber streetlights and the occasional blue neon of a draft beer sign in a tavern window were the only sources of illumination on the block. All the stores were closed and dark and there was no one on the streets.

Bix pointed to an ominous-looking warehouse with gray, de- caying walls crammed with graffiti. He pointed to a distinctive piece of graffiti depicting a cracked human skull with sunken, evil-looking eyes.

"Punishing Skulls," Bix said, like a tour guide in the depths of hell.

When I told Bix I'd never heard of the Punishing Skulls, he raised his eyebrows and explained to me with a sigh that the Punishing Skulls were a widely-known, much-feared street gang who'd really torn up the studio the day they were on "Wake Up, It's Morning."

I wanted Bix to turn the car around. Before, the streets looked dark. Now they looked dark and dangerous. I didn't need to run into anyone who punished. I punished myself enough, with a low-impact mental torture that was relatively harmless. I was good at it and it required no assistance.

"Maybe we caught this city on a bad night," I told Bix, squinting down alleyways, looking for the glint of anything threatening—a set of brass knuckles, a straight razor, a bicycle chain.

Bix waved me off and kept driving, slowing down by dimly lit doorways, looking for a sign that said 3-D.

"You can't always tell," Bix said. "These places don't always jump out at you."

I didn't want anything jumping out at me in this neighborhood. I really wanted to go home. But suddenly Bix's foot shot down on the brake and my knee smashed into the glove compartment. Bix pointed to a painted sign that said "Dead Cat Club." Below it, in different, sloppy handwriting it said "under new management."

"Let's give it a shot," Bix said.

"A shot's not going to cure it," I said.

"Come on," Bix said.

I looked anxiously up and down the empty block.

"But there are no cars here."

Bix jumped out and I followed, far enough behind to let me run back to the car if there was trouble, but close enough to Bix to make it sort of appear like I was traveling in a group. When we reached the front door, Bix fingered a flyer tacked up in the entryway. It was the same flyer I had in my pocket.

"Looks like the place," Bix said. He seemed pleased.

Bix rapped on the door. There was no answer.

"Maybe there's a password," I said, hoping that there would be one and we wouldn't know it and have to go home. Bix knocked on the door again and then simply pushed it open. "What are you doing?" I asked.

"Goin' in," Bix said.

I walked in behind him, hovering over his back like a baby gibbon. I looked over his shoulder and saw that the room was empty. There was a large, vacant area, a dirty tile floor with lots of missing tiles and cracks. It led up to a stage in the back of the room. Onstage there was a piano, a couple of guitars, amps, lots of cords and wires and a few empty beer bottles near a drum kit. There were no musicians.

"Maybe it's tomorrow night," I said.

"Terrific," Bix said, with disgust. "The flyer says this place is open every night."

There was a long Formica-covered bar lacking barstools which ran the length of the right side of the room. A raspy, threatening voice, sort of like an evil Andy Devine, came from behind the cash register at the end of the bar.

"Whatcha lookin' for?" the voice wanted to know.

"Hi," Bix said, like the first person to arrive at a company picnic. "We're looking for the 3-D Club. We hear there's supposed to be some music here."

A short, round man approached us from behind the bar, wiping his hands on a dirty white bar towel. My mind flashed:

bouncer. Not only because he looked like the kind of guy who would throw you out a door or window, but because he looked as though he might, if dropped, actually bounce. He was wearing black pants and a t-shirt that said STAY OUT. In smaller, lowercase letters followed the words "all night." The message wrapped around his corpulent body like an announcement on a blimp hovering over the Superbowl. A thin, oily mustache drew a line over his upper lip.

"You're in the right place," he said, pushing a squat finger along his mustache, "but at the wrong time."

Whenever I'd heard this line in a movie, the person to whom it was directed was usually killed.

"Let's go," I said.

"What time do you open?" Bix asked.

"Around one," said the bartender.

"No kidding," said Bix. He was thrilled and smiled at me in anticipation. "Can we get a beer?"

"Not here," said the bartender. "Not until one. Take it up the street a ways."

Bix and I walked back to the car.

"What do you want to do?" I asked, though I already knew what Bix wanted to do.

"Where did that guy say the nearest bar was?"

"He said up the street a ways." I tried to make it sound far.

"Well let's walk around and see what we can find."

"No," I said. "Let's take the car."

We got back into Bix's Duster and drove a few blocks until we spotted a bar with no name that had a red neon OPEN sign blazing in the window. Bix pulled over to the curb, put the car in park, looked at me and shrugged. I shrugged back and we went in.

The bar was sparsely populated with what looked like a few locals and regulars. Two guys in baseball caps were playing darts between shots of bourbon. There was a couple at a table in the corner forestalling a night of passion by getting drunk and doing the kind of rubbing, stroking and groping that no ensuing sex act could ever live up to. It's been a while, I thought, unable to keep from staring at them. Sometime soon I would think of the two of them and have better sex alone than the two of them would have together. Bix and I parked ourselves at the bar and angled our barstools so that we could sneak glances at the couple from time to time and see how their foreplay was progressing.

Bix ordered a couple of beers from a slow, middle-aged bartender whose dour expression told me he was supposed to have gone home hours ago. He dredged a couple of beers from the cooler under the bar and slapped them down in front of us with the lethargic motion of a dump truck unloading wet sand. Well, it was late, after all. I wanted to take whatever energy I had left, which wasn't much, jump up on the bar and deliver some kind of impassioned, Jimmy Stewart-esque speech:

"Folks! Listen up! For God's sake, let's go home! We're decent people! We should all be in bed!"

Bix nodded towards the hormonally over-happy couple in the corner and clinked his beer bottle against mine.

"Women. Eh, Mal?"

I nodded knowingly, but I wasn't sure what he meant. Neither of us had anything to brag about. The ladies in my life consisted of a dental assistant who worked on a hot line who probably wanted nothing to do with me, a post-punk dirge singer who probably wanted nothing to do with me and an ex-girlfriend who certainly wanted nothing to do with me. Bix's love life wasn't much better. Bix was in the middle of a long distance romance with a woman named Delores from Dallas. Eighteen hours away. They saw each other four or five times a year.

"We meet in Missouri sometimes," he said, as casually as if it were a stroll to the corner to buy a newspaper.

It was a situation I couldn't comprehend. I'd been with Lena for seven years. I spoke to her every day on the phone. Often we spent evenings on the phone, silently sometimes, me doing a crossword, she doing her nails, but still together somehow. Connected. Maybe we'd been overexposed. Ran out of stuff to say. But if Lena had moved to Dallas would I have met her in Missouri? I didn't think so. No, I needed someone to be with me most of the time. Someone to hold at bedtime. Someone who had the same bedtime as me.

Bix was happy to supply me with several reasons why I shouldn't get involved in a long-distance relationship, from the complicated:

"You never know if you're still a part of her life."

To the purely practical:

"You never know if you're going to have enough gas to make it through Arkansas without stopping."

"But," Bix emphasized, "the sex is great."

How could it not be, I thought, after being apart for so long? Maybe all I need is some sex. I stole another look at the couple necking in the corner. Their hands had disappeared into the folds of each other's disheveled garments. An inebriated glaze had settled over their eyes, a filter which kept them attractive-looking to each other throughout their drunken pawing. They didn't look happy, exactly, but they didn't look as though they were concerned about it one way or the other. Maybe I need another drink, I thought. No. Have to keep sharp. Well, awake, anyway. I thought about the time and I looked at the vacant spot on my wrist. I really need to find my watch, I thought. On the wall behind the bar was a digital clock with an illuminated diorama depicting a Seminole Indian in a canoe, paddling upstream towards one in the morning. I pointed the Seminole out to Bix.

"Let's go," I said.

As we approached the 3-D Club again, the street was jammed with cars. They were lined up on either side of the street in front of the place, bumper to bumper. A quick search down the side streets uncovered a similar river of cars. It was as if the Pope had suddenly arrived to give his blessing.

"This is great!" Bix said and he gunned the car down the street looking for an opening where he could wedge his Duster. We finally found a place four blocks away and started to walk back. There were people splashed all over the streets where there had been none before. People were in front of the club, yelling. People were hanging out of cars, yelling. Basically everyone was yelling. I don't know what they were yelling about. I stayed close to Bix, prepared to forget our years of friendship and use him as a shield, if necessary.

Most everyone was fashionably unkempt. Hair uneven, long on one side, cropped short on the other side like wheat at harvest time. Oversized shirts with rips in them, done on purpose. They wore dark clothes to match their mortician's expressions. My expression was somber too, but while they jumped around in the streets, I kept my hands jammed deep in my pockets and tried not to be noticed.

Unfortunately, Bix and I looked like Midwestern college recruiters from the suburbs. Bix was in blue jeans and a football jersey. I had on a white button-down shirt with the sleeves rolled up, and tan pants. We weren't exactly inconspicuous. Suddenly I wanted to be inside the club, in the middle of a dark crowd, where just my head would be conspicuous.

Bix was already pushing himself inside and I stayed as close to him as I could. The 3-D Club had been transformed from an empty room into a thick mass of smoke, bodies and noise. A pre-recorded tape was playing a dance beat which thumped rhythmically and felt like Missus Calabrone's broom handle against my apartment floor.

I fished for my wallet and tried to find three dollars. I didn't want to hand out a five or a ten or any denomination that would require making change. I wanted the transaction to require as little interpersonal skills as possible. I found three singles and looked around desperately for someone to hand them to, but no one came forward.

Suddenly I felt someone tug at my forearm. Hard. This is it, I thought. I'm about to be singled out and thrashed within an inch of my life for no particular reason other than the fact that I was wearing tan pants. I couldn't see where my arm had been taken or who had taken it. Then I felt something pressed, hard, into the back of my hand. My God, I thought, I'm being injected with something. I'll wake up tomorrow with no memory and a warrant out for my arrest. I jerked my arm back. The three dollars was gone from my fist and there was a red blotch on the back of my hand. Blood? I held my hand up to my face and inspected it more closely. It was red ink and it looked something like a cat.

I spotted Bix a few bodies ahead and pushed my way towards him. He was only about a foot away, but lacking sharp elbows and some upper body strength, I found it something of a struggle. I guess he saw a frazzled, dazed expression on my face.

"You okay?" he asked.

"I guess so," I said.

"Hey, did they stamp your hand with a dead cat yet?"

I looked at my hand again. The cat was on its back and I now saw it had two little crosses for eyes.

"What's this for?" I asked.

"You can't come and go without it. They're still using the stamp from when this was the Dead Cat Club."

Bix began to make another remark but was cut short by a man's voice which suddenly boomed over the sound system.

"All right!" he hollered. "I'm Big Grunt. You ready to party?"

The crowd roared back with enthusiastic approval.

"Okay, here they are," Big Grunt yelled. "All the way from Tonawanda, New York. Give it up for Dream Research!"

A spotlight lit the stage on fire and there was a tremendous crash of low register electric bass and bass drums. A scorching guitar made its first assault and immediately burned the little hairs on the inside of my ears. If I'd wanted to tell Bix something, the opportunity had just passed forever.

The members of Dream Research, a trio whose blond-haired lead guitar player doubled as lead singer, screamed and gyrated and stalked the stage spewing out acid lyrics about bad relationships and spitting on the first three rows in the process. I was about eight rows back, so I wasn't in the direct line of fire. The vibration that went from the bearded bass player's electric bass through the floor and up into my testicles was almost pleasant, in a frightening, health-threatening kind of way. I even tried to decipher some of the lyrics, hoping to relate to them on some level. It was something about a girl who'd done . . . something that had made the singer of the song so angry that he was going to do . . . something. I wondered if I could make it fit with the story of a projectionist whose ex-girlfriend was marrying a cardiologist and how the projectionist was going to do . . . something. But it was all so loud I really couldn't make heads or tails out of it.

I endured it for a while, letting the tsunami of sound wash over me. Sooner or later, I thought, it's got to let up. But it showed no signs of letting up. It was relentless, to the point where I felt the sky was going to open up and unleash hailstones the size of grapefruits. I had to get out for a few minutes. I pushed my forefinger into Bix's side to get his attention. Then I used the same forefinger to point to myself and then point to the door. My forefinger was fast becoming the most important part of my body. Bix nodded like he understood.

I pushed through the crowd and the tangle of sweaty bodies pushed back. Everyone except me was facing the stage, so I was moving against the flow. It was like trying to roll a car out of the mud, forward a bit, then back, then forward a little more. I finally squeezed through a door and stumbled out onto the street. The night air was thick, but at least I didn't have to share it. I saw the lights of an all-night grocery. I prayed I could make it there and back without encountering any Skulls. I was alone and wearing a white shirt. Asking for it, in other words.

I ducked inside the grocery store, located a pack of spearmint gum and brought it to the counter. Behind the counter was a woman in her fifties with blonde stringy hair, reading *Chopper Quarterly*. She was wearing a halter top and had a small coiled rattlesnake tattooed on her shoulder. She's probably a Skull, I thought. Or the mother of a Skull.

I put the spearmint gum on the counter and laid a dollar bill next to it. The woman behind the counter glared at me.

"You from the 3-D Club?"

I wasn't sure how to answer. I thought maybe there was a discount on gum and other sundry items if you mentioned the 3-D Club. Then I noticed she was looking at the dead cat on the back of my hand. I pulled my hand away sheepishly and buried it in my front pocket.

"Just gum," I said.

"I don't want you punks hanging around my store!" she said sharply. This is it, I thought. I was worried about being taken out by some young street gang and now I would be beaten to death by some middle-aged female biker-grocer. She snatched up my dollar and gave me back forty-seven cents. I took my spearmint gum and hightailed it out of there.

I returned to the club. Someone grabbed my arm again on the way in, but this time it was only to make sure I had a dead cat on the back of my hand. Funny thing about a dead cat, I thought. Makes you welcome in some places, unwelcome in others.

But in the fifteen minutes I'd been gone, the 3-D Club had changed yet again. The smoke remained, but the crowd and the noise had thinned out somewhat. The pre-recorded dance music was back on, so I assumed they were between sets. I found Bix near the bar, bending his elbow with a draft.

"You missed the Soiled Sheets," he yelled, much louder than

was necessary and I realized his hearing had been impaired. I hoped it wasn't permanent. "They did only two songs. Cover versions of 'Nice 'n Easy Does It' and 'Little White Duck.' Then they left the stage and everyone booed. It was great."

Bix was clearly enjoying himself. This is not the response I'd hoped for. Bix was supposed to have found the whole thing objectionable so that I'd never find myself in this situation again. But apparently the high frequency in the music had seared away a great many of his brain cells. He was now bobbing his head like the rest of the crowd.

The house lights went out and the crowd quieted in anticipation. From the darkness a bass began a slow throbbing line, a walk that brought you to the edge of a cliff and gently, with no remorse, pushed you off. The drummer joined him, brushing his high hat in slow syncopation. Tsh. Tsh. Tsh. Then a piano began to play mournful, death knell chords. Chords that said: You just missed your last bus home.

A white spotlight stabbed the stage and the woman I'd seen in the bookstore approached the microphone. She was dressed in a long ivory dress with spaghetti straps and a loose neckline that yawned at her cleavage. A black scarf wrapped around her neck made her look like she was being strangled by a python. With the spotlight trained on her, she was quite literally glowing, giving off her own reflected light, like the moon. I looked up at her, my jaw slack, a small satellite in her orbit.

She cupped the microphone in both hands and began to sing the saddest, most gut-wrenching version of "Cry Me a River" I'd ever heard. I'd heard the song when I was younger, but never rendered so tragically. This was God's wrath, mother's guilt and lonely afternoons all rolled into one. I stood there, knees trembling, re-experiencing all the empty moments of my life. The time I'd gotten lost in a department store as a child. The times I prayed and heard nothing in return. The first Sunday afternoon I spent alone, without Lena after I'd broken up with her.

Tears didn't come easy for me. They started somewhere in the region of my heart, made a difficult journey through my chest and then got trapped, painfully, in my throat. There the tears would remain, stuck against a hard, impassable dam. Unreleased. Unsatisfying. And because tears had accumulated in my body for more than thirty years, I feared once the torrent was unleashed, there would be no stemming the flow.

I looked over at Bix. He was still nodding and bobbing, his internal needle apparently still stuck in the groove of the last song. I guess he hadn't made the transition from metal-thrash versions of Burl Ives songs to post-punk ballads. Anyway, he was nowhere near being on the verge of tears. I wasn't anxious for Bix to see me start sobbing. We had bonded as males, yes, and had told each other some personal things, his more interesting than mine, to be sure. Nothing we shared, however, warranted crying on each other's shoulders.

So I pushed through the crowd again and ducked into the men's room. I locked myself inside a stall and faced the toilet. I imagined myself weeping so tremendously that my tears would fill the bowl. My head would pop off and a great whoosh, like an opened fireplug, would come forth, spewing out a lifetime of my salty, bitter tears. I would literally cry a river. But the tears didn't come. They choked my throat so hard I thought they'd strangle me, but they never broke through to the surface.

I stayed in the men's room, removed from the immediacy of

the performance, while the Circadian Rhythm Section continued in their funereal vein. It was still painful, but in a more muffled, muted way. Diluted enough to stave off another attack of catastrophic despair. I lined the toilet seat with paper, fearing there were germs present strong enough to eat through my tan pants, and sat down. I'll just hang out here for a bit, I thought. My head drooped down suddenly and my neck snapped back up like it'd been yanked in a noose. I rubbed my neck and then my aching throat. Exhaustion. That must certainly be a part of it, I thought. I had no idea what time it was anymore. I felt the area where my wristwatch had once been, as if it might appear like a genie if I rubbed it. I imagined it must be around two or two-thirty in the morning.

What was I doing here? At this time of night I should be in bed, lying awake, not in a toilet, sitting awake. I yawned one of those yawns that felt as though it was going to split my face like a carved pumpkin. I decided to close my eyes for a moment. The last thing I remembered were dismally seductive strains of "Beautiful Dreamer" seeping in under the door of the stall.

I woke up looking into the face of the post-punk dirge singer.

"You ought to get a real bed," she said.

I stretched my face and opened my eyes wide.

"What time is it?"

"Four-thirty."

"Jesus," I said. I looked around and, with some dismay, realized I was still in the men's room. I quickly checked to make sure my pants were still up. They were.

"Where's Bix?"

"Bix?"

"I came here with a friend of mine."

"Oh. That guy. He found you asleep in here after the last set. But he was, like, really afraid to wake you because you were whimpering. He was afraid you were having some kind of nightmare and he didn't think it was a good idea to wake you."

I stood up and quickly learned that there's nothing to be gained from sleeping on a toilet. Every muscle in my body that was kinkable had kinked.

"I'll have to remember to thank him," I said, rubbing a knot out of my neck. "Where the hell is he?"

"He went home."

"Home? No, that's not possible. He couldn't have gone home."

"Relax. It's okay. I told him I'd drive you home."

"I couldn't ask you to do that," I said. "I live about an hour west of here."

"Hell, I'm further out than that," she said. "I can take you, no problem."

"What are you doing in the men's room?"

"Oh, everybody's been in here. Everyone wanted to see you sleeping and whimpering. It was really something."

"Oh good," I said. I made a mental note that this had probably been the lowest point in my life. I wanted to remember it, so that all future bad experiences could be put in perspective.

"I got in here about an hour ago," she said. "I recognized you from the bookstore. Probably because I already knew what you looked like asleep. Although, I've got to say, you don't look much different sleeping than when you're awake. Anyway, I told your friend—what's his name?"

"Bix. How did you know he was my friend?"

"You guys look kind of similar. The same haircut or something. And he was telling people not to touch you or anything. But he was really trashed and he had a long drive home. So I told him I knew you and that I'd met you in the bookstore and that I'd take you home and that he could take off."

"So he took off?"

"I told him it was okay."

"And what about you? You're not too trashed to drive?"

"Me? No, I just did a couple lines. I'll be up for hours yet."

More good news, I thought.

"Maybe I'll just get a cab. Is there a phone around here? Some place I can call and wait for a cab?"

"You can't wait around here. I've gotta lock this place up. There's an all-night grocery on the corner if you want to hang out there."

I looked at the dead cat on the back of my hand.

"No, I've been there. They don't want me in there."

"Catch a ride with me, then. C'mon, I could use the company."

"All right," I said.

I followed her out of the men's room, down a dark hall that opened into an alley. She locked the back door of the club and lit a cigarette. As the match flickered, she looked kind of sexy again. She was the kind of woman who looked better in low light, I decided. She had a red Pacer with a spider web crack on the passenger's side of the windshield. We got into her car, she cranked it up and we zoomed off into the darkness.

She drove fast. Really fast. I held on, my fingernails discreetly piercing the vinyl seats while the seat belt dug into my abdomen. No one stopped her. Even highway patrolmen were asleep behind their billboards at this hour. *The Hour of the Wolf*, I thought. Bergman said it was the time when demons had a heightened sense of power and vitality, when nightmares came to one. And here I was, accepting a ride with someone I hardly knew, some female demon who'd just ripped me to shreds with her singing. I looked through the spider web crack in the windshield at the dark, empty highway. Maybe Bergman was right. Maybe God was a spider God.

"Does your radio work?" I said, cutting through the silence.

"No, damn it," she said, clicking it on and off and punching the dead dials. "I'm going to rip the fuckin' thing out and put in something nice some day."

"That's okay," I said, "I'd rather just listen to the sounds of acceleration."

She pressed harder on the gas and used the end of one cigarette to light another.

The only good thing about her proclivity towards warp speed was that I was getting home in half the time it'd taken Bix to drive us into the city. The sooner the better. We didn't talk again until we got off the highway and into town.

"You want to stop somewhere and get some breakfast?"

"Breakfast? No, I don't think I can do breakfast," I said.

I was hungry, but the haunting image of this woman pulling my sleeping head out of a plate of scrambled eggs was too much for me. My eyes were no longer blinking, they were closing for three minutes at a time and then opening again. It didn't seem to matter to her. She kept drivin' and smokin'.

As dawn approached and a dim gray light filled the car, I could see her face again. Her makeup had melted, under the

spotlights at the 3-D Club I guess, then oozed a bit before drying again. It gave her face a waxy, surreal quality. As if I was
being driven by a character from Pirates of the Caribbean at
Disneyland. There was something still seductive about her, however, that the cruel light of morning could not diminish.

Maybe it was her energy, somewhat drug-induced but seem-
ingly inexhaustible. She had enough horsepower for both of us.
If her car died out, I could imagine her hiking the rest of the
way and still rearranging the furniture when she got home.
Maybe I could find happiness somehow, just being dragged along
in her wake. Like those dogs they put on water skis, who appear to be smiling even though they don't know what's going
on.

"I really appreciate this," I said.

"I don't mind. Like I said, I like the company."

"I haven't been great company," I said. "I haven't said much
at all."

"That's okay," she said. "I know you've got that weird sleep
thing happening."

"I'm told there's nothing clinically wrong with me," I said.
"I'm going through a transition, I guess. From being a day person to a night person. I'm told there's nothing wrong."

She nodded. "Yeah. The transition is the worst part."

"Yes," I said.

"I go through that with my hair."

"What?"

"Go through transitions."

"Oh."

"So I know where you're coming from."

We cruised into my neighborhood just as the sun was pressing an impudent wedge into the corner of the horizon. I'd hoped to avoid this moment, when Friday night suddenly became Saturday morning. My body shuddered as if the whole of me were yawning. I pooled the last of my resources to stay awake long enough to point out which building was mine. She pulled over to the curb in front of it and turned off the engine. If she'd left the car idling I might have hopped right out, but there was something about the fact that she'd killed the engine. Maybe she wanted me to invite her up. I wasn't ready for that. And she didn't look tired enough for me to feel compelled to ask. I had already begun to absently unbutton my shirt as if I were already inside, preparing for bed. I caught myself and started to redo the buttons. She pressed her hand against my fumbling fingers.

"Don't," she said softly. "Leave it open."

My hands moved away and her index finger traced a line from my throat to my stomach.

"Maybe we could have lunch," I said.

"Mm hmmm . . . ," she said, still finger painting on my torso.

I wondered if she was waiting for me to kiss her. I leaned over and planted a soft one on her lips. Then I withdrew.

"Now I'll kiss you," she said. She leaned into me, her body angling around the Pacer's gearshift. She kissed me hard, like a boar rooting for truffles. Parts of my body that had gone to sleep began to wake up abruptly. It was a long kiss, passionate and frightening. When I couldn't breathe any more, I pulled away. She leaned back and savored me, her eyes sparking like a short in the wire of a broken vacuum cleaner.

"Now you kiss me again," she said.

"Couldn't we work out something we could do together?"

"I like doing this," she said.

"I don't think I have the energy."

"Kiss me again," she said. "I like taking turns."

"Couldn't we do it like darts?" I asked. "You do three, then I'll do three?"

She smiled, sighed and gave me three long, wet kisses. Two on my chest and one dead center on my lips. I slumped back, feeling like a punctured dart board.

"When would you like to have lunch?" I asked.

"Now," she said. "I'd like to have lunch now. Would you like lunch now?"

"I can't do lunch now," I said. "I still have to do breakfast. And I'm not sure I can do breakfast."

"How about noon?"

"Noon? You mean today noon?"

"Yes."

"Can we make it a little later? I need to sleep for a couple of days."

"I forgot. You have that sleep thing. Okay. One o'clock then. Do you have a car?"

I pointed to a green 1969 VW microbus parked up the street.

"I use that sometimes," I said. "But it may need a jump." I may need one too, I thought.

"There's a place near the tracks by my apartment. Can you get to the train?"

I nodded again.

She told me to take the train three stops west. Get off and go to a restaurant just east of the tracks called The Crossing. Make sure I check the Saturday train schedules because they're different from weekdays. Meet her there at twelve-thirty. It sounded more complicated than it was, as if I was going to rendezvous with a woman in a trench coat named Frederica at the station and slip her a ceramic rooster containing microfilm. But at the moment it was easier than getting directions to her home and trying to get my VW started. I stumbled out of the car and walked around to her side.

"This was fun," she said.

I wasn't sure what part of the evening or morning she was referring to and there wasn't much point in finding out. Whether it was our torrid embraces or seeing me sleeping and whimpering in the men's room, all in all it had been a satisfying evening for her and one I doubted I could ever recreate. She drove off and left me standing in the street, cheerlessly facing the sunrise.

Everything was louder at five in the morning. My footsteps clunked and squeaked up the narrow wooden staircase to my apartment. I locked myself inside and made sure all the shades were pulled tight. I hadn't removed my shoes and they tapped along the hardwood floors until I heard Missus Calabrone's broom handle rap on her ceiling. I cursed myself for waking her, took off my shoes and shuffled into the kitchen.

I took my shirt off and draped it over the kitchen chair. I stretched and rubbed my hands along my sides and over my chest. I felt a lingering trace of lipstick and saliva. I thought about indulging in a little onanistic pleasure while the memory of those kisses was still fresh in my mind, but knew I was too exhausted to work up the proper head of steam. And if I did that, I wouldn't have any energy left to eat, and at the moment the desire for food was higher on my hierarchy of needs. Or was it? I went back and forth in my mind, a sandwich on one hand, the post-punk dirge singer on the other. No. I told my-self. Eat. Maybe after you eat, you'll have the energy to do it.

I opened the refrigerator, pulled out a loaf of bread and put two slices into the toaster. I didn't have the upper body strength I needed to push them down, however. Nor did I care to wait the two minutes it would take to make toast. So I took the bread back out of the toaster. I took one slice, folded it, then stuffed it, whole, into my mouth. I walked down the hallway, not really chewing but sort of moving the bread around my teeth and gums. I heard the familiar hum of angry insects. I spotted an early-rising, wayfaring yellow jacket climbing up the wall. I observed it for a moment and then, reflexively, swat-ted it with my remaining piece of bread. The bread stuck to the wall and I left it there. I was too tired to feel revulsion. I walked back to the living room and sat down on the couch. I fell asleep sitting up, head back, white bread still stuffed in my cheek.

chapter eight

I woke up at seven and couldn't get back to sleep. I turned on the television, curled up on the couch and watched Saturday morning cartoons, hoping to get drowsy again. Upsetting things were happening on all the networks. A family dog was blamed for everything the cat did. A duck blew up and had to reattach his beak. I switched channels for several hours, trying to find something to lull me back to sleep, but there was nothing, and instead of turning it off, I watched until eleven a.m.

I got up, showered and dressed, dragging myself through the process of preparing to go out. I was exhausted but I kept going, fearing that if I stopped I might get stuck in some sort of eternal zombie-like trance. I got out my Walkman and looked for a tape to listen to on the train. It was only a fifteen-minute trip but I needed something with rhythm, the right kind of music to keep me moving. Besides, after last night I was anxious to hear something familiar. My music.

I once had a dream that I couldn't commence with sex until I'd found the appropriate music to accompany it. I'd finally had it narrowed down to "You Can't Always Get What You Want (But Sometimes You Get What You Need)" by the Rolling Stones and "Slippery, Hippery, Flippery" by Roland Kirk, but by the time I'd made my choice, the dream was over. Since the dream, I'd become neurotically obsessed—with finding the right music for the right moment. It was a malady that came with being a film projectionist, I guess. Everything needed to be set to the proper background score.

My music was arranged seasonally and meteorologically rather than by artist. Thus I'd find myself listening to Miles Davis in October doing "Autumn Leaves" and listening to Charlie Parker in April doing "April in Paris." Most of the music in my collection was introspective—jazz, blues, and classical. You'd never, for instance find me frolicking through my apartment listening to "The Lovely Month of May" from *Camelot* no matter how nice a day in May it was. Nor would you find me walking in "A Winter Wonderland." Particularly not on a day like this. In my apartment it was "Hotter Than July," but I couldn't find my Stevie Wonder tape. So I went south, into the next continent, for my music. Brazil. It was hot in Brazil. Maybe even hotter than my apartment.

I pulled out a tape of Milton Nascimento and snapped it into my Walkman. Then I stuffed the other staples of social interaction into my pockets. Keys, change, handkerchief, comb, lip balm, spearmint gum, Binaca and my wallet. I suddenly appeared awkwardly loaded down, like a marsupial with triplets in her pouch. I pulled a large t-shirt over my head and let it dangle down, hiding some of the bulges.

As I descended the staircase, I spied Missus Calabrone in her curlers and her blue terry-cloth robe. She was sweeping around the parkway where there was nothing to sweep. Not a good sign. She was waiting for me.

"Just a minute, Malcolm," she said, like a prosecuting attorney prepared to lay some damning evidence on a witness. A prosecuting attorney who smelled like clam sauce, I noted as I approached her.

"I don't care what time you get in, Malcolm, it's none of my business."

I nodded, certain that there would be more to follow. There was.

"But there are people in this neighborhood, decent people, who *do* care. And I don't want them seeing you coming in at strange hours and have them think I run some sort of . . . smut house."

Smut House. Malcolm Cicchio is Charles Dirt in . . . Smut House. See . . . a man who dresses like a marsupial. See . . . a man who comes in at strange hours. Smut House. A Smutty Production.

I wondered if Missus Calabrone was truly concerned about the hours I kept. Interesting, I thought. *The hours I kept.* If only I really could keep an hour or two. Save them up. Redeem them later. More than likely, Missus Calabrone was more concerned because she'd seen me getting my chest kissed at five in the morning.

"No one will think it's a smut house," I said.

"You come and go," she said. "People talk. You don't know."

"I'm sorry I got in so late," I said.

"So *early*, you mean. Early in the morning."

"Yes. So early. I'm sorry."

"I can't have people coming in my building at five in the morning."

"Lots of people get up at five in the morning," I said. I wasn't prepared to name them or point out where they lived, but they were there, statistically, for me to use.

"They're going out," she countered, pointing her broom handle menacingly in my direction. "You, you're coming in at that hour."

"You're right," I said. "I was coming in. I'm sorry. I'll try to be going out next time."

"All right then," she said. "It isn't me. I don't want you to think it's me."

"No," I said, " I don't."

Her eyes suddenly zeroed in on the back of my hand.

"What's that on your hand there?"

It was my dead cat stamp. Apparently it hadn't washed off in the shower. I licked my thumb and rubbed at it.

"I spilled something on it," I said.

"You didn't spill it on my floor?"

"No. No. I spilled it last night. I spilled all of it on my hand. Nothing on your floor."

She shook her head. One of her curlers flew off her head and shot onto the lawn, frightening away a cardinal.

"I don't care what people do," she said. "But my late husband . . . if he was alive you'd be getting more than just a good talking to."

What would Mister Calabrone have done, I wondered? She probably idealized him as the kind of husband who would have thrashed me with a broom handle. But I bet he was really a little paisan who would have invited me into his kitchen, poured me a tall glass of homemade vino and pressed me to tell him all the details of last night's adventure. And if my story wasn't wild and steamy enough to match those of his youth, *then* he'd thrash me with the broom handle.

"I'm late for a train," I said.

"All right then," she said. "I'm glad we had this talk."

"Me too."

I walked six blocks to the train station, bought a westbound ticket and boarded. As the train started up and I settled back in my seat I thought, wow, this is really strange. Here I am on a train about to meet her for lunch. Then it struck me. Her? My God. Who was she, anyway? I had no idea what her name was. It seemed indecent, somehow, to have a rendezvous with a person whose kisses put my brain into a sucking vortex, but whose name was a complete enigma. She didn't look as if she'd have an average name like Mary, Edna or Susan. She could only be Bronwyn, Arazou, or Kendra. At the moment, however, she was a stranger. A post-punk-dirge singer-with-no-name who'd become my mystery date.

I put the headphones of my Walkman over my ears, pushed the play button and let the musical waves of Brazil wash over me. The melodic strum of guitar, the gently insistent throb of the tumbadoro and cuica. Then the haunting, resonant voice of Milton Nascimento filled my head. I didn't understand a word of Portuguese, but it didn't matter. In his native tongue Milton could be singing about sleep deprivation, scorching summers, yellow jackets in the wall and women without names. Yes, I decided, that's what he was singing about, by God. It was soothing. I fought the urge to close my eyes, fearing that while my brain was in Brazil, my sleeping body would end up on a train headed for Ogden, Utah.

I arrived at my stop, got off the train and located the diner just east of the tracks. I'd cooled off for a few minutes on the air-conditioned train, but the short walk to the restaurant had my clothes sticking to my body again. I went in and looked around but didn't see her, even though I was a few minutes late. I took a booth near the back so that I could scope out the entire restaurant and watch for her arrival. A middle-aged waitress promptly appeared at my table.

"What can I get you?" she asked. Her starched white uniform was spotted with little daisies. It was much too bright, floral and cheerful for my eyes.

"Just coffee," I mumbled , trying to blink some sort of protective film over my eyes.

"Coffee? In this heat? It's not good for you. You should be drinking something cold."

"I know, but I like coffee."

"How about a nice iced tea?"

"No, just coffee."

She smiled knowingly. "Up late last night?"

I nodded. "My circadian rhythms are off," I grumbled. "And I'm trying to make a transition from being a day person to a night person."

"Well, I admire that. I admire people that can decide on something and do it."

"I didn't decide to do it," I said. "It's just doing it to me."

"Well, good luck anyway, sir," she said, her voice dripping with syrup. I could have told her that my heart was going to explode in sixteen months and it wouldn't have melted her smile one little bit. "Would you like to hear our lunch specials?"

"Not right now," I said. "I can't handle anything special. I'd just like something ordinary. An ordinary cup of coffee. No cream. No sugar."

"Is there anything else I can get for you?"

"Have you seen anyone in here who looks like she might be named Bronwyn, Arazou or Kendra . . . something like that?"

She thought a moment. "Our cashier's name is Fern," she offered.

"That's all right, thanks," I said.

When my date hadn't arrived by one-thirty by the restaurant clock, I went ahead and ordered a grilled cheese sandwich. And more coffee. Sitting for such a long time in the same place made it increasingly difficult for me to stay awake and alert. I'd made a pact with my mind and body to make me passably sociable between one and two in the afternoon in return for a total collapse later. Once the hour had elapsed, however, the deal was off and I wasn't able to sustain the self-induced flow of adrenaline. I felt myself getting woozy again.

She finally glided in around one-forty. She was wearing a white t-shirt and a pair of short blue jean cut-offs which looked as though she'd cut them off herself. The shirt seemed to be big enough, but it was pulled tight from being tucked into the jeans. It seemed to be saying: I don't know if we've met yet, but I'd like you to meet my breasts. She had red thongs on her feet and painted red toenails. There was no polish on her fingernails. I liked that she'd taken care of her toes rather than her fingers. Feet inherently need more attention than hands.

She spotted my slumped body in the booth, smiled and came over. She zoomed in and planted a kiss on my neck. I tried to respond but reacted too sluggishly, managing only to kiss a mouthful of wet hair. I smelled sweet strawberry shampoo and retreated. She sat down opposite me, took off her sunglasses and smacked her feed-bag purse down next to her. I felt the vibration roll through my body.

"You already ate?" she asked, noticing the crust and crumbs on my plate.

"I thought we said one o'clock," I said, trying to straighten up.

"One?" She laughed. "I couldn't have said one. I had to get some sleep."

"Up late last night?" I said.

She smiled at me again. Her freshly-washed hair was hanging down in damp, clinging strands that caressed her face. Without makeup she had a pale, albeit clear complexion, about the color of oatmeal. I'd never cared much for oatmeal. As a boy I remembered staring at it, waiting for it to turn into something else. My mother often dumped several heaping spoons of brown sugar into it to make it more to my liking. Maybe that's what this situation needed—my mother's hand descending from the heavens to dump some brown sugar on this woman.

"Did I really say one o'clock?" she asked.

I nodded.

"How long would you have waited here for me?"

"I don't know." I didn't tell her I'd already browsed the late-night snack menu.

She looked at my coffee.

"Did you order drinks yet?"

"Drinks? No."

She looked around for the waitress and waved her over.

I was not a Noel-Coward-three-martini-lunch-cocktails-on-the-observation-deck kind of guy. Drinking in the afternoon seemed like a frivolous, self-indulgent thing to do. Rather like masturbation. And since in my depleted energy state I could only allow myself one frivolous self-indulgent vice, daytime drinking was out. Maybe I could convince the post-punk dirge singer to skip the drinks and masturbate with me. There was nothing thus far to indicate she wouldn't think it was just another fun date. Whatever we were going to do, however, we'd have to do it soon. My left leg was asleep and the rest of my body was about to follow suit.

She ordered two beers when the waitress arrived at our table.

"I told him he should be drinking something cold today," the waitress said.

I pitched my menu like a tent in front of me and pulled the waitress inside for a powwow.

"Keep the coffee coming," I whispered. "And I'll have one of these." I pointed to a non-alcoholic beer on the menu.

"Nothing to eat for you, ma'am?" the waitress asked.

"No. I just had some Fruitie Kazooties at home."

The real beer and the pseudo beer arrived in tall frosted mugs. I put my palm around the mug to let the chill revive a portion of my body and to conceal the embarrassingly pale amber fluid I was drinking.

"Down the hatch," she said, and smashed her mug against mine. I wasn't prepared for the toast and felt porcelain break in the back of my teeth. I watched her take a hearty pirate's swig of beer and I mirrored the movement with a drink of my innocuous brew.

"What are you drinking?" she asked. She snatched the mug out of my hand and took a drink. Her face pruned. "Ugh. Tastes like tomatoes or something."

She flagged down the waitress again.

"Get him a real beer," she said. The waitress gave me a helpless look and I nodded my assent.

"I thought you weren't a drinker," I said, when the waitress had left.

"This isn't drinking." She laughed. "Good God. You've never seen me really drink. This is just lunch."

"I'd thought that purely alcoholic lunches qualified one as a drinker. They must have changed the rules on me again."

"I told you, I had a bowl of Fruitie Kazooties. With milk. Twelve essential vitamins and minerals. I'm going to be feeling

'Rootie Kazootie all day,'" she said, giving lip service to the breakfast cereal ad. "Didn't you have breakfast?"

"I had some toast. Well, bread. A slice of bread." I thought about the other slice of bread, presumably still sticking to the wall of my apartment with a dead yellow jacket underneath it. That image, combined with the image of her beer being sloshed around in her stomach with a bowl of Fruitie Kazooties was making me a bit nauseous.

"I'm trying to wake up, actually," I said.

"What for?" she asked, smacking her lips. "It seems to me like you just sleep whenever you want to anyway. "What's with this sleep thing, anyway? Do you have narcolepsy?"

"No. I don't think so. The doctor doesn't know what's wrong."

"So you're like an . . . oddity of nature."

"Um . . . yes, I suppose." I didn't care for the description, but it seemed indefensible.

"I get off on that paranormal stuff."

"I was hoping to get to a place in my life where I wouldn't have to consider being 'paranormal' a compliment."

"Oh no, don't get me wrong. I don't think it's a bad thing."

"It's not a good thing, I can tell you that."

"Yes, but isn't it amazing, you have this sleep problem and then you run into me?"

"Amazing? In what sense?"

"I'm a singer with the Circadian Rhythm Section and your rhythms are off."

"Yes. Indeed. The thing is, I do need to be awake sometimes. For my job."

"You have a job?" she said incredulously.

"Yes," I said. "I run a movie theater. There's not a lot I have to do, but I do have to be able to at least turn the key in the front door and be able to thread up the film in the projector."

"A movie theater? No kidding? Can you get passes for new movies?"

"It's not that kind of a theater," I said. "I show foreign films. Classic foreign films."

"You're kidding. How come?"

"How come? I don't know. Some people like them. I like them. I guess I don't cater much to what's popular."

My new, more potent beer arrived and she crashed into it again with her mug. An inch of beer spilled out of my glass. If I can keep her toasting, I thought, maybe I can spill most of my beer on the table.

"Here's to ya," she said. "You and me, we're very alike. I don't cater to what's popular. I don't give a shit what people think of my act."

"I suppose that's a good thing."

She smiled. "So, what did you think of the show last night?"

I took a long draw on my beer.

"I only heard the one song, really. 'Cry Me a River.'"

"What did you think?"

"It was beautiful. In . . . in an agonizing, wrenching kind of way."

"Yeah, it's a nice song," she said. "Our bass player wrote it."

"'Cry Me a River'?"

"Yeah. Kevin wrote that. He said it was based on something that really happened to him."

"No. No, I don't think so. Kevin didn't write that."

"Yeah, he did. I was there when he was laying it down. I even helped with the lyrics."

"You did?"

"Yeah."

"'Cry Me a River'?"

"Oh yeah. He was working on it, had the "cry me" part and was looking for something big, so that you'd know it meant a lot. So we kicked some things around and I said, like, 'Cry Me a Pyramid' and he said, no, he was looking for something with water, because, you know, it's tears, right? So I think I said 'ocean' first, then I said 'river' and he liked that and said that sounded more like what it should be."

"I don't doubt it happened that way," I said. "I just think someone else did it first."

"You mean the Soiled Sheets? They're always ripping off songs, doing cover versions."

"No, I mean a long time ago."

She thought for a moment, then shrugged and nodded.

"I don't know. It's possible, I suppose. He pulled that shit when he said he wrote 'All of Me.'"

"Your arrangements are original," I said, trying to say something nice while changing the subject.

"The way I sing it? Yeah, that's what I do. That's what post-punk dirges and ballads are all about. I sing what I feel."

"Do you feel an extraordinary amount of despair?"

"Nah. But that's a sad song. 'Cry Me a River.' It's about crying. If it was a song about laughing I'd probably be laughing up there."

"I didn't see you crying onstage."

"No, it's . . . what is it? Evocative. Right. That's what it's all about. Making *you* cry."

"I whimpered, actually."

"Cried, whimpered, whatever. Same kind of thing. It's evocative."

"So the group allows you to contribute . . . ?"

"Oh sure. But musicians can be real assholes. Especially in a group. Real head trips. Egos. They feel threatened. When you're trying to be creative and someone else is trying to show he's more creative than you. But they let me do my thing. My singing. I mean it's okay to come up with some little thing. Like a tambourine part. Ringo used to do that."

"Ringo? You mean Ringo, like in the Beatles?"

"The Beatles, right. The Beatles used to let Ringo make up his own little tambourine parts. On account of he wasn't good at writing songs and they felt sorry for him. So they let him do his own thing with the tambourine. That was okay. But they only let him have one drum solo. Ever. Like George with that sitar stuff. I mean, sure, it's great, a few songs, fine. But you can't have a whole sitar album. I mean, you could, but then it wouldn't be the Beatles, you know what I mean. But the ego thing is so strong. Everybody wants to do their own thing. That's why the Beatles didn't make another album for so long."

"I thought it had to do with John being dead."

"Right. That's what I mean. What are you left with? Are you going to have a whole album of tambourine and sitar solos? Forget it."

"Uh huh."

"My aunt was at Woodstock. She saw all this happening. Tempers, the whole ego trip. Right on stage in front of half a million people. It's really tragic. Especially for drummers."

"I don't think the Beatles performed at Woodstock," I said politely.

"No, not the Beatles. But all those other groups. And then what happens? A few years later? Fifteen, twenty-minute drum solos. And what happens to Ringo? Solo career, right? But he never takes another drum solo in his life."

I nodded fervently because I couldn't bear the thought of her trying to explain it to me again. The moral had something to do with making sure you never become a drummer.

"That's a shame about Ringo," I said.

I wasn't fully aware of it at the time, but knowing that the Beatles never performed at Woodstock and that drummers had it tough were the last two coherent thoughts I would have that afternoon. I looked at our beers. Hers was still nearly full. Mine had only a few suds ringing the bottom of the mug. She had been talking and not drinking and I'd been drinking and listening, or trying to listen, anyway.

She continued to drone on about anything that happened to roll around in her brain. But I was very comfortable with this conversation, kind of like an interview, in which I'd say four words and she'd give me four paragraphs. I wanted to know more about her and I didn't want her to ask me anything else that would make me feel insecure about my life, which meant I didn't want her to ask me anything at all, really.

I knew I was going to fall asleep again. I reached down and felt for the Walkman which was pressed against my thigh. I'd been high-pressured into buying an expensive model, with auto-reverse, a graphic equalizer and one-touch recording. The salesman hadn't successfully explained the graphic equalizer to me but he had been able to put into my head that a higher-priced, recording Walkman, a "mobile message center at my fingertips" was something I couldn't afford to be without. "It eliminates the need for a brain," he'd told me. I was sold.

I surreptitiously moved the Walkman onto the table, next to the napkin dispenser. The cassette inside was ninety minutes long, forty-five minutes on each side, consisting of Brazilian music from my archives. It was a good tape. But it was expendable in an emergency like this. I took one last opportunity to say, "I see what you mean" in response to a premature eulogy for Keith Richards.

"People will never know," she said, "how really painful it was for him to write 'Happy.'"

She didn't seem to be taking any notice of the fiddling I was doing with the Walkman so I discreetly hit the record button. The remarkable little capstan drive began to pull the tape around the small plastic reels, recording her voice and leaving me free to fly on automatic pilot. Later that evening, I planned to play back the cassette tape and find out what I'd missed. If anything.

Internally, I went to sleep at that point, enveloped in some kind of silent void. But on some other physical plane I remained there, awake, having drinks with her. I watched her lips move, mouthing dialogue to a film I could no longer hear. It was like looking at some actress from the twenties, pale makeup and all, in one of those silent films I used to watch in high school.

Outwardly, I was still somehow able to nod, smile and respond to what she was saying, although my answers were something akin to those found on the bottom of an eight-ball fortune teller: "yes," "no," "these things are not knowable." Eventually the dreamlike world and the real world collided into an indistinguishable yellow blur, an amber wave of brain. Then, darkness.

* * *

When I woke up again, she was gone. The waitress told me she had paid the bill. I saw three dollars lying on the table. I added another two, a small fee for sleeping in a public place. I gathered up my Walkman, stumbled out of the restaurant and caught a train for home.

I got back to my apartment and went upstairs in the late afternoon heat. I stripped, went into the shower and turned on the cold water. Missus Calabrone promptly thumped with her broom handle. One shower a day. It was in my lease. I stayed in the shower a moment longer, then shut off the water and came out. I toweled myself off and began to sweat anew. I picked up the phone and dialed Bix's number. It rang five times before a zonked, disoriented voice picked up.

"Hullo?"

"Bix?"

"Mal, is that you?"

"Yeah, it's me."

I heard him stretch and yawn and give the kind of appreciative grunt that indicated he was glad to be alive. And glad to have slept into the afternoon.

"Hey, pretty wild last night, eh, Mal?"

I despised him for still being in bed and, above all, waking up refreshed and in a good mood. This was not the game plan. He was supposed to have hated the 3-D Club, hated the music, lost sleep, woken up grumpy and regretful. Then he'd have told me I was crazy for getting mixed up with a post-punk dirge singer and I could return to getting my circadian rhythms back on track in a more conventional manner.

"What time is it, Mal?"

"I don't know." I squinted at the kitchen clock. It said four o'clock. "It's late. Late afternoon. It's practically evening."

"Thanks for getting me up."

"Don't mention it," I said. "And thank you for abandoning me in the neighborhood of the Punishing Skulls."

"That woman said she'd take you home. What was her name?"

Uh oh.

"I don't know."

"Did you get home okay?"

No, I'm in a bar in Tangiers with tattoos all over my body.

"Yes," I said. "I guess you could say I got home okay."

"So what happened?"

"Happened? Nothing happened. We talked a little on the way home. Well, she talked, anyway. I didn't talk much." I didn't tell Bix that she'd given me a kiss that could suck the life force out of the universe. I didn't like to talk about such things. And I hoped she wasn't the type to suck the life force from the universe and tell. "We met for lunch today."

"No kidding? Atta' boy, Mal. What's she like?"

"I'm not sure."

"What did you talk about?"

"I don't know. Drummers. Ringo, I think."

"Ringo?"

"I don't know. I've got to listen to the tape."

"What tape?"

"I taped our lunch today."

"You videotaped it?"

"No. Audio. I used my recording Walkman."

"Did she know you were taping her?"

"I don't know. I don't think so."

"I think that's illegal, Mal."

"I don't think she'll go to the cops. She's a thief. She stole a book on substance abuse for her drummer."

"Did she say that on tape?"

"No. I don't know. Why?"

"I don't think you can use it in court if she didn't know you were taping her."

"I don't want to use it in court. I'm just using the tape for myself. My own private home use."

"Did you call to get my advice on this?"

"No. I wanted to wake you up."

"I'm awake. Ready to face the day," Bix said energetically.

"The day is facing in the other direction," I said.

After I got off the phone with Bix, I sat down at the kitchen table and pulled a magnet pen off the refrigerator. On a blank space on the back of an envelope I wrote:

Hours slept in 3-D Club men's room: 1:30

Hours slept at the restaurant: 1:30

Hours slept on couch: 1:40

Total hours slept: 4:40

Something was wrong. By my calculations, I'd been cheated. I was still supposed to be getting at least six hours of sleep in a twenty-four hour period and now it was closer to four-and-a-half. Maybe I was supposed to get another hour-and-a-half here at the kitchen table. I pulled my chair out a little, extended my legs and closed my eyes. Nothing happened. No, this isn't fair, I thought. I'm supposed to be losing a minute of sleep each night. But not more than that. I was already falling asleep with bread in my mouth. It was the kind of behavior that invited embarrassing fatalities.

I wondered, with all these random catnaps, if my brain knew we were still in the same twenty-four-hour cycle. Or has a new circadian rhythm already taken effect? If I could just sit down and have a little talk with my brain, one on one, perhaps I could get it to listen to reason. If I could motor up to the left side of my brain, park on the corpus collosum, arrange a meeting with the neurons and sensory tracts, I could say, "Look, I know I've been sleeping in book stores, men's rooms and restaurants, but that's all over now, I promise." I wouldn't even beg for the return of a normal night's sleep. I'd just ask for my hour-and-a-half back. Please.

While I mulled this over, I brewed a pot of coffee, poured a cup over a jelly jar filled with ice, downed it and went to the Arcadia Filmhaus.

"What's that on your hand?" Ginny asked, recoiling as I handed her paycheck to her that night.

I looked at the stamp on the back of my hand. I was hoping by now that the image would have faded or blurred and the ink stain would have taken on the quality of a Rorschach test, the whatever-you-think-it-it, that's-what-it-is look. But no, it was still clearly a dead cat.

I knew Ginny had some affection for cats. One evening she'd called in and told me she wouldn't be able to make it because there was a thunderstorm and Muffy, her cat, wouldn't come out from behind the umbrella stand. She said she'd have to stay home all night and try to coax the animal out with liver treats. So when Ginny saw the cat on my hand I wanted to lie and tell her it was an animal she might not have such tender feelings for. One whose demise she might not find so objectionable. A capybara, perhaps. Maybe I could convince her that the capybara was endangered and that I'd contributed to the cause and that they'd stamped my hand to show that I was a concerned citizen.

"It's a capybara," I said.

"A what?"

"A capybara. They're endangered."

"It looks like a cat," Ginny said.

"It is a cat," I confessed. Then I gave a little chuckle, shrugged and said, "Someone stamped it on my hand at a club last night." I thought perhaps she might find the situation innocent and amusing enough to join me in the chuckle. Maybe this would break the ice and years from now we'd see each other on the street and I'd say, "Remember when I had the dead cat on the back of my hand?" and she'd throw her head back and laugh and say, "Remember when you used to masturbate in the projection room?" and we'd go somewhere for coffee.

Instead, she looked crestfallen and her eyes darted to the floor. "A man on my block was arrested for abusing a cat," she said.

"I didn't do anything to any cats," I said. "Honestly."

"I have to go make popcorn now," she said solemnly.

The seven o'clock screening of *High and Low* played to four people. It was time to order another film. I had to change the film and marquee every few weeks or I feared someone from the city would come around to check up on me and make sure I was really showing films and not seducing young women or killing cats.

Before the nine o'clock show I went down to my office and pulled the film catalogue off the shelf. I skipped the popular stuff and thumbed my way directly to the back, where the foreign films were listed. The turnout for *High and Low* had surprised me. Usually my goal was to choose a film that I liked, but that no one would come to see. This wasn't easy. Once, I'd ordered what I presumed was an obscure Canadian film and it subsequently won a prize at Cannes the week I screened it. I had to form a ticket line, help Ginny at the candy counter and clean up all the Jujubes in the theater afterwards. Never again. But you never knew for sure. Another time, I'd taken a chance on a film called *Das Draht,* which turned out to be a twenty-minute industrial film about the making of wire. A few people came anyway.

Well-known films like Bergman's *Seventh Seal* and *Persona*, which I'd shown earlier in the year, pulled in hardly anyone. I think a lot of it had to do with video. Most Bergman films had become available on video and I guess people would rather rent it for three bucks and watch it at home than pay four bucks at my place and have to deal with Ginny's attitude. There just wasn't much of a market for large-screen Swedish despair anymore. But now I wanted to draw a few people in, to impress Anne. *Wild Strawberries* seemed a good bet. Anne liked it and she was a dental hygienist. And people liked to go to film events, things with live actors, cheese and schnapps. It was worth a shot, anyway. So I ordered *Wild Strawberries* to coincide with Soren Sonderby's visit to America, a few weeks away.

I looked down from my projection booth at nine-fifteen that evening into an empty theater. I told Ginny she could go home. She made a phone call and ten minutes later a kid in a day-glo tank top, a Piston's cap and a sneer pulled up in a shiny black Jeep convertible and honked the horn twice. Ginny grabbed her purse and darted out the door without saying good-bye.

High and Low was already threaded up, so I turned it on and let it run. I got some corn chips out of my office, poured myself a Sprite at the candy counter and ducked into the theater. I sat in the eighteenth row, just left of center. This was the way to do it. Like an aging Hollywood matinee idol spending his days watching his old films in his private screening room. In the dark and all alone. Bliss.

But it was no good. I couldn't concentrate. The lonely sound of the projector upstairs, the sound of my corn chip crunches echoing off the walls. It made me unbearably self-conscious. I needed something. Someone. I got up, went up to the projection booth and turned off the film. Then I went back to my office and dialed D-I-A-L-O-G-U.

"Dialogue, this is Anne. How may I help you?"

And once again the voice was speaking to me. The voice that could melt the peaks of Kilimanjaro, the voice that could convince a dozen Zen monks to throw in their robes and buy plaid jackets. The voice of salvation. And once again, I dissolved like a wet wafer.

"It's me again. Malcolm."

"Malcolm. Yes. Hello."

Just hearing her voice helped to flush out the nest of shrikes that were fluttering in my head. I suddenly wished I'd had the presence of mind to have recorded her simple words into my Walkman with one of those telephone suction microphones. *Malcolm. Yes. Hello.* My name, an affirmative response and a cheerful greeting. *Malcolm. Yes. Hello.* If I could only play those words on an endless tape loop when I needed them. It might

ease me through the difficult times. But I was already experiencing too much of life on a taped delay.

"It's good to hear your voice," I said.

I made some small talk, then casually dropped in a remark
about how I'd spent some time with a woman the night before
at the 3-D Club. I was careful to describe the experience with a
lack of specifics. I wanted Anne to know I was interested in
such things, like women, and that such things were interested
in me. Maybe even make Anne a little jealous, though I doubted
that eventuality. Even so, I was careful not to tell Anne that the
woman I'd spent time with sang post-punk dirges, got fired up
on coke, and drove too fast. I didn't tell Anne that I didn't
know the woman's name. I thought these colorful details might
give Anne the wrong impression about the type of woman I
was interested in dating. It might make Anne think I was desperate in some way. I wanted to make it clear to Anne, however, that I could see room for improvement. And that my idea
of improvement included Anne.

"We clash on some issues," I said, in a nonspecific summa-
tion of my feelings for the post-punk dirge singer.

But before I could re-address the matter of getting together
for pie and coffee, Anne had already locked into her take-a-
sad-song-and-make-it-better mode.

"There must be something about her," Anne said. "Why do
you think you're attracted to her?"

Attracted? It seemed much too strong a word. I was fasci-
nated. Intrigued. Bowled over, perhaps. But attracted? So far
her greatest attributes were the fact that she could stay up late,
was a good kisser and kept her toenails well-manicured. It
seemed shallow. And discussing these facts certainly wouldn't

win me any points with Anne. I pretended to give the matter some serious thought, then sighed deeply as if searching my mind for the most succinct answer.

"Attracted . . . hmmm . . ."

"Perhaps something unusual happened?" Anne asked, trying to be helpful. "Something that hasn't happened with anyone before."

Yes, I thought. Everything. Everything I did with the postpunk dirge singer was different from anything I'd done before. But nothing I felt comfortable telling to Anne. Then I remembered the crying thing. It seemed innocuous enough.

"I cried," I finally said.

"You cried? You cried when you were with this woman?"

"Not with her, no. But I cried when I was near her. I was in another room." I didn't mention that it was while I was sleeping in the men's room. Details.

"That's good," Anne said. "It sounds like you're not afraid to express your emotions."

"It was more like whimpering, actually," I said. "So I guess you could say I'm not afraid to express my whimpering."

"It's good you're getting your feelings out," Anne said. "Do you think you're in a better place now? A better place than you were with Lena?"

"Hmmm?" I felt my palms grow moist. Ah yes. Wasn't the whole idea of getting out of one relationship so that I would eventually find myself in a better one? Lena had done that. She'd moved upward on the desirable mate totem pole from neurotic projectionist to successful cardiologist. But where was I headed? More specifically, where was I headed with this type of conversation with Anne? I'd been circling her airfield, waiting for clearance and now I didn't feel as though I was landing on her carrier as much as plunging suicidally into her deck.

Where had I made my mistake with Anne? I shouldn't have fallen into the trap of allowing her to listen to my problems. You can't have problems around people who actually think they can solve them. But without my problems I didn't have much to offer in the way of conversation. Instead, I clammed up.

"You're not saying anything," Anne said.

I remained tightly sealed.

"Do you feel angry?"

"I don't really get angry," I said.

It was true. I never really got angry. It took too much energy. It sapped strength away from things I felt were more important, like walking, making breakfast, or swatting yellow jackets. And even swatting yellow jackets had nothing to do with anger. I knew the yellow jackets didn't have it in for me personally. I didn't think so, anyway. When I killed them, I did it quickly, before some ridiculous sense of remorse overcame me. And certainly before I had a chance to get angry. Was I angry at Lena? Nah. Let her have her cardiologist if that's what she wants. About the only person I knew I was mad at was Anne for not wanting to get together with me. But I knew I couldn't tell her that. When I told Anne I didn't get angry she just tacked more books onto my reading list—*Back Off!* and *The Big Book of Rage.*

"Stay with your feelings. These are good feelings you're having. This is an important time for you," Anne said.

My feelings, my real feelings, the ones I was communicating with all the fluidity of undercooked potatoes being pushed through a strainer, were the feelings of frustration towards this phone conversation. If I could only get past it, I knew there was a woman behind this wall of self-help books that I wanted to know better.

All I really knew about Anne was that she cleaned teeth by day and comforted souls by night. So, at her behest, I stayed with my feelings and said, "I feel a little funny talking about these things with you. I think it's because I don't know a lot about you. I'd like to know more about you, Anne."

"It's important for us to stay client-focused," she said, like a board director at a corporate conclave. "This isn't about me, it's about you. Like I said, this is an important time for you."

Yes, I thought, it's important that in my last sixteen months, more or less, before my heart explodes, I spend some time getting to know a woman like you.

"Yes," I said. "But part of what I'm about is wanting to know what you're about. I mean, I let you put a poster in my lobby. You told me you might be interested in coming to my film festival. We know each other a little. Doesn't that give me some slack in this area?"

"Okay, Malcolm, " she said, loosening a bit. "What would you like to know?"

"I don't know. What's your favorite kind of column?"

"Column? You mean like Doric, Corinthian or Ionic?"

"Right."

"Doric is low proportions, shaft without base?"

"Yes."

"I think I prefer that."

"Really? I would have seen you as more the Ionic type. Slender proportions, spiral ornaments."

She laughed. "It's a toss-up, I guess. Anything else?"

"Yes. Are you coming to my film festival?"

"I don't know, Malcolm." She paused. This time it was a good pause. A pause that refreshed. "Are you really showing *Wild Strawberries*?"

"I'm going to have a really good print for the screening," I said. "And did I mention that I'll be serving cheese and schnapps?"

"Yes."

"Did I mention I'd be having a Bergman actor as a guest lecturer?"

"Yes, I think you said something about that."

"So, is there a possibility?"

"There's a possibility. I'm on call a lot at the hotline as a volunteer, so I can't say for sure."

"It's good you keep busy," I said, wishing I could be more productive with my own time.

"There's never enough time to do everything I want to do," she said.

There it was in a nutshell, I thought. She was still trying to figure if I was important enough to include in the things-to-do column of her life.

"You know what you need?" I said.

"What's that?"

"A watch without hands. You know. Like the clock in *Wild Strawberries*."

And then, suddenly, just as things were starting to go my way with Anne a little bit, I felt a wave of nostalgia and loss.

"I have to go now," I said. "I'll talk to you later."

I sat in the projection room staring at my wrist. I remembered what had happened to my watch.

chapter nine

Having and eventually losing my watch had something to do with my having seen Lena naked in the daylight on my desk at the Arcadia Filmhaus one afternoon. Early on, in the first year of our long relationship, Lena and I had enjoyed an unparalleled season of uninhibited sexuality. In memory, times like these seem to loom larger and last for years, but, in actuality, it lasted only about three months, then it dropped off considerably. After a spate of relentless carnal pleasures, Lena and I settled into a groove in which we deluded ourselves into believing we still maintained an adventurous sex life. In fact, it was only a mechanical completion of a few predetermined acts. By the time we reached this mundane plateau, we'd come to convince ourselves that not doing it face to face, or doing it while the "Tonight Show" was on, was still within the realm of "adventure." This belief sustained us for many years.

But in that frenzied first summer of ours together, Lena's erotic sense of daring knew no bounds, nor geographical boundaries. Thus, it was not unusual that we found ourselves on the slippery hood of Lena's yellow Camaro in a vacant Big Boy parking lot. Or on top of the washers in her friend's apartment, feeding quarters into the slot to keep the spin cycle going. Or, even in her mother's living room on Memorial Day, with her mother in the next room making potato salad, explaining how some people put in too much mayonnaise and how she puts in just enough so you know it's there.

All these events were initiated by Lena. I was far too shy to suggest a re-creation of any scene I'd memorized from the letter pages of *Penthouse*. I was young and Lena was only the second woman I'd ever had sex with, so I was just glad to be part of the program. Not that I didn't consider, at one point, sending my own letter to *Penthouse*, since my sex life was beginning to take on that quality that makes lonely men envious.

The point is that I was pleased, though not altogether sur-prised, when one day I found Lena naked on my desk at the Arcadia Filmhaus. We'd stopped there one afternoon on the Fourth of July when the theater was closed. Our ultimate desti-nation was a backyard barbecue, hosted by some of Lena's friends, but first I needed to retrieve my wallet, which I'd left at the theater the night before. I located it in my office, near the coffeemaker, after an extensive, self-absorbed search. When I turned around, Lena's clothes were draped over the film reel racks and she was reclining, naked, on my desk.

I sat down at my desk, quite calmly, and opened her legs as if I were opening the afternoon mail, separating the flyers from the bills. But this particular envelope, hers, was not one I'd ever opened in daylight before. And as I did so, the late afternoon sun streamed in through the venetian blinds laying tracks of light across her body. There was a warm red glow between her thighs. In that moment, my sense of time and space suspended and I became transfixed. All lewd thoughts and carnal desires left me. A whole new world was opening itself up to me and my

only thought was: What a vast and wondrous universe this is!
So many secrets. So many possibilities. So many folds.

I remained there, between her legs, for what seemed like an
eternity, meditating on this lotus flower of enlightenment. Then
she roughly shoved my head forward and had me perform something that was oddly anticlimactic and disappointing, especially
after the incredible feeling of serenity and well-being that had
preceded it.

Later, at the barbecue and in the days that followed, I had a
strong desire to relate this exquisite moment to someone. Not
in an ugly, testosterone-gone-wild sense. Not among the group
of beer-swilling men huddled around the Grillmaster, inhaling
the smell of burning sausages. Not while knocking off my fifth
beer of the night, crushing the aluminum can with my fist, belch-
ing and announcing: "Did I ever tell you fellows about the time
Lena was naked on my desk in the daytime?" No.

It was when I saw children crying. Couples arguing. People
eating alone in restaurants. The elderly, the homeless, the ter-
minally ill. I wanted to communicate with the sad and the suffering, the bewildered and beleaguered. I wanted to tell these
people: "I've seen a woman naked on my desk in the daylight
and I can tell you, the world is a wonderful place after all, full
of folds and possibilities."

Unfortunately, that feeling of bliss was short-lived. After that
would come years of boredom, arguments and misunderstand-
ings, and in all that time the afternoon matinee at the Arcadia
Filmhaus never repeated itself. No matter how good things were
at times, I never again saw Lena in that special way, that special
light. I saw her when she changed into her bathing suit and I
saw her plenty of times in the cruel bedroom light of post-sex

clean-up time. But it was never the same as that time in the Arcadia Filmhaus.

Years later, after we'd broken up, when I'd come to think that perhaps it had something to do with the unique circumstances of the moment, I found myself on a date with another woman on a Fourth of July. I was standing with her in a long line at a Dairy Queen, waiting to order a couple of dip cones. More in an attempt to make conversation than for information, she asked me what time it was. I didn't have my watch, so I asked a man in a fishing hat behind me in line and he told me it was three-fifteen and I passed this information along to her. Then I looked up at the angle of the sun, the way the shadows were being cast by the giant soft cone on the roof of the Dairy Queen, and I suddenly wondered if the light was coming through the blinds in my office at the Arcadia Filmhaus the way it had years earlier. I wondered if that unique moment from years ago had something to do with the time of year, the time of day, the angle of the sun and the fact that it was the Fourth of July. A perfect equation of elements. And then I wondered if I could convince this woman, whom I hardly knew and had never slept with, to get out of line, drive across town to the Arcadia Filmhaus, let me set her up on the desk naked and see if there was something really special about it or not. But then the line moved forward, she was ordering and the moment passed. And the opportunity never arrived again.

But I came to realize that the event was not specifically connected to the Fourth of July or the angle of the light coming in through the blinds in my office or even sex, for that matter. It was rather a golden, once-in-a-lifetime moment. A moment of discovery. A moment where the world unfolded and presented all of its opportunities. In that moment, everything was exactly as it should be. I did not long nostalgically for some event from the past, nor did I ache for some eventuality in the future. I was in exactly the right place at exactly the right time. For one brief, shining moment, everything was right with the world.

A few years after I'd seen Lena on my desk and we were still dating, we went to a sidewalk cafe in the city for dinner. We were relaxing, eating good food, drinking good wine and having one of those evenings that later we could reflect on and say, "but there were some good times, too."

In a whimsical moment brought on by the wine, I asked Lena what she thought was the most significant moment in our relationship. Without hesitating, she said it was day I accompanied her to the veterinarian to put her ailing thirteen-year-old Miniature Schnauzer to sleep. Then she asked me, I think perfunctorily, which moment I thought was the most significant in our relationship. I hadn't really expected her to bounce the question back in my court and I had no answer ready. But I gave it some thought and finally said:

"I think it was when I saw you naked on my desk on the Fourth of July and felt everything was going to be all right with the world."

Not only did Lena not remember it, forcing me to give her several details about her clothes on the film reel rack and so forth, but she was utterly disgusted to learn that of all the things I could have thought of, this is the one I'd chosen as significant. My eleven-year-old Springer Spaniel had been put to sleep when I was eleven, and that had been a traumatic and defining moment in my life, but it had nothing to do with Lena. Then I wished I'd said, "It was the day when I realized I wish you'd been there when I was eleven and my Springer Spaniel died." But that didn't sound right either. And then I wished I'd simply said, "Yes, it was when your Miniature Schnauzer died for me, as well." But it was too late. She left the rest of the meal on her plate and we rode home that day in silence.

About a month later, after I'd forgotten about the incident at the sidewalk cafe, Lena bought me a wristwatch. It wasn't my birthday or anything, she just bought me a watch because I didn't have one and she said I needed one.

There was nothing unusual about the watch, it wasn't gold, it didn't display the date or anything. Just a simple Timex watch with regular numerals and a black leather band. But I was grateful and I told her so and I put it on and I admired it and I showed it to friends and family and waitresses and bank tellers. But something was still wrong. Lena gave me the feeling that I hadn't reacted properly to the gift and eventually she told me as much, saying with a sigh:

"The watch was something special. Doesn't it feel like something special to you?"

I knew she was referring to our discussion a month earlier at the sidewalk cafe. I wanted to tell her that yes, the watch was a wonderful, sweet, unexpected gift, all things that I truly felt. But it was, in fact, nothing compared to seeing her naked on my desk that afternoon. This time I knew better, however, and I nodded, smiled and admired the watch and said:

"Yes, this really is very special."

And I thought that would be the end of it.

But something was still wrong, in Lena's mind I guess, because she kept bringing it up. "Do you like your watch?" "You didn't expect it, did you?" "I love when you wear the watch I gave you." Then I realized she was determined to force the watch to become a symbol of a bond between us. But moreover, I think she was trying to use the watch to displace my memory of seeing her naked on my desk.

What I couldn't tell her, could never tell her, was that the thing I liked most about the watch was the fact that it reminded me of the very thing she was trying to drive from my mind. And she must have known, intuition or something, because she still wasn't satisfied and told me she was going to have it engraved.

Lena removed the watch from my wrist and told me she was going to take it to a jeweler and engrave it with some meaningful sentiment. But I never saw it again. By this time I'd had the watch for several months and had gotten used to having it. When I started asking Lena when I'd have my watch returned to me she would dance around the question, saying she'd forgotten to take it to the jeweler's. Too busy one week, she hadn't had a chance to get over that way the next, and so on. Eventually I stopped asking about the watch. I just assumed, in time, I'd get it back. But I never did.

Years later, when Lena and I broke up, I gave her back her Paul Simon album and she returned my Cat Stevens album, but in the process of getting everything back to its rightful owner the subject of the watch never came up. By that time I'd buried the watch somewhere in the back of my mind. But the idea that I'd eventually get it back stayed with me and, for that reason, I refrained from buying another watch. And although Lena never told me what she'd done with the watch, I created a kind of selective memory around its whereabouts. I knew it hadn't been stolen and that it wasn't really lost. But occasionally I searched my apartment for it, thinking perhaps somewhere along the line Lena had returned it to me and I'd just forgotten about it and misplaced it. But she hadn't and I hadn't.

When I remembered all this, as I did when Anne mentioned the clock in *Wild Strawberries*, I began to wonder about the watch again. I was a compulsive saver. I still had pens, clothes and canned goods from the seventies. But Lena was not this way. She saved very discriminately and was neat and organized with her things. Her socks stayed in her sock drawer and never ventured into her underwear drawer. Her stuffed animals were arranged on the bed in the exact same way every day, from smallest to tallest. So it was unlikely that the watch had gotten lost, mixed in or mixed up with something else.

So where was it? I knew that if I could give her bedroom a quick search I could find it. Like in those spy films where the hero finds the missing microfilm while the femme fatale is in the shower, and he's got about seven or eight minutes, depending on how thoroughly the femme fatale washes. In seven or eight minutes, tops, I could find my watch. I saw myself snatching up the watch in my fist and shouting "Aha!" Never in my life had I been able to shout "Aha!" Not about anything.

I knew then that I wanted the watch back. I didn't want Lena back. Just the watch. So that evening, after I'd talked to Anne and closed up the theater for the night, I went home and thought about calling Lena. I hadn't spoken to her in a while but her phone number was still scratched into my brain as if someone had taken a nail to a brick wall.

It was eleven-thirty that night when I sat down in my kitchen in my underwear and began to stare at the phone. It was too late to be calling anyone, especially an ex-girlfriend who was engaged to be married. I knew that Lena's mother would probably be out of the house. She worked the graveyard shift at Denny's. At least Lena would be alone, I thought.

I used to visit Lena around this time of night. Sometimes I'd park down the street in my car with the headlights extinguished and wait for her mother to back out of the driveway in her huge boat of a Chrysler LeBaron. Then I'd move in like a commando on a night mission and stay for an hour or two, or however long my mission took. Her mother never knew about these late-night forays into her daughter's bedroom. I don't think she knew, anyway.

I picked up the phone and dialed quickly, knowing that I would chicken out if I hesitated. Lena's mother answered the phone.

"Hello?"

"Hello. May I speak to Lena, please?"

"Who's calling?" The voice was disapproving and suspicious. Everything you'd expect from the mother of an ex-girlfriend.

"This is Malcolm," I said. "How are you this evening, Missus Karponski?"

I tried to sound polite but I'm sure I sounded like one of those guys who tries to sell real estate over the phone. The kind of voice that fully deserves to be hung up on.

"You shouldn't be calling here, Malcolm."

"Why not?"

Missus Karponski clucked her tongue. "Malcolm. Lena's getting married in a few weeks."

"Yes, I know. That's fine. That's not why I'm calling, though. May I speak to her, please?"

"I don't think she'll want to speak with you."

"Could you ask her, please? I'd really appreciate it."

"Do you know what time it is? It's very late."

"Yes, I know. I thought you'd be gone by now."

"I'm late," Missus Karponski said tersely, "and you're making me later."

"I don't want to hold you up," I said. "If you'd just let me speak to Lena."

She sighed. "Well, it's none of my business, I guess. Hold on."

Missus Karponski dropped the phone onto a hard surface and the noise reported back sharply in my ear. I heard the television on in the background. An actor who sounded smooth and authoritative was telling someone else to halt or he'd shoot. I tried to register the way the word "halt" was said, so that I could report back to Bix on it, but then there was a lot of shooting, so the actor's "halt" apparently hadn't been that effective anyway. As Lena approached the phone I heard her mother telling her that it was me, Malcolm, yes *that* Malcolm, and no, she didn't know what I wanted and yes, she'd told me how I shouldn't be calling and no, I'm not going to tell him that, you tell him that. It made me a tad apprehensive.

"Malcolm?" Lena's voice was just as disapproving and suspicious as her mother's. Something in the genes.

"Yes, it's me. Hello."

Lena left a space in the air you could have filled with ten thousand airplanes.

"Malcolm," she finally said, as if just uttering my name was an affront to her senses, "what do you want?"

"Did you call me?" I asked. It was a pretty feeble response but I hadn't expected her to get to the heart of the matter so quickly. "I was just getting in," I continued, "and my phone was ringing and I went to answer it and there was no one there. So I thought it might have been you."

"No, Malcolm, it wasn't me."

"Oh."

"How could you possibly think it was me, Malcolm? Don't you know anyone else?"

"Sure. Of course. But I thought, if it was you, then it must be pretty important since we haven't spoken in a while and you never call me. So I figured I'd better call right back to find out what was going on. I couldn't imagine you'd just call for no reason."

"But I didn't call."

"No. But I thought you might have." I cleared my throat. "Anyway, how are you?"

"I'm fine."

"Good. Good."

"You shouldn't have called, Malcolm. I'm getting married in a few weeks."

"Yes, I know. I already had this conversation with your mother."

"I can't stay on the phone. Andrew is supposed to call soon."

Andrew? Why not 'Andy'? Lena had always called me 'Mal' and only used 'Malcolm' when she was angry at me, which she apparently now was. If she's using his full first name, I thought, she can't be all that happy with him.

"So this Andrew. Is he a nice guy?"

"Of course he's a nice guy, Malcolm. I'm marrying him."

"So he doesn't rough you up or anything?"

"Don't be silly. He's a perfect gentleman. He's a doctor."

"Yes. Well, the two don't always go hand in hand. Who was that doctor in Ohio? Doctor Sheperd? The one they say killed his wife. No one will ever know for sure. You can't be too careful. Looks can be deceiving. Look at Ted Bundy. Nice guy, a real charmer."

"Andrew is very nice. Very normal."

There was something that suggested comparative abnormality in me, but I let the remark pass.

"Aren't you seeing anyone, Malcolm?"

"As a matter of fact, I am."

"What's she like?"

"I don't know that much about her yet. I have a tape I have to play."

"A tape? Is this one of those video dating services?"

"No. It's an audio tape. I didn't meet her through a dating service, I met her in a bookstore. We had lunch and I taped our conversation."

"Does she know you were taping her? I think it's illegal. I don't think you've thought this thing out."

"No, it's not that. It's just that I'm having a little trouble staying awake when we're together, so I taped it. I'm going through something, I don't know what exactly. A French doctor, a specialist, told me there's nothing clinically wrong with me. I think it may have something to do with my circadian rhythms. And I've got these yellow jackets living in my wall . . ."

" . . . Mother told me she saw you in Sears and that you have yellow jackets. For God's sake, Malcolm, move out of that place."

"Well, it's bad, but it isn't as bad as it sounds. I'm sure it's not as bad as your mother made it sound. It's not like the place is crawling with insects. Just yellow jackets. And they live in the wall, and only one or two at a time come out. The thing is, Lena, I don't think I could handle a move right now. I'm having enough trouble just moving around. In general, I mean. Even the yellow jackets have trouble getting around. I think it's the heat."

"It's not normal living with yellow jackets like that. And you shouldn't be calling me, telling me about your problems with yellow jackets. That's not normal either."

"I didn't. I didn't call you to tell you I have yellow jackets. I'm just telling you. I have yellow jackets."

"So why did you call?"

"Why is it so strange that I should call? We were together for seven years, Lena. I mean, I know we argued a lot, but there's no reason we shouldn't still talk to each other. I mean, Lena, there are people who have been in far more stressful situations than you and I. POWs, for instance. Plane crash survivors. They still get together and talk."

I was getting away from the point a bit. Ask her for the watch. Ask her for the watch and get off the phone.

"I really have to go," Lena said. "Andrew is going to be calling me and I don't want to have to explain that the line was busy because I was talking to you about yellow jackets and plane crash survivors."

"Does Andrew know about me?"

"Of course. I don't have any secrets from him."

"What did you say about me?"

"This is really sad, Malcolm."

"No, really. I'd like to know."

"I told him we had some good times early on and then we argued a lot and then we broke up."

"That's it? That's seven years in a nutshell?"

"I haven't had the time or the inclination to tell him everything we ever did or discussed."

"Did you tell him all the places we had sex?"

"That's it. I'm hanging up."

"No, I'd just like to know. You said you told him everything."

"Everything that was important."

"Does he know how large my penis is, for example?"

"I'm hanging up."

"No, I'm just curious, that's all. I don't think I like the idea of my personal life being told to him. Then he tells it to someone else and then it gets retold and it never stops. It's like *Roots* or something."

"It's not important."

"Not important to whom?"

"Malcolm. You're being ridiculous. I'm hanging up the phone."

"Wait a minute, Lena." I took a deep breath. Easy, boy. "Look, Lena, I'm sorry. I apologize. Forget what I said. I'm not trying to give you a hard time. Honest."

"Why did you call me, Malcolm? What is it that you want?"

"What do I want? My watch. I just want my watch back."

"What watch? What are you talking about?"

"My watch. A Timex watch with a black leather band. The watch you gave me."

"Did you lose it?"

"I don't think so. I think you have it." I posed it as a suggestion rather than an accusation. It made me feel as if I was still sort of in control. Like a car with no brakes but a good steering wheel.

"What makes you think I have it?" Lena asked.

It was a classic non-denial denial. Lena had majored in political science, the gateway to a career in radiology. She'd written a paper on Nixon's innocence in the Watergate affair and had learned a thing or two about how to avoid implication through slippery rhetoric. Lena's politically evasive response confirmed in my mind that she knew where the watch was and that she wasn't about to hand it over.

"I want my watch," I said firmly. "Do you know where it is, or not?"

If she could play Nixon, I could play Woodward and Bernstein. One of them, at least. The shorter one.

"I have to get off the phone," Lena said. "It's ridiculous for you to call me like this."

She wasn't going to loosen up. The more I shone a bright light on her, the more Lena dried up hard, like pottery clay.

"All right," I said. "I guess we can discuss the watch some other time."

"Malcolm, listen to me. I don't want to discuss the watch with you. I don't want to talk to you any more. I'm getting married soon."

"I know that. Does that mean you don't have any time for me?"

"Not unless you're a florist, a caterer or a musician."

"These florists and caterers and musicians, did you spend seven years with them? Did they all get watches too? I suppose I'm not invited to this wedding."

It wasn't that I wanted to go to the wedding, really. It would be too strange, I thought, to watch someone I'd once seen naked on my desk get all dressed up in a bridal gown and marry someone else. I just didn't like be excluded, or worse, restricted. And I still wanted my watch back.

"I'm getting off the phone," Lena said. "I'm putting down the receiver."

"I'll talk to you later, Lena."

"I wish you wouldn't," Lena said, and she put down the receiver.

I hung up the phone and sat in my underwear in the dark for a while, sweating. Was it the heat, I wondered, or the after effects of talking to Lena? I felt like a moth getting dangerously close to a candle's flame. Working myself into a lather and being confrontational hadn't helped matters any. How was I going to survive the hot summer months if I couldn't even keep my cool emotionally? I thought about what Lena had said about my living with the yellow jackets. Maybe she was right. Maybe it was abnormal to be co-habitating with them and eventually it would all close in on me. The heat would melt the wallpaper paste and the yellow paper would slide down the walls like hot mustard. Then the yellow jackets would invade like an angry wave and feed off my limp, lifeless body for several days until Missus Calabrone found me.

I got up from the kitchen table and filled a dishtowel with ice. Then I went into the living room, sat down on the couch and ran the ice pack over my legs and temples. It was still too early to attempt a shot at bedtime. The only thing to do was sit in the dark and stay as still as possible. My Walkman was on the coffee table in front of me. I fumbled for it in the dark and pulled the tape out of it. I got up, turned on my stereo, slipped the tape into the tape deck and hit the play button. I sat back on the couch and closed my eyes.

I was expecting to hear the voice of the post-punk balladeer and the chatter I'd missed when I'd fallen asleep in the restaurant. Instead, classical piano music burst forth from the speakers. I got up quickly and turned the volume down.

The music wasn't anything I recognized from my own archives. It was a beautiful tenor voice, a woman's, accompanied by piano. I looked at the tape through the little illuminated window. The tape was a stranger. But it was soothing, so I left it on.

By now I'd figured out that the post-punk dirge singer must have changed the tape in my Walkman after I'd fallen asleep. She was tricky, that one. But as I listened to the music I was thinking about what she must have thought of me for recording our lunch. I thought about how she might be listening to the tape now. I wasn't really paying attention to the music. So it wasn't until the next song, "Cry Me a River," that I suddenly realized who I was listening to.

I couldn't bear to hear her sing "Cry Me a River" again, so I rewound the tape to the beginning and listened to the classical piece again. It was stunning. Her voice had the same crystal resonance but with a bit less despair. It felt like God's music, her voice a perfect instrument, plucking notes from the heavens off sweet angel harps. Just the kind of thing you'd expect to hear at a wedding. It took a few seconds more before the thought returned to the door of my brain and knocked more insistently. Wedding. Didn't I know someone who was getting married?

I pulled the tape out of the machine and turned on the light in the living room. The tape had a label on it, written in red ball point, which said: *Demo: Darlene Bleeker.* It was followed by her phone number.

Darlene Bleeker? Darlene? It certainly wasn't the exotic name I'd been expecting. It was close to being normal. Average. It sounded like it could be the name of a woman who gave forecasts on the twenty-four-hour weather channel. "Residents of the Northeastern portion of the United States will need to carry an umbrella today. A cold snap in Barcelona. Italy, wear a jacket. I'm Darlene Bleeker."

Now that I knew who she was, now that I could attach a name to the face, I felt Darlene Bleeker starting to become more real to me. I sat and listened to the rest of the tape. It ran about thirty minutes long and alternated between post-punk dirges and ballads and classical selections. An obvious effort to display her versatility. I fast forwarded through the dirges and ballads, which I found too painful to listen to, and listened carefully to the classical pieces. It seemed like two different people. Between the two, I figured there must be one person in there that I wanted to be with, and I suddenly felt compelled to see her.

It was midnight on a Saturday. A good time to catch her at the 3-D Club. I dressed, went downstairs and jumped into my VW bus. I turned the key and cranked it hard but the motor did nothing but whinny like a horse that had just been gunned down. I smelled gasoline fumes and realized that in my haste, I'd flooded the engine.

I sat for a while, leaning my body against the big round steering wheel, trying to remember why I'd purchased such a useless behemoth. I'd bought the beast off a used car lot a few months after I'd broken up with Lena.

I'd admired the round, pop-up toaster look of VW buses since the sixties. The owners of these vehicles were bearded men with long hair and aviator sunglasses. They had sheep dogs panting happily in the passenger seat. Drivers of these vehicles seemed to know what words like "leisure" and "off-time" meant.

"It's a hippymobile," Lena complained whenever I'd expressed a desire to have one. "I won't be seen driving around in a hippymobile."

After Lena and I broke up, I started looking around for one in earnest. I checked the want ads and eventually found one that said:

> Deadheads: Cruise the open road in this
> free spirit 1969 VW Microbus. $1000
> drives you to the nearest nirvana

At the time, I wasn't aware what a deadhead was. It sounded like a pretty accurate description of me. Moreover, I assumed the ad implied that it was something of a low-maintenance, worry-free vehicle. Something anyone could keep running, even a deadhead.

So I laid out nine hundred and fifty dollars, thinking I was getting a real deal. When I drove it off the lot I tried to put one of my cassettes into the stereo but the tape was swallowed up in a giant hole that turned out to be an eight-track player. I opened the glove compartment and found a couple of grimy, weathered eight-tracks by the Grateful Dead. Lena had been right. It was a hippymobile.

Undeterred, I tried to get into the spirit of things, or rather, the free spirit of things. They stopped making eight-tracks in the seventies, so it was pretty much the Dead or nothing, but I played them anyway. I cruised around looking for women hitchhiking in tie-dye shirts and headbands, looking to have my very own summer of love.

But I was nothing more than a tragic man-out-of-time. One of the eight-tracks got jammed in the player and repeated "Casey Jones" endlessly. Trouble ahead. Trouble behind. Trouble ahead. Trouble behind. It might have been interesting if I'd been high on exotic mushrooms somewhere out in the middle of the California desert, but I was an art house movie theater manager driving around in the suburbs and I found it irritating. So I ripped the eight-track out of the dash, leaving brown entrails of tape behind, and never used it again.

Then things started going wrong with the bus. I replaced the alternator, mended the radiator and changed the fan belt in the first few weeks. Instead of driving me to the nearest nirvana, the bus was being towed to the nearest VW mechanic.

"This takes me back," the old German mechanic would say, as he lovingly regarded the useless, rusty parts he removed from under the hood of my bus. As he grew more sentimental, I wrote larger checks.

Thank God, I didn't need to rely on the bus much. My microcosmic world was usually a short walk away. I'd convinced myself that I was keeping the bus for aesthetic and sentimental reasons but the truth was I couldn't give it away, let alone sell it. Sometimes, however, when the moon and stars were in the right position, or if the Dead were in town, the thing would start up and run just fine. I prayed tonight would be one of those nights.

I turned the key again and stomped down hard on the gas pedal. Nothing. I did it again, but this time I jammed the key in the ignition harder, like I was bending someone's arm behind his back. The engine gave in to the torture and suddenly vroomed alive. I floored it. I watched in my rear view mirror as a huge cloud of toxic white smoke billowed and then disappeared into the darkness. I put it in first, let the clutch out and screeched away into the night. Here I come, Darlene Bleeker.

When I got out on the highway, however, I started thinking what things would be like at the 3-D Club at this time of night.

There'd undoubtedly be another mob scene at the club. And there might be people who recognized me as the whimperer in the men's room from the night before. Besides, it was only midnight. Too early to be able to talk to Darlene.

So I suddenly found myself taking an exit and heading towards the southwestern suburbs. To Lena's house. Every time I hit a pot hole, the Darlene Bleeker demo cassette jangled in my breast pocket. I wasn't sure why I'd brought the cassette or what I was planning to do with it. I thought maybe I could use it as a bartering tool. Maybe trade her the world's best wedding singer for my watch. I didn't really know. For now I was just driving. Maybe a plan would come to me later, when I needed it.

Lena's house was at the end of a tree-lined block on a quiet suburban street. It was the kind of house you see on the news all the time that looks really normal on the outside but turns out to be the scene of some ghastly beheading or something. I'd been to the house hundreds of times, both during the day and at night, and it always gave me that same impression.

I stopped my car halfway down the block and stared at the dark house. I didn't want to pull in the driveway, have Lena look out through the living room curtains, see me and call the police. I put the car in park and turned off the engine. Her mother's car wasn't in the driveway, so I knew Lena was alone. All I was doing, I told myself, was visiting, unannounced. People did it all the time. The only difference was that it was after midnight, she was alone and I was parked halfway down the block watching her house. It felt a bit more like I was stalking her, but I shrugged off this feeling.

I sat for a while more, just staring at the house. Sweating. Looking at the clock on the dashboard grow later and later.

What was I doing? It was a question I asked myself a lot, so I didn't pay too much attention to it.

I got out of the VW, walked up the street and arrived at her front door. There was a sign above the door that I'd been told meant "welcome" in Hungarian, but in its native language, illuminated only by moonlight, it looked like a sign you'd find at Dracula's castle. I pushed my hair out of my face and knocked. I tried to make the knock sound friendly, but it's impossible to make a knock sound friendly after midnight.

I saw Lena look through the curtains with a bewildered expression on her face. When she saw that it was me, her eyes rolled up into her head. She opened the door, sighed heavily and stood inside the foyer with her arms crossed. She didn't invite me in so I just stood there.

"This is really too much, Malcolm," she said, shaking her head.

"I know," I said.

She had on a green nightshirt that I recognized. It had a zipper up the front that ran from her clavicle to her shins. The teeth of the zipper were a little off track just a few inches under her breasts. I recalled many nights when I had to stop, right at that point, and fiddle with that zipper until I could continue. I thought of Lena now, without me, putting that nightshirt on every night and getting tripped up in the exact same spot. I pictured Doctor Andrew Buntrock, cardiologist, getting tripped up in the same spot, fumbling with it just as I had. It seemed absurd, thinking of everyone getting tripped up on the same zipper, for generations to come.

"You scared the hell out of me," Lena said.

"I'm sorry," I said. "I tried to knock friendly." I showed her what I meant by repeating the gesture on her front door, but it just looked silly.

Lena's eyes followed my hand as I put it back down by my side. She was looking at the dead cat on the back of my hand. I looked down at it. It was faded, but it was still a dead cat. It looked like one of those cartoons where the cat dies and the transparent cat body with a halo and wings rises up out of the dead cartoon cat body.

"What is that?"

"It's a dead cat," I said. "Can I come in?"

She didn't answer but moved away from the door and walked into the kitchen. It wasn't exactly an invitation, but I followed her in. Funny thing about a dead cat, I thought. Gets you in some places, keeps you out of others.

It was about forty degrees cooler in Lena's kitchen than it had been outside. Lena and her mother always kept the house brisk, no matter what kind of electric bills this incurred. It was a welcome excess. I sat down at the kitchen table.

"It's nice and comfortable in here," I said. "It's still godawful hot outside."

"You can't stay," Lena said. She leaned against the stove and kept her arms tightly crossed.

"I know." I said. " I won't stay. I just wanted to stop by."

"Why?" She asked it very directly. It wasn't one of those whys you could dance around or ignore.

"I don't know," I said. "I just wanted to see you again before you got married, I guess."

"This isn't good, Malcolm," Lena said.

"I just wanted to see you, that's all. I mean, pretty soon you'll be married and you'll own a home in some far western suburb

I've never heard of. Or maybe Doctor Buntrock will get transferred to the cardiology wing of some hospital in Missouri and you'll be having kids and I won't know where you are or what you're doing."

"That's how it's supposed to be," she said. "That's what's supposed to happen. You aren't supposed to know where I am, or what I'm doing."

"Why?" I tried to make my why just as direct as hers but it was lacking somehow. Maybe because there was no real commitment behind it. I was getting used to the fact that Lena might indeed move to Missouri some day with Doctor Buntrock and name her kids Andrew Jr. and Lenette. I just didn't like the way she was so neatly closing the book on our past.

"You're the one who ended it," Lena said. "Have you forgotten that? You're the one who said you didn't want to see me any more."

"People always say that when they're breaking up. It doesn't mean that person doesn't want to see the other person ever again. It just means . . . for a while. I said it like I meant it so that I'd be taken seriously."

"I took it very seriously."

"Right. I meant it then. I don't mean it as much now."

"Well, it still counts."

Still counts? It was a phrase I hadn't heard since the fourth grade. I'd said it and it still counted and now I couldn't take it back. There was a big script in the universe that demanded continuity. You couldn't deviate from it. If you did, there'd be chaos and the natural order of things would be destroyed and everything would change. Chappaquiddick would never have happened, Ted Kennedy would be president, there'd be thirteen planets instead of nine and pigs would live in trees.

I tried to recall what I'd said when I'd broken up with Lena. I didn't recall saying anything about never wanting to see her again. I remembered saying something like "this isn't working out," and that breaking up seemed like "the right thing to do." She didn't fight me much about it, either.

Lena had broken up with me a few times, when she thought she'd met someone better. But eventually the infatuations would wear off and she'd come back to me. And I took her back. But when I broke up with Lena it wasn't because there was someone new in my life. In fact, nothing was particularly wrong when I did it. I just thought it might feel good to break up with her for a change. Or maybe I wasn't clear on the rules and thought it was just my turn to break up with her. In any event, once it happened we never got back together again. I'm not sure why. Maybe because when you're not exactly sure why you break up, it's even harder to get back together. There's no place to begin. Nothing to patch or mend. Nothing to apologize for.

"What are you doing with yourself these days, Malcolm?"

"Right now I'm in the midst of coordinating a film festival," I said. It sure sounded like something important.

"You? You're having a film festival? Where?"

"What do you mean, 'where?' At the Arcadia Filmhaus. I'm showing *Wild Strawberries* for three nights only in July."

"You showed *Wild Strawberries* a few years back, didn't you? And no one came."

"Some people came," I said. "Besides, this is different. I've got a Swedish film actor coming in to lecture on Bergman."

Lena pushed out her lower lip, conceding that she was impressed, even though I knew she didn't care much for foreign films. It was one of the many things we'd wrangled about when

we were dating. My interest in world cinema, which Lena ini-
tially considered an attractive bit of eclecticism on my part,
turned sour after a few years. She would harangue me about
what she considered to be my stubborn resistance to show mainstream films.

"Everyone shows mainstream films," I once said. "The
Arcadia fills a void."

"The Arcadia *is* a void," she argued, citing my nearly negli-
gible ticket sales. But I wasn't interested in commercial success.
It was probably one of the reasons Lena had chosen a cardiologist for a husband, instead of a projectionist. And besides, com-
mercially successful films were usually too loud. Too many car
crashes, gunfire and explosions. I was having enough trouble
sleeping as it was. How was I supposed to catch a nap in the
projection booth with a loud cacophonous soundtrack waking
me up?

"So when is this so-called 'film festival'?" Lena asked.

"It's the last weekend in July. Friday, Saturday and Sunday."

"The last weekend in July?" Lena smirked. "I'm getting married that weekend. On Saturday. Gee, that's a shame, isn't it,
Malcolm? Because I really would have liked to have come. I'm
sorry I can't be there to support you."

I tried to remember the last time I'd found Lena's sarcasm
witty and amusing. Sexy, even. It seemed like a very long time
ago. Maybe it was good that Lena was getting married that
weekend. I'd be busy, well, busier than I normally would be,
and it would take my mind off the event.

"Actually," I said, "I'm expecting a good turnout. We're going to have cheese and schnapps. Have you already sent out
your wedding invitations?"

"They went out a month ago. Why? You didn't think I'd invite you, did you, Malcolm?"

"No. It's not that. I was just thinking. I wouldn't be surprised if some of your friends wanted to go to this film festival. It's going to be the place to be that weekend. I just wouldn't want to cut into your wedding plans."

"I wouldn't worry about it, Malcolm."

The perspiration on my forehead was drying in Lena's air-conditioned kitchen. I wiped away the last of the sweat on my temples with the back of my hand.

"Still hot?" Lena asked.

"I'm starting to cool off, thanks," I said.

"Do you want something to drink?"

"What do you have?" I asked, trying to go with this uncharacteristically hospitable mood Lena had suddenly channeled into.

She ambled over to the refrigerator, opened it. She pushed some bottles and cartons around and took out something in a bowl with plastic wrap over it. She sniffed it, made a face and set it on the counter.

"Spoiled?"

She nodded. Then she rattled off a list of soft drinks. Lena and her mother were volume consumers of carbonated beverages.

"Coke, Tab, Fresca, 7-Up, 50/50, Orange Crush . . ."

I spotted a plastic pitcher on the top shelf.

"Is that your mother's lemonade? With real lemons and sugar?"

"Yes. Is that what you'd like?'

"That'd be great, thanks."

Lena pulled a tall glass down from the kitchen cabinet, filled it with ice and poured the lemonade into it. She put the lemonade down in front of me, returned the pitcher to the refrigerator and closed the door. She hadn't poured any lemonade for herself. I was kind of hoping she would. In summers past, we'd spent many nights out on Lena's back porch swing, naming the constellations, sipping her mother's lemonade. If Lena had joined me, it might have bonded us in some way, both tasting the same thing at the same time. But instead she leaned against the stove again and stared at me.

I began to feel as though her accommodating me was only a subtle psychological tactic. Like when a lunatic is holding hostages in a bank and the police give him anything he wants. They don't do it because they like him, they just want to move things along and pretend to cooperate while they arrange for a sharpshooter to pick him off. Like Sonny in *Dog Day Afternoon*.

It was probably this paranoid apprehensive feeling that caused what happened next. As I picked up my glass of lemonade and drank down a big gulp, it went down the wrong pipe. Or whatever it is when you feel yourself choking and it's clear you did something wrong when you drank.

With the glass of lemonade still clutched in my fist, I bolted up and made a dash for the sink. I knew I was about to hack and spit and I didn't want to do it all over Missus Karponsky's embroidered kitchen tablecloth. But before I could get to the sink, Lena leaped from her position at the stove to intercept me. Even though she worked as an x-ray assistant, a job which rarely sees the kind of code blue situations that the emergency room of a hospital does, she must have known something about what to do with a choking victim. She'd probably seen one of those diagrams with choking stick figures like you see in hospitals. Or maybe she saw it on one of the many TV hospital shows. Anyway, I don't think there was any real compassion to the act. She just knew what to do and did it.

As Lena grabbed me from behind and tried to get me into position for some kind of rib-cracking, Heimlich hug, I shook my head and struggled to get away from her. Unfortunately, in these situations you can't communicate to the other person whether or not you're in serious trouble because your throat is temporarily constricted. So when I struggled to get away, she tightened her grip on me and said something like "easy . . . easy . . ." as if I were one of those giant African elephants on Wild Kingdom being steadied for a stab with a tranquilizer dart.

But I wasn't about to get my ribs cracked over a little bit of regurgitated lemonade. I wrenched myself partially free but Lena still had a solid grip on my right shoulder. As I moved forward, she pulled back hard. My body swung around at about three hundred and sixty degrees and I whomped back into her body, leading with my lemonade. The ensuing effect was not unlike one of those water slides at an amusement park. You start out completely dry and then you dive and crash in a great spray of liquid and suddenly you're drenched.

There was lemonade everywhere, but most of it had emptied onto the front of Lena's green nightshirt. Her concern about my choking, which had now stopped, became secondary. She clutched the front of her nightshirt, pulling the cold, wet, sticky material away from her breasts. Then I reacted.

I didn't stop to think that grabbing her zipper and yanking it down would be an inappropriate thing to do. In the back of my mind I guess I was confident that if anyone could get Lena out of her wet nightshirt quickly and efficiently, it was me. I did, after all, have years of experience and some expertise in this area. I'm sure it seemed to Lena like a feeble attempt by an ex-boyfriend to get her out of her nightshirt. Something that some greasy rogue would do with the unsuspecting heroine in a film. The kind of guy you wouldn't mind seeing get run over by a train.

She screamed. I'd known Lena for years and had heard all sorts of sounds come out of her, but this scream was something else altogether. I once saw a dog get broadsided by a kid on a ten-speed bike and the dog, which survived and hobbled away, made a bloodcurdling howl upon impact. It was something like that with Lena. But she also made a hateful face no dog could ever make. The sound she made and the look on her face frightened me to the extent that I recoiled, backpedaling into the living room, dripping more lemonade onto her carpeting. Lena dashed for the bathroom with her wet green nightshirt gathered around her semi-exposed cleavage. She slammed the door and I heard the little push-button click of a spring lock. It was a sound I'd heard many times before at the climax of arguments we'd had in her home. It was such a familiar noise that it made me feel a bit more at ease. Almost welcome.

I went to the bathroom and put my ear to the door. I heard the water running in the sink. I imagined Lena naked, squeezing lemonade out of her green nightshirt into the sink. I knocked. I tried to knock with that friendly knock I'd used at the front door, figuring it would sound friendlier now that she knew it was me. It didn't.

"Go away," Lena snarled.

"Are you okay?"

"Just go away."

I went away. I walked down the hall and went into Lena's bedroom. It looked exactly the same as the last time I'd seen it. Lena wasn't big on rearranging. Once she found the most efficient location for her bed, nightstand, dresser and bookcase, she put them into position and left them there. The wooden legs of her bed disappeared into ever-deepening holes in the shag carpeting.

Lena had her tape deck on a shelf of her bookcase and two pint-sized six-inch speakers on the shelf above it. She'd left less than half an inch between the two speakers. Some people just don't get the idea of stereo, I thought. She had a dozen or so cassettes stacked up next to the speakers. I scanned the tapes quickly to see if she still had any tapes of mine that I could repossess. When I didn't find anything, I looked again just to see if there were any tapes I'd purchased for her which she hadn't fully appreciated that I could now justify taking back.

I ejected an Elvis Costello tape Lena had in her tape deck and put it back in its case. *Trust.* Then I took the Darlene Bleeker demo tape out of my breast pocket and slipped it into the deck in its place. It wasn't a particularly ingenious act. Lena would find the tape and know I'd made the switch. But no matter how she felt about me, I knew once Lena heard the Darlene Bleeker demo tape, she'd be bowled over by it. Enough to want Darlene to sing at her wedding. Then, somehow, I'd get into the wedding on Darlene's coattails. After that, I didn't know what I'd do. It wasn't much of a plan, but then I didn't have much of an idea what my purpose was either.

Next, I looked for my watch. I made a swift, thorough search of Lena's dresser drawers and jewelry box and came up empty. I looked in her closet, in some shoe boxes, but all I found were shoes. There was a limited number of possibilities and I'd pretty much exhausted them in a matter of minutes.

I scanned the room again. It was painful to imagine the watch sitting out somewhere, in plain view, while I looked everywhere but the right place. My eyes moved across Lena's stuffed animals which were lined up at the head of the bed, arranged by height. Egberto the egg at one end and Julian the giraffe at the other, flanking an assortment of bears, bunnies and pigs, all stuffed and staring at me with shiny-black lifeless eyes. I felt kind of sorry for them. Until the arrival of little Doctor Andrew Buntrock Jr. and little Doctor Lenette Buntrock, the stuffed animals were destined to be shoved into cardboard boxes and stuffed up in an attic somewhere.

Other remnants of childhood were also on the bed. A cross-stitch design of an Indian Princess that she'd made as a Girl Scout and a copy of Doctor Seuss's *Sleep Book*.

Apparently Lena wasn't ready to give up everything from her past, just the part that included me. Why couldn't she think of me as a remnant from childhood?

I picked Egberto the egg out of the line-up and turned him around. I opened the little zipper on his back and poked through his stuffing with my index finger. Egberto was not smuggling a watch. I methodically gave this same rude search to every stuffed creature on the bed, from smallest to tallest. I came up with nothing but a lot of lint and fuzz on my fingertip.

Lena was still quietly stewing in the bathroom. I knew from experience that she was likely to stay in there until I left. Sometimes, after an argument with Lena, I'd leave and watch her house from the street and I'd see the bathroom light go out shortly after I'd departed.

I looked at the clock radio at Lena's bedside. It was one-eighteen. I looked at the hairy creature yawning on the cover of the Doctor Seuss book and I yawned in response. I stretched out on the bed and put my head down next to Egberto the egg.

Lena's mattress was just as I remembered it. Soft and yielding. Nothing like the limp, ragged mattress in my hide-a-bed. I rolled onto my back and stared at the ceiling. I listened to the hum of the air conditioner and closed my eyes. It felt good. I bet I could get a good night's sleep in Lena's bed, I thought, as long as Lena wasn't in it. Perhaps I could convince Lena to let me sleep here occasionally. I turned on my side and nestled into her pillow. Then I suddenly got a vision of Lena walking in, seeing me stretched out on her bed and giving another one of those canine yelps. It sobered me. I got up and went back down the hallway. I pressed my ear to the bathroom door. I could hear Lena turning the pages of a magazine.

"I'm going now," I said softly.

I didn't get a response.

"I'm sorry," I said. "I didn't mean to upset you." I leaned my ear against the door again and listened. I didn't hear her turning pages any more. I didn't hear her moving about. I imagined her sitting on the toilet, naked, listening to my voice and staring off into space.

"Are you all right?" I asked.

"Just go," she finally said. "Please, just go."

"All right," I said. She sounded exhausted. I went back into her bedroom and made sure everything was the way she'd left it. Except, of course, the new tape in her tape deck. I went down the hallway and let myself out the front door, locking it behind me. I stood in the street and watched the bathroom light go out. I got in my VW bus and headed east, to the city.

chapter ten

Sweat chased down the front of my body like hot otters on a water slide. Just off the highway I saw a sign above a bank displaying a temperature of ninety-one degrees. Ninety-one degrees at one-forty-five in the morning. It was eight degrees hotter than it had been that afternoon.

Even in Death Valley the temperatures dropped down to jacket weather by midnight. So there was something unsettling about it getting hotter overnight. I thought about the Twilight Zone episode where the earth's orbit gets screwed up and sends us in the path of the sun and oil paintings melt and mercury bursts out the top of the thermometer.

I'd hoped that once I was out on the highway, cruising along at fifty-five miles an hour with the windows open and the vents aimed at either side of my head, I might cool off. But the air was steamy, like a blow dryer/vaporizer, and all it did was make a crest of my hair at my widow's peak, while the back of my hair stayed plastered down with sweat.

Occasionally I'd catch a glimpse of myself in the rearview mirror and staring back at me was a swarthy-looking individual with Woody Woodpecker hair.

But as I neared the 3-D Club and started searching for a parking space, I noticed I wasn't as apprehensive as I'd been the night before. Maybe it was because I knew what I was getting myself into this time. It was still a stupid endeavor, to be sure, but at least I knew that going in this time. There was some consolation in knowing that I had my own vehicle and could turn it around whenever I wished. My VW was not a particularly reliable form of transportation, however. There was always the possibility it would die on me and I wouldn't be able to get it started again. And then there was the chance that the Punishing Skulls would jump out from an alleyway and carry off my microbus with me in it. Then torch me and my VW in some kind of ritual neo-Nazi VW sacrifice. I hoped I could appeal to their neo-Nazi sensibilities by pointing out that if Hitler were still alive, he'd probably be driving a VW. Or some German car, anyway.

These fears aside, I didn't experience any real trouble getting into the club that night. Someone grabbed my arm on the way in, but was apparently satisfied with the faded image of a dead cat on the back of my hand and let me in without further incident. I got a cold beer and parked myself in the middle of the crowd. With all the sweat covering my body and all my hair pushed up in the middle I felt unkempt and disheveled enough to blend in with the rest of the crowd. I listened to the Soiled Sheets run the voodoo down. They were performing "My Funny Valentine" in their most sincere, bang-your-head-against-the-nearest-hard-surface style.

Amid the throng, I thought I spotted the drummer from the Circadian Rhythm Section. When I saw his blond head disappear through a doorway at the back of the house, I began to shuffle in his direction. I had to kind of shuffle in rhythm to make any progress. Rhythm was not something I was particularly blessed with, so it took some time. When I got to the back of the house, I passed the men's room where I'd slept the night before. Beyond it was the hallway leading to the alley where Darlene had escorted me out. On either side of the hallway were several doors. Some of the doors were open and appeared to lead into small offices. I wondered how there could be any offices in a place like this. I couldn't imagine anyone typing or filing here.

As I passed one office, I saw a guy behind a desk with his feet propped up on it. He was thumbing through a copy of some music magazine. He had his long hair tied in a ponytail but he looked older than most of the people I'd seen there. There were some long, wiry gray hairs that straggled loose, refusing to be combed back with the rest. He had on thick, rose-tinted glasses and a madras shirt. I leaned my head into the office and cleared my throat to get his attention.

"Excuse me," I said. "Did you see a guy pass by here? A drummer for the Circadian Rhythm Section? Actually, I'm looking for their lead singer. A woman named Darlene Bleeker."

When the man behind the desk saw me, his eyes caught fire and he bolted upright in his chair.

"My man!" he squealed. He threw the magazine across the room and rushed up to me. He gripped my shoulders and pinned me against the wall. "You're the guy! You're the guy!"

His eyes were gleaming from behind his thick glasses. I couldn't imagine he would try to kill me with all these people around. Then again.

"You're the guy," he kept repeating.

"I'm not," I insisted. I didn't know what he was talking about but whatever it was I didn't want to encourage him. Even if I was the guy, I knew I didn't want to be the guy.

"Man, I know you. You're the guy. You're the guy that pulled that gig in the men's room. That was you. I want to talk to you."

He pulled me away from the wall and pushed me into a caneback chair. He sat opposite me on the edge of the desk and flailed his arms in my direction.

"I saw it," he said. "I saw the thing you did."

"I didn't do anything," I said.

"Hey, no, don't get me wrong. I'm not trying to shake you down. I dug it. The whole angst trip. Pretty wild."

"Angst trip?"

"Angst trip. Nose dive. Passion Play. However you want to personalize it, it's cool with me. I'm Ricardo Pisces. I run this place." He took my hand in both of his and pumped it vigorously.

"Look, I'm sorry I fell asleep in your men's room. I didn't mean to."

"Fell asleep? No. More than that. Whimpering. Moaning. Crying out for man's sins. The whole angst thing in a neat little package."

"No, no, I was just sleeping, that's all . . ."

" . . . I can dig it. Dreams of Angst. Somnambulistic Suffering." He punctuated these phrases with his hand, pecking the air like a crow in a corn field. "I've never seen people lined up like that. It's a hell of an act."

"It's not an act," I protested. "Really. I fell asleep. I've got some kind of problem with my sleeping. I'm losing at least a minute of sleep a night."

"Details, details . . ." he said, savoring my every remark. "It's got potential."

"I'm just looking for Darlene," I said. "She plays with the Circadian Rhythm Section."

"Post-punk ballads? Yesterday's news. People like you burn out in this business faster than a match in a fucking monsoon. You've got to grab it while you can."

"What do you mean, people like me?"

"Performance artists, midnight ramblers, anarchists. You're in the spotlight and then you're gone. The trick is to turn it into something bankable before it busts. Something commercial."

"I don't see how sleeping in the men's room could be called commercial."

"You think I don't know that? It's all bullshit. I know that. Once it can be recognized as commercial, it's in the pot, nine days old. That's the paradox. Paradox de l'arte. Only when something is so clearly non-commercial does it have its peak commercial potential. Stay with me on this."

"I'm not really interested."

"Not really interested? What kind of bullshit squeeze play is that? If I'd been standing at the door to the men's room last night charging ten bucks a head, you'd damn well have been interested."

"It's not the kind of thing I want to do on a regular basis. Thanks, though."

I saw Darlene flit past the door of the office.

"I have to go," I said.

"We could start with a sixty-forty split. Then play around with the numbers when you get really hot."

"Hold that thought," I said, and I bolted for the doorway.

"Think about your future," he yelled after me.

I chased Darlene down the hallway. She was wearing a black mini skirt, a tight black short-sleeved turtleneck, black nylons and shoes. I'm sure she was always ready for funerals, but what the hell did she wear to weddings? I called Darlene's name down the hallway. She didn't stop walking, but turned in my direction and backpedaled. She looked surprised.

"Malcolm? What the hell are you doing here? I'm going on in a few minutes."

I dashed down the hallway and caught up with her. Her face looked pained. "What is it? What's wrong?"

"My fucking head is splitting," Darlene said. "I feel like I could rip it off my shoulders and hurl it into the crowd."

Now there's an act for Ricardo Pisces, I thought. Sixty for him, forty for her and the head raffled off at the end of the night.

"I think I have some aspirin in my glove compartment," I said.

Darlene stopped in her tracks. "You're a saint. Let's go."

She took my arm and led me out to the alley. I'd kind of expected to run out to my VW, get the aspirin and bring them back to her. Particularly since she was about to go on stage. But it felt safer being out on the street with her on my arm, so I didn't mention it.

I saw two pairs of eyes shining halfway down the alley. Too tall to be rats.

"Skulls," Darlene said.

"Let's go back," I said instantly.

"They'd better not fuck with us," Darlene said. "I've got a headache."

"Hold up," one of the Skulls said. The taller one.

I froze. The shorter of the two pulled something out of his pocket. So it ends here, I thought. In an alley outside the 3-D Club. My mother will never understand when she sees it on "Eyewitness News." I stood in front of Darlene wondering why I was choosing to die first. Did it really matter? My bravery would go unheralded anyway when they found our bodies in one neat pile.

The shorter Skull flicked his fist and his Zippo lighter flashed in my eyes. He looked past me at Darlene. His face lit up.

"Hey, it's Darlene from the Circadian Rhythms," the shorter one said, snorting. "Man, your group sucks!"

"Who is this?" the taller one asked the shorter one.

"Darlene Bleeker, man. She was on 'Wake-Up, It's Morning.'"

"Should we fuck with her?" the taller one asked the shorter one.

"Don't," I said. "Please . . ." The Punishing Skulls had never heard me talk before so they couldn't have known my voice didn't naturally skip into different registers when I spoke.

"Shut up," the taller one said.

"Naw, don't fuck with her," the shorter one said. "Too many people know her, man. She's been on television."

"We've been on television and people still fuck with us," the taller one said.

"Let's fuck with the other one," the taller one said.

"Are you somebody?" the shorter one asked, holding the lighter close enough to my face to singe my nostril hairs.

I thought about lying. Saying something about how I was the next hot thing, the guy who whimpers in his sleep in the men's room.

"I'm with Darlene," I said. "I need to get her some aspirin.

You guys don't have any aspirin on you, do you?" I guess they were used to people pleading for their lives, something they could channel their hostility into. But given a direct question they responded very politely. They checked their pockets and pulled out some pills.

"No . . . no, I ain't got nothing here for a headache," the taller one said.

The shorter one showed me what he had in his hand. He pushed some of the pills around in his palm.

"I don't think so, man. I don't think any of these are aspirin. But you're welcome to take a couple, whatever they are."

"That's okay," I said. "Thanks anyway."

The two Skulls nodded at us as if to say "Have a nice evening" and we beat it out of the alley and out onto the street. I led her to my microbus and opened the passenger side for her. Then I jumped in on the driver's side. Pools of near-death sweat collected around my neck.

"This thing is yours?" Darlene asked incredulously, her neck craning to see the far reaches of the bus.

"Yeah," I said, breathing heavily.

She continued to look around, checking out the interior. I pulled my sweating back away from the vinyl seat with an uncomfortably audible *thwock*. I reached over her legs to get at the glove compartment and brushed against her black nyloned knees. I arched my wrist awkwardly to avoid touching her legs as I rummaged through the glove compartment. While I was pushing things around, Darlene reached in and pulled out a Grateful Dead tape.

"Eight tracks?"

"They came with the vehicle."

"Time warp," she said, shaking her head.

"I was trying to create some kind of summer of love for myself," I said, pathetically.

Darlene smiled and tossed the eight track back into the glove compartment. I found the aspirin and fumbled with the child-proof lid until I'd pried it open. I tumbled out a couple of white tablets and held them out for her in my palm.

"Do you get a lot of headaches?"

"I don't take aspirin," I said. "I can't swallow pills. These are guest aspirin."

Darlene took my left hand, the one with the aspirins in it, and slowly drew my middle finger towards her lips. She kissed my finger gently, then began to draw the digit into her wet mouth. I pulled my hand back carefully, but still dropped the aspirins onto the carpeted floor of the VW.

As I reached down to retrieve the aspirins, she put her hand on my chest and pushed me back into my seat. I felt myself get reattached to the sticky wet vinyl. It was pretty clear what was happening. It was just the kind of loose spontaneous act that I'd been missing since my early days with Lena. Maybe this would be the thing that would finally burn away the memory of Lena naked on my desk. Make me forget about my watch. Make me forget about time altogether.

But no. My summer of love had arrived on the wrong evening. It was like a sauna in the bus and I was too hot and grimy to consider engaging in any activity that required putting my skin against anything, particularly more skin like mine.

One part of my body, however, disagreed with this conclusion and stood up in protest. Darlene must have sensed it because she began to move in the direction of the protester. At that point, reason stepped in to have a chat with me. I considered the devastating power of her kisses. With all the sleep I was losing, one of those kisses could kill me. Not metaphorically, like people who say it'd kill them to get up at five in the morning, but really, genuinely, kill me. And at the very least, I pictured myself driving home all sticky. I pushed her away.

"Isn't there an angry mob of disillusioned youth waiting for you?" I asked.

"They'll do the show with me or without me," Darlene said. "The audience doesn't care."

"What about you? Don't you care? Don't you need that feedback from the audience to validate you as an artist?" Rattling on like a public radio announcer helped me lose my erection.

"Naw," she said. "I don't care what anyone thinks."

"What about your headache?"

"This will take my mind off it," she said. "I've always wanted to make it in one of these hippymobiles." She moved towards me again.

"No, really," I said. "You should try the aspirin." I pushed her away again.

She backed off and sighed. "Okay," she said.

I abandoned the two aspirins that were somewhere on the floor of the VW and got two new ones out of the glove compartment. I held them in a fist so Darlene couldn't do anything funny with my finger again. When her hand was cupped under mine I opened my hand and let the tablets drop into her palm.

"I don't have any water," I said. "Maybe you can get some water back inside the club."

"I don't need any water," she said, popping the pills into her mouth. She swallowed and the pills went down. She didn't even flinch. It was pretty impressive. "My throat is naturally smooth and lubricated," she said.

It was the kind of sentence a man waits an entire lifetime to hear. I suddenly wondered if I'd made a huge mistake by pushing her away. Maybe what she had to give was worth dying for.

But while I was blaming the heat and sweat and general discomfort for my wanting to pass on sex with Darlene, the truth was there was an awful lot swimming around in my addled brain. Even if I'd been well-rested and freshly showered, I don't think I would have wanted to do it. Maybe it was because I'd just been with Lena and still had her on my mind. Or maybe it was because when Darlene drew close to me I was wishing it was someone more like Anne, the hotline volunteer. Maybe it was because I was thinking of everyone *but* Darlene.

On the other hand, Darlene didn't seem too broken up over the fact that we weren't going to do anything. Her first choice to cure her headache had been sex in a VW bus. But a couple of aspirins were just as good, I guess.

"I'm going back inside," she said. "Are you coming?"

"No," I said. "I couldn't bear to listen to another set like the one you did last night."

"You told me you thought my singing was beautiful."

"When did I say that?"

"Yesterday. At lunch. I have the tape if you want to hear it again."

"No, that's okay." I said. I swallowed uncomfortably and sank back into my seat. "I'm sorry I taped our conversation. That was a really stupid thing to do."

"S'all right," she said. "I thought it was kind of sweet. Are you taping us now?"

"No," I said. I tugged on my earlobe a few times. "I do remember what I said about your singing. I said it was beautiful in a wrenching kind of way. I think that's what I said."

"It's supposed to be emotionally moving. Is that such a bad thing?"

"I don't know. It is for me. I can't put myself through that."

"I don't know why not. It's good to get upset sometimes."

"I come by it naturally. I don't need to seek it out."

She shrugged it off. "Whatever. Can't please everybody. People at weddings love me. They come up afterwards and tell me how much they love the way I spill my guts with the classical stuff."

"I *really* enjoyed the classical music you did on the tape," I said, much too quickly. "I'd *love* to hear you sing at a wedding."

All the way into the city I'd thought about the demo tape in Lena's tape deck and had tried to figure out a subtle way to approach the subject of weddings with Darlene. When it came up naturally within the course of the conversation, something I hadn't banked on, I pounced on it with all the subtlety of a cheetah mauling a gazelle. And if that wasn't bad enough, I added, "Please let me know the next time you sing at a wedding? Could you? I'd really like to hear you when you sing."

"Sure," she said, slightly taken aback by my sudden display of enthusiasm.

I noted her reaction and composed myself back into the bland, nondescript individual she'd come to expect. She looked at me quizzically, but I didn't return her look. I sat stone-faced and stared at the dash.

"So what are you going to do now?" she asked. "Are you going home?"

"I don't know," I said. "I'm not due for a nap for several hours yet."

"Why don't you stick around? You don't have to stand around in the club. You could hang out in the back of the house for a while. Meet some people."

I thought about Ricardo Pisces lurking back there in one of the offices. My mind flashed back to times in high school when I'd dive into my locker pretending to look for books when the career counselor came down the hall.

"No, thanks," I said. "I already met some guy in there who wants to talk to me about my future. I'd like to avoid him if I can."

"I could hide you in the back," she said. "Somewhere where no one would bother you."

"Not tonight," I said. "Let me call you."

I didn't think I'd actually call her, but I wanted to make sure we exchanged phone numbers so that Darlene would have *my* phone number. So that Darlene would call me after Lena called her, after Lena heard Darlene sing on the tape I'd left in Lena's tape deck. It was kind of complicated, but there was a good chance it would work out like I'd planned. Or sort of planned, anyway.

I reached into my glove compartment and found a ballpoint pen and a deposit slip from my bank. I wrote my phone number on the back of the slip. I put my name over the number in case she forgot whose number it was. Or who I was. Then I tore off just the portion that had my name and phone number, so she couldn't use the slip to take money out of my bank account. I didn't think she actually would, but . . .

"Here's my number," I said, handing her the slip.

I tore off another small piece of deposit slip for her to put her number on.

"You already have my number," Darlene said. "It's on the tape."

"Oh," I said. "That's right."

She looked at the number I'd given her and then up at me.

"Malcolm," she said. "Is that your name? Don't fall asleep at the wheel, Malcolm."

She jumped out of my VW bus. I watched her nylon legs stream up the street and back into the alley.

chapter eleven

A few weeks passed. *High and Low* played out to the end of its run to empty houses, and near-empty houses with a smattering of repeat customers. Toshiro just wasn't packing them in. I'd seen Toshiro Mifune in the flesh once, at a real film festival, a retrospective of his work. He was introduced after a screening of *Rashomon*, in which he played Tajomaru, a bandit whose vitality made him seem larger than life. When the film ended and the curtain parted, however, an extraordinarily short Japanese man in a suit came out, smiled and nodded. It was Mifune. He was nothing like his screen image, but the packed house didn't seem to mind. They cheered anyway.

I didn't expect a packed house or any cheering when Soren Sonderby appeared at the Arcadia Filmhaus. But I was hoping for a respectable turnout. I'd put an ad in *The Reader*, but I certainly didn't expect anyone would come based on name recognition. If it hadn't been my own festival, I don't know if I would have come.

During the lull before my film festival, I just kind of let the wheels turn on their own for a bit. I waited for Lena to hear the tape of Darlene singing which I'd provided her with. I waited for Lena to call to tell me how grateful she was (she never did).

And I waited for Darlene to call me about the wedding. I hadn't decided whether I would actually ride on Darlene's coattails and crash Lena's wedding—it seemed a tacky thing to do. Whether or not I would sink to that level kind of depended on the success or failure of the film festival. The advertisement in *The Reader* promised three successive nights, Friday, Saturday and Sunday. But if no one came on Friday, I could probably bank on the fact that no one had paid any attention to the ad and then I could do whatever I wanted. Sonderby's room was paid for, in any event.

There wasn't much I had to do to prepare for the festival. On Thursday morning I received a print of *Wild Strawberries* from Film-o-Rama. The next thing I had to do was change the letters on the marquee outside. I didn't like this task. It required the big ladder. The big ladder was a really big, big wooden ladder, frighteningly enormous. It probably dated back to the construction of the theater, left in the storage room because it was too big to move anywhere else. I took the big ladder out of the storage room and set it up on the sidewalk, then got the big black letters.

I looked up at the marquee and shuddered. It was a dizzying enough experience just getting up on the ladder, but it was particularly precarious in the late afternoon sun. I was afraid I'd pass out from the heat, plummet and splatter on the sidewalk. The letters to *Wild Strawberries* would re-form and spell the cryptic phrase BIRD WRIST ARE SWEL on my mangled corpse.

There was a diner a few blocks west of me, Dale's Good Eats, and I'd seen the manager there stay on the ground and change the letters on his outdoor sign with a long stick with a claw on the end of it. I couldn't begin to think what kind of a store would carry a tool like that, I'd never seen one in a hardware store. So I was forced to use my big ladder and try not to look down.

My fear of heights may have caused an unconscious choice to choose films with short titles so that I could avoid being up on the ladder for too long. I noticed that I showed films like *High and Low*, *Ran*, *Persona* and *Diabolique*, but avoided films I liked equally well, like *The Bitter Tears of Petra Von Kant*, *The Garden of the Finzi-Continis* and *The Cabinet of Doctor Caligari*. No one ever asked about my short film titles. There weren't that many people who would ask, however. *Wild Strawberries* had fifteen letters. A bit long, I thought, as I counted them out.

I tried to bribe Ginny into assisting me with the marquee. I waved a crisp, new twenty-dollar bill in front of her face and told her it was hers if she'd just hold the ladder and toss the letters up. It would in no way involve Ginny actually getting up on the ladder, and Ginny was clear on this point:

"I could never let anyone see me up on a ladder," she said. "I wouldn't be able to go back to school the next day if anyone saw me."

I couldn't imagine what shame could be connected with this activity. I wondered what sort of future we were in for if the youth of today castigated its peers just for being up on a ladder. Then again, kids could be cruel and there wasn't always any underlying logic attached to it.

"We could do it at night, after dark," I suggested.

Ginny's eyes grew saucerlike.

"Never mind," I said. "I'll go up the ladder. You hold the box of letters."

She's not getting the twenty, that's for sure, I thought as I shakily ascended the ladder.

We were about halfway through the task when I spotted Anne coming up the street towards the theater. I wanted to get the job done quickly so that I could descend the ladder, regain my composure and greet Anne with some degree of cool. But all I'd finished was WILD STRAW. Ginny was having trouble finding the letters. Never mind the difficulty she was having throwing them underhand and still within my reach.

"Throw me a B," I barked down to her.

"B?" Ginny repeated. She repeated each letter before sailing it up to me.

Anne stopped underneath the marquee and looked up at me. She blocked the afternoon sun from her eyes and waved. I waved back carefully, gripping one hand firmly on the ladder.

"Hello," I called down.

"Hello," she said. "Is it *Wild Strawberries?*"

Ginny nodded and told Anne something about how she should go on "Wheel of Fortune." I think she meant it sincerely and wasn't being sarcastic. I couldn't tell for sure from my crow's nest perch.

"Wait a minute," I said. "I'll be right down."

"Go ahead and finish," Anne said.

"Do you want to do it?" Ginny asked her. "You know all the letters."

"Sure," Anne said. Ginny was probably conning her, anything to get out of work. But I was glad when she went back inside the theater and let Anne take over.

Anne tossed the letters up to me without my having to shout them out like a foreign film cheerleader. When we were finished, I came down the ladder slowly while Anne held it steady for me. She couldn't hold me steady, however, and I wobbled and jerked down the ladder. I grunted down the last few steps and thanked her.

"Did you come by to see me?" I asked, smiling.

"No," she said.

"Oh," I said.

"I'm on my way to the hotline."

"Now? It's too early, isn't it?"

"We're having a meeting this afternoon to discuss longer hours for the fall."

"Isn't it a little soon for that?"

"It'll be here in a few months and we want to make sure we're fully staffed. There's more depression in the fall and winter months."

Something to look forward to, I thought.

"Sort of like department stores putting out their Christmas stock right after Hallowe'en," I remarked.

Anne nodded.

"When are you going to show *Wild Strawberries*?" she asked, blinking up at the marquee.

"This weekend," I said, wiping some sweat out of my eyes. "Friday, Saturday and Sunday is the actual festival when Soren Sonderby will be here. Are you going to come?"

"I don't know. I'm still thinking about it."

"You shouldn't think so much. Why don't you just say you'll come and show up. I mean, what is there to think about?"

"I'm still not sure this is appropriate," she said, reddening just enough to make me feel encouraged.

"I'm sure it's appropriate. You'll have a good time, I'm sure."

"I have to get to my meeting," she said, still remaining noncommittal, and started to walk away.

"Let me walk with you," I said.

Anne stopped and turned around. "It's nothing personal, Malcolm," she said. "But we're not supposed to have any physical contact with the people who call the hotline."

"I don't want to touch you, I just want to walk with you," I said. Actually, I wouldn't have minded touching her. Just holding her hand, maybe. But I didn't say so.

Anne sized me up again.

"I guess it's okay," she said.

I ran inside the theater and told Ginny I'd be back in ten minutes. She let out one of her big audible sighs and rolled her eyes up. But she didn't object. I think Ginny may have been amazed that I had any real human friends. She probably thought I went home most evenings and had cocktails with something inflatable.

I caught up to Anne and walked with her.

"I'm sorry about the rules," she said. "They just do it to protect us."

"It's okay," I said. "I know how these things go. Like you can't walk up to the drive-up windows at the bank. I guess they have that rule so drivers won't hit pedestrians. But this is not nearly so dangerous. Just walking together."

"I agree," she said. "I don't see any harm in walking together. But I don't know if it would be appropriate to talk about your problems."

"Good," I said. "I don't want to talk about my problems."

Maybe Anne was starting to see me as a person without problems, or a minimum of problems or even just the accepted amount, whatever that was. So I didn't tell Anne that I was waiting for Darlene's call so that I could crash Lena's wedding.

I didn't know if I could explain it anyway. Besides, when I was with Anne I wanted to forget such things and be a normal, average person. The kind of person who barbecued on Sunday and recycled aluminum.

We walked and spoke about the weather, how it was an unusually hot summer with no relief in sight. Occasionally, Anne would look over at me and smile and I'd smile back. I was self-conscious about my teeth and hoped I'd brushed well. It's something you think about more when you're with a dental assistant.

When I returned to the Arcadia Filmhaus, I pulled a poster for *Wild Strawberries* out of a mailing tube from Film-o-Rama and put it up in the glass display case. Ginny happened by, glared at the sad face of Victor Sjöström staring balefully into space and said:

"I thought this sounded familiar. Our teacher made us watch this one."

There was something in Ginny's tone and the words "made us watch" that led me to believe the class hadn't enjoyed the film. I pictured the poor teacher nailing up barbed wire around the doors and windows, pushing his glasses forcefully up the bridge of his nose and warning the class: "If anyone tries to leave during the dream sequences . . ."

I was sitting at my kitchen table in my underwear eating chocolate pudding late Thursday night when Darlene called. I was beginning to think, since Lena's wedding was Saturday, that maybe Darlene wouldn't call. But when the phone rang around midnight I had a good idea it might be her. I wasn't psychic, I just didn't get that many phone calls that I wasn't expecting. People didn't call me out of the blue. They knew that if they caught me in an introspective mood they might get an earful of my life history, starting as early as the third grade. Even people who sold subscriptions and collected for charities were not immune to this. I think eventually my phone number was put on a list of people you'd never want to call, no matter how badly you needed money.

So when the phone rang, I knew it'd probably be Darlene. I sat at the kitchen table and watched it ring a few times before I got up to answer it.

"Hello?"

"Malcolm? You really are a shithead, you know that?"

"Darlene? And how are you this evening?"

"Yeah. Darlene. I thought you were going to call me."

"I was," I said. "Time slipped away."

"Time, my ass. You haven't come to see me sing at all in the past few weeks."

I made up something about being really busy in the last few weeks. Preparations for the film festival, I said, though in actuality the preparations amounted to next to nothing. "Besides," I said, "I told you, I have some problem listening to you sing. It makes me too sad. You're really very good at what you do, though."

"Is that supposed to be flattery? You're lucky I didn't throw your number away."

"I'm glad you didn't," I said, spooning more chocolate pudding into my mouth. I wasn't trying to be smug, it's just that when things turn out as you predicted and that's about all you have going for you in your life, you want to get as much mileage out of it as you can.

"Some chick called me," Darlene said. "X-ray technician's assistant. Marrying a cardiologist. Big bucks. Someone palmed a demo tape off on her."

"Wow, pretty strange," I said, continuing to feign as much surprise as I could. For a minute I thought Darlene might blow the whistle on me. Maybe she'd ask what I'd done with the demo tape she'd given me. Or even ask for it back.

But instead she said: "No, not so strange. I leave tapes everywhere. Bars, phone booths, johns, automatic tellers . . ."

If this was true, then Lena could have eventually come across the tape on her own. Not particularly likely, but possible certainly. Anyway, it took some of the zing out of my covert operation.

"So when's this wedding?" I asked. I pulled a magnetic pen off my refrigerator and pretended to prepare to write the information down. Even thought I knew when the wedding was, it was important to go through these feigning motions on the phone to make it sound realistic.

"It's this Saturday."

"Mmm hmm, Saturday," I said, miming a motion with my pen.

"Hose it down a minute, pal," Darlene said. "I haven't invited you yet. Maybe you couldn't listen to me sing the ballads and dirges, but you could have called me. Or stopped by the club."

"I know. I'm sorry," I said. Now I was feigning sincerity. This feigning business took a lot of work. I paused to let my apology gel. Then I asked: "May I accompany you to this wedding?"

Darlene let me sweat it out in silence for a few more seconds. Then she asked: "Have you got a decent suit?"

chapter twelve

The following morning I was posted at the airport terminal, awaiting flight twenty-two from Stockholm. I was holding a makeshift cardboard sign that said WELCOME—ARCADIA FILMHAUS FILM FESTIVAL. As they debarked from their flight, I noticed a lot of healthy, good-looking Nordic people. Soren Sonderby was not one of them.

Sonderby was old, I'd expected that. But he dressed like a man still in his twenties. More specifically, he dressed like a man in his twenties might have dressed in the 1970s. He had on a pair of green and white wide-flared trousers and a white polyester shirt, specked with little blue anchors. His frame was small, he couldn't have weighed more than one-twenty, yet he moved as if he was dragging an enormous weight behind him. Maybe all those anchors.

The nautical attire continued on his head, with some kind of ragged blue fisherman's cap. When he saw my welcome sign, he removed his cap and waved it in my direction. Part of a poorly-manufactured brown and white toupee came up with his cap and he quickly patted it back down into place on top of his head. Keep the cap on, I thought.

"Soren Sonderby?"

"Yes," he said, and he smiled, showing me two or three of the four or five teeth left in his mouth. I prayed that he'd packed the rest of his teeth somewhere in his SAS carry-on bag. He didn't make a great first impression, I thought. But he'd just gotten off the plane from a long flight from Sweden, so I gave him the benefit of the doubt. He didn't say anything as I helped him get his bags and he remained silent until we reached the airport parking lot.

"They still make these here in America?" he asked when I opened the passenger side of my '68 VW bus.

"No," I said, "this is a classic." He got in and pushed down a cracked bit of leather on his seat that dogeared upwards as he sat down. "Original leather interior," I said.

"So this is America," Sonderby said, looking out the passenger window.

"Well," I said, cranking the ignition hard to fire up the VW, "this is just the parking lot. It's part of America. This is the Midwest, actually. It's small town America."

"But still part of the United States?"

"This parking lot? Or do you mean small town America? In either case, yes, it's all still part of the United States."

He didn't look at me much as I drove, which was fine, but he stared out the passenger window as if looking for something. I think he may have been anticipating some site or landmark that he could distinctly identify as American. I don't know what he expected to see—the Grand Canyon or Mount Rushmore or the White House or the entrance of Disneyland, maybe all of these. None of them, however, would be included on the trip from the airport to the motel. Just a flat Midwestern landscape, highways and buildings. I didn't have the heart to tell him that the scenery he was looking at now would probably remain the same for his entire trip.

Sonderby told me the name of the town he was from in Sweden. I didn't recognize the name of the town and I was confused about whether he lived there currently, or had been born there. No number of questions seemed to be able to clear up this matter. I realized then that I knew very little about Sweden. Nearly everything I knew about Swedish culture came from watching Bergman movies, mostly from the fifties and sixties. But these films didn't tell me anything about the history of Sweden or who ruled the country. Was it King Olaf? Olaf was a four-letter answer to a recurrent crossword clue that had something to do with Sweden. But I didn't imagine King Olaf was still in charge. I didn't embarrass myself by asking.

"We're very excited to have you here," I said, as though I represented a group of excited people rather than just myself.

"It seems much warmer here," he said. He wiped his brow repeatedly, but held his cap on his head.

"I'm sorry about the heat," I said, suddenly realizing that I was talking a little louder than normal. I think I was doing it because Sonderby was a foreigner, even though he spoke English well and there was no logic in the idea that being louder would make me any more intelligible. "It's a particularly hot summer. But the theater and your room are both air-conditioned."

"Where am I staying?"

"I've reserved a room for you up at the Quality Nook," I said. "I would have put you up at my place, but I have no air-conditioning and a nosy landlady. And I have yellow jackets living in my wall."

"Yellow jackets?"

"Yellow jackets," I said. "Do you have yellow jackets in Sweden? They're like bees. They're in the wall of my apartment." Sonderby looked bewildered, perhaps even frightened. He may have been rethinking his whole trip to America now that he realized there was no Disneyland and bees lived in people's walls. I tried to ease his mind.

"The yellow jackets aren't everywhere. Just in my apartment. In fact, I think they're *all* in my apartment."

"And my hotel . . . ?"

"Motel," I said, "It's a mo-tel. No, I'm sure there are no yellow jackets in the walls of your motel."

"Is it a nice hotel?"

"It's a very nice mo-tel," I said. "It's an American motel. A kind of motor inn," I said, trying to make it sound like something delightfully American.

"Is there a good bar in this mo-tel?"

"I think they may have one of those refrigerators in the room that you can buy drinks from. Kind of like a vending machine for drinks. Though I haven't actually been there myself. I'm told it's very nice."

Sonderby looked at me as if he were still waiting for an answer to the liquor situation.

"I'm told there's an ice machine on your floor," I said.

We pulled up in front of the Quality Nook. It didn't look like much from the outside and the motel wasn't in the best of neighborhoods. I got Sonderby's suitcase out of the back of my VW bus and quickly ushered him inside. Unfortunately it didn't look like much from the inside, either. Peeling wallpaper on the walls in bright, splashy and ultimately depressing colors. Green velvet flowers against yellow stripes. The lobby apparently hadn't been redecorated since Nixon was in office. Then again, Sonderby's clothes were from the same era, so perhaps he wouldn't notice.

As Sonderby walked up to the front desk I wandered about the lobby. Amid some dreadful oil paintings of toreadors, there was a framed photo of the Quality Nook manager, Dave Zenk. He appeared to be the same man who was checking Sonderby in. Same white short-sleeved shirt, same green and blue checked tie. Next to the photo of Dave Zenk was a framed letter addressed to the manager. It was from the FBI. It complimented Quality Nook, and Dave Zenk in particular, for the superb way in which they'd handled a potentially dangerous hostage situation at the motel. Maybe I should have gone with Best Rooms instead of Quality Nook, I thought. I should have paid the extra five dollars and put my mind at ease about Soren Sonderby being taken hostage.

We walked down a musty hallway to room twenty-one, which was decorated exactly like the lobby, with the same green velvet wallpaper. There was nothing else distinguishable about the room: it had a bed, a night stand, a closet, a bathroom and a television set. There was no mini-bar. Luckily, Sonderby was distracted by another appliance.

"Ah," Sonderby said with a grin. "American television."

I wasn't sure if he meant the set itself—perhaps television sets were manufactured badly in Sweden or shaped like fish. More likely I think Sonderby was looking forward to American television programs. Reruns of "LaVerne and Shirley." There was a remote control, bolted down to the night stand with an excessive amount of hardware. I hoped it was a color television at least.

He invited me to stay while he unpacked. He pulled a large bottle out of his luggage, held it up and smiled. The universal gesture for alcohol. Ah, I thought. Sonderby's brought his own mini-bar. But the bottle wasn't shaped like a regular liquor bottle. It looked more like a bottle of mouthwash or some kind of cleaning product. It reminded me of the liquor that the old man brought to Ingrid Thulin in *The Silence*.

"A little nip, eh?" he said, indicating that I should join him.

"Uh . . . yes, certainly," I said, wanting to be accommodating. "Shall I get some ice?"

He handed me the bucket and I went down the hall and filled it with ice.

When I returned, he'd put his teeth in, which I counted as a good sign. He seemed more sociable with his teeth in. Maybe he just put them in when he drank, but I hoped I was wrong.

"I'll be serving schnapps at the screening tomorrow night," I said.

"Yes, " he said. "I just wanted a little something now."

"Oh, no," I said. "I wasn't admonishing you. You go ahead and drink. I was just mentioning the schnapps. I don't know if I can find this brand of . . . whatever this is." I took the bottle, tried unsuccessfully to pronounce the name on the bottle. He snorted and laughed at my attempt.

"You Swedish people certainly make use of your consonants," I said.

I poured some of the stuff into glasses I found in the bathroom and dropped in a couple of ice cubes.

"Skoal," he said, which was one of few Scandinavian words I knew, so I echoed it as I clinked his glass against mine. I felt the sting on my tongue and that should have warned me not to swallow it. I could almost see the hot lava trail it burned down my throat and into my stomach.

"My God," I gasped.

He laughed again. I held the bottle up to the light, looking for . . . what? I didn't know. A little Swedish worm at the bottom of the bottle, perhaps.

"I have a little trouble getting to sleep at night," he said.

"Really?" I said. "That's interesting. I'm having a sleep problem myself." I pointed to the bottle. "Does this help?"

He shook his head. "I'm just getting old. Need a little lubrication to quiet the engine down before bedtime."

"Right," I said. "I understand." But it wasn't exactly bedtime. It was only eleven o'clock in the morning. I wondered if he knew that. Maybe with the time difference between here and Stockholm he thought it was bedtime.

"How is the time change affecting you?"

"I set my watch when I was back in Stockholm," he said. "This will help me get over jet lag." He poured another three inches of the colorless poison into his glass and drank it. I waved off a second helping and sat down on the edge of the bed, still feeling aftershocks of the first drink.

"If there's anything else I can do for you while you're here . . ."

He nodded.

"So, I've been wanting to ask, what was it like, working with Bergman?"

"Bergman is Bergman," he said brusquely, in a tone that left little room for conversation.

"Yes," I said. "Yes, of course. Indeed."

I wasn't about to argue with him. But I hadn't flown him all the way over here just to make a positive identification of

Bergman for me. Bergman is Bergman? What the hell was that? I was suddenly apprehensive about the old person sitting on the bed, whom I'd just imported from across the Atlantic. If he was really somebody, why had Bergman never used him again when he tended to use the same repertory group again and again? Did it have anything to do with his drinking these large quantities of this colorless liquid?

"I imagine you have lots of stories about Bergman," I said.

"What can one say about Bergman?" he said, sighing deeply.

"Well, I'm hoping there's something," I said, chuckling nervously, hoping he would understand the irony and laugh. He didn't.

"I never married . . ." he said, out of the blue.

"Oh?"

"I had someone once. Yah, a sweet thing, she was. But I let her go." His voice, suddenly filled with rancor, trailed off a bit at the end.

"I'm sorry," I said.

He didn't seem to be a really happy person. Maybe he's tired, I thought. The long flight, jet lag. I was always tired, so I couldn't always tell if someone was tired as the result of something, like a long flight or from drinking colorless liquids, or just normally tired, like me.

"I'd better get going," I said. "You need to rest up for tonight."

"You're welcome to stay," he said, sweeping his hand out, offering to share his deluxe accommodations with me.

"No, I have some things I have to take care of," I said. "By the way, as you know, the film festival is for three days. Friday through Sunday. But I may have some scheduling conflicts on

Saturday, so I want to leave that date open. My thought is that we'll see how tonight goes and then maybe take a night off to assess the situation and then resume again on Sunday. How would that be?"

"You're going to take a night off from a three-day festival?"

"To assess," I repeated. "We want to see how many people come, how the schnapps and cheese move, things like that."

What I didn't tell Sonderby was that if the thing was a bust, I was going to Lena's wedding with Darlene. I might have explained the whole thing to him, but I thought it might only make him drink more, and I didn't want that. I wrote down the name and address of the theater, told him to be there before seven, American time, and gave him money for a taxi.

As I walked down the musty hallway with its ragged carpeting, I realized how much I didn't want to be there. Sure, my apartment was not air-conditioned and had yellow jackets in the wall, but this was a different kind of depressing. I wondered if I came off like this— cranky. The word crotchety came to mind. Then I wondered— was I looking at a Swedish version of my future? Maybe it wasn't even a distant future. I mean, how different was my life from Soren Sonderby's?

As I drove away from the motel, I started looking for a place to buy a suit. I didn't have a lot of color-coordinated clothes, let alone a decent suit. I didn't even have clothes that could be mistaken for eccentric chic. My closet was filled with a lot of bland tan pants and white shirts with sweat-stained collars. It might be a nice touch, I thought, if I was dressed up for the film festival. And it might impress Anne if she happened to come. Also, I was thinking in the back of my mind about Lena's wedding. If I decided to go with Darlene and crash Lena's wedding, I would need a suit that made me look a bit less like a crasher. I wanted to look like the dashing ex-boyfriend, the one that got away.

I needed one of those fancy Italian tailored suits that I'd seen in commercials for Tony's Cool Suits for Stylist Gents. Knowing about Tony's was one of the advantages of being an insomniac. By staying up late and watching television until my eyes felt like fishing sinkers, I could tell you who you could call to get carpeting today with no payments until January. I could tell you who to call to have your car towed away for free and still get twenty-five bucks for it, no matter what condition it was in. I could tell you what number to call where lonely women in short skirts and men in bicycle racing shorts were sitting by the phone waiting for your call. And I could tell you where you could get an inexpensive good-looking suit.

Tony Riccarelli, the owner, general manager and spokesperson for Tony's Suits for Stylish Gents, was not a particularly impressive figure. He was a small, mustachioed gentleman, probably in his mid-sixties. Not unhandsome for his age. He looked a little like my Uncle Emil, so I felt I had to pay attention to him, even if I didn't listen to him. In his self-produced late-night commercials, Tony would frown at the camera ever so slightly, more to suggest concern than anger and point at your shins, saying, "Hey, don't be a newt. Get yourself a decent suit." Apart from this snappy line, Tony's crack team of advertisers had come up with the tag line, "When you think of cool suits, think of Tony." And I, vulnerable zombie that I was at three in the morning, was hypnotized into doing just that.

Actually, I didn't think of Tony so much as the guy who

came out during the commercials to model the cool suits. He was a virile-looking young Italian, probably Tony's son or nephew. A self-assured guy who would inherit the business in his mid-sixties and end up pointing at people's shins. He'd come out with a blonde on each arm and just stand there in the suit. Not really modeling. Not even smiling.

It's not that these women were stunning. If I adjusted the contrast on my television, black roots would spring up out of their blonde heads. And it wasn't the fact that he had a woman on each arm. I realized what they were doing. They figure most guys are lucky if they have one woman on their arm for any length of time. When you saw two women, you made a psychological association that it might have something to do with the suit. They might as well have had a hundred women, since all they were doing was feeding some male-ego, two-girls-for-every-boy fantasy. But I guess they hold the line at two women because if they had more than that you wouldn't be able to see the suit.

But the idea of more than one woman didn't do anything for me. While it was true I had quite a few women on my mind lately, I never hoped for any more than one of them at a time. Once, when I was in college, I'd gone to a party, gotten myself drunk on something orange and liquor-colored, staggered into a bedroom and collapsed onto the bed. Soon after that, a girl in roughly the same condition staggered in and joined me on the bed. And then another girl, also in a similar state, staggered in and joined us. As we began to drunkenly grope, paw and pet each other, I delighted in the idea that an endless parade of drunken women might stagger in and join us. But I soon found the activity of just the two women disorienting and unpleasant.

Sort of like trying to drink a cup of coffee while you're in an airplane that's taking all sorts of loops and dives. I know a lot of it had to do with being young and drunk, but I never wanted to find myself in that situation again.

So when I saw this young Italian guy with a woman on each arm, I wasn't envious. I was just amazed he could stand there with two women and deny himself one of those moronic, devilish grins. It made me think perhaps he knew something I knew. Maybe he'd had two women, maybe even the two women in the commercial, and it hadn't been so hot. Or maybe he was just one of those smug jerks who never smiles. Especially when there's a camera pointed at him. But the thought that he might be unhappy with two women was the reason I thought of Tony's Suits for Stylish Gents when I thought of suits.

I might not have done anything about the suit situation, I might have skipped the idea of getting a suit and, in turn, forgotten any ideas about crashing Lena's wedding and got on with my life, but Tony's Suits for Stylish Gents was only a few blocks down from the motel where I'd booked a reservation for Soren Sonderby. It wouldn't hurt to just look, I thought.

The store was actually squeezed between an espresso café and a cannoli bakery in the heart of the Italian district. Even though it was a small storefront, they'd managed to cram the entire name, Tony's Suits for Stylish Gents, on the display window. There were some Mediterranean-looking mannequins in the window. Olive-toned wooden dummies with black mustaches, dressed in cool suits.

I walked in and cased the joint. The surroundings were close. Claustrophobic. Hot. None of the cool suits looked all that cool hanging from the wire hangers. The big brass anti-theft rings attached to them like handcuffs didn't help any.

Tony Riccarelli, whom I recognized immediately from the commercial, emerged from the back room. A cigar dangled from his mouth, dropping flecks of ash onto a piece of pin-striped material he had in his hand. Tony was wearing a conservative dark blue suit. Something the owner of a funeral home might put on. He had sense enough to know he was too old to wear one of his own cool suits. Tony was muttering to himself. I wasn't sure if he knew I was in the store. But when I wandered off to look around he addressed me.

"Need a suit?"

"Yes," I said.

"What's the occasion?"

"I'm not sure. I think I need an all-purpose, multi-occasion suit, something that could be worn to a film festival or a wedding."

"Your wedding? You don't want those suits there," he said, nodding to a rack just beyond where I was standing. He was making a beeline for a rack of clothes just to his left.

"No, it's not my wedding," I said. "I'd just be a guest. Sort of."

Tony put on the brakes and changed directions, aiming his cigar towards a rack on his right. He sized me up quickly, squinting over the top of his nose, then he turned his attention back to the rack. He rifled through the suits, the hangers going clack clack clack like an Italian carbine.

"You a friend of the bride or groom?" he asked, without looking up.

"Bride, I guess."

Tony smacked away at the suits like a sergeant doing a drill inspection. Pushing aside those suits he considered unfit. Not up to snuff.

"Close friend?"

"It's an ex-girlfriend," I said.

"Oh." This appeared to stump him. He stopped beating the suits and leaned against the display tree. He took the cigar from his mouth and tapped his lower lip with his index finger, muttering, "Ex-girlfriend . . . ex-girlfriend . . ."

"It doesn't matter," I said. "I just need something kind of hip-looking. The woman I'm taking to the wedding said I had to have a nice suit."

He fixed me with a stone-face glare.

"What are you, late thirties?"

"Early thirties."

"Let me tell you something. You don't let any woman tell you you've got to have a nice suit. We'll get you a nice suit, don't worry. You'll be fine. But don't go telling this woman you bought this suit for her. You just tell her you had the suit already but you forgot about it. You don't even have to tell her why you forgot about it. And if she asks, you tell her 'Never mind.' You don't let her, you don't let *any* woman tell you how to buy your clothes. Okay? We understand each other, eh?"

"Yes."

"All right. How about brown? Brown's a good color for you."

"That sounds fine."

"You don't want a black suit because you're too pale," Tony said, searching through the rack again. "Brown's good if you're pale."

Tony unlocked a brown suit. He shook it out as if the arms

might have been tired from being shackled to the display tree. He pressed the suit against my body.

"You a thirty-six?"

"Thirty-eight."

"Then let's go with a forty or forty-two."

He went back to the suits to hunt for a larger size.

"Forty-two? That's kind of big, isn't it?"

"I'll tell you something," Tony said, leaning into me. "I don't tell everyone this, so pay attention. Three things. Good material. Good color. Good size. And the right size for today is big. A son-a-mon-bitch that hangs on you. I know it sounds stupid. Ten, fifteen years ago, you don't have to tell me. Tight. Tight clothes. Pants you can't get your balls into. Today? Just the opposite. Just try and find your balls in these."

Tony pulled a large brown suit off the rack and draped it over the display tree.

"There's a nice one," he said.

He pulled a fabric tape measure out of his back pocket and started to measure me.

"I've seen your commercials," I said, trying to make conversation while he measured my inseam.

"Oh yeah? What's the matter? Can't you sleep?"

I nodded.

"I get a lot of insomniacs. And referrals from insomniacs."

"I'm losing about a minute of sleep a night," I said. "Have you ever heard of circadian rhythms?"

"Oh, sure," he said. "What a racket those things make. Those God damn son-a-mon-bitches all over the yard. I had to have a guy come out and fog. Then I had to rake 'em up. Madonna, you never saw such a mess!"

Tony gave me the big brown suit and pointed me to a dressing room. The dressing room was about the size of a phone booth. Just enough room for one body, one suit, one mirror on the wall and one hook on the back of the door. I hated trying on clothes. It exhausted me to get myself dressed once a day. Anything more than that could push me over the edge. I put the suit on. It felt ridiculously huge. Like I was a lone spud in the bottom of a giant potato sack. When I had the jacket on and my pants zipped up, I turned to face the mirror.

The sleeves extended down past my hands and hung lifelessly at my sides. The legs were puddled around my feet. I looked like I'd been a big man at one time and had shrunk or melted.

Tony spoke to me from just outside the door of the dressing room.

"How's it look?"

"It's a little big," I said.

I opened the door of the dressing room and slithered out.

Tony pulled me to him by the back of my collar, like I was a bad puppy. Then he slapped at my back and sides as if I was being punished for something. But he didn't seem concerned by what he saw. And he didn't tell me to take it off, which is what I'd expected. He tilted his head this way and that, stuck up his lower lip beneath his cigar and nodded a lot.

"Don't hunch," he said.

"I'm not hunching," I said.

He played with the suit some more. Pulled on the sleeves. Ran his fingers under the lapels. Folded the cuffs of my pants a few times. "It's good. It's good. A few alterations, that's all. When I'm done, it'll be a nice suit like you want, eh?"

"Can you do that now?

"Now? No."

"When can I have it?"

"When do you need it?"

"I need it now. I was going to wear it to a film festival to-night. Don't you have any suits that are ready to go?"

"Do you want to look good, or do you want to look like some imbecile who bought a suit off the rack?"

"Well, I want to look good, but there's only so much I can do with what God gave me. I don't want to get into this suit thing too deeply, you know. I don't want to spend beyond my looks."

"What's the matter with you? You're a good-looking kid. A little tired-looking maybe, but you still got a lot to work with."

"So when could I have this suit? If I can't have it tomorrow, I'll have to forget about it."

"You can have it tomorrow. Can you pay me today?"

"Um . . . yes. Certainly."

"Then you can pick it up tomorrow."

I nodded. Tony started marking and pinning the suit. I felt a little uneasy standing there while he did this. I guess it's some sort of homophobic thing. But I figure if a man is touching my legs, I'd better talk about something. Otherwise, he'd wonder what I was thinking. I knew it was stupid, but I did it anyway.

"So, is that your son in the commercial?" I asked.

"Vince? No. He's my nephew. My luck, two daughters, no sons. Madonna."

"Those two women in the commercial, the . . . blondes, those aren't your daughters, are they?"

"Nah. Models. From an agency. Overpaid."

"Oh."

"Bet you like 'em, eh?"

"Sure," I said. It was the homophobic thing again. Tony touching my legs. It seemed necessary to heartily agree that big-haired peroxide blondes were right up my heterosexual alley.

"Your girlfriend, she's pretty, eh?"

I wanted to explain to him that Darlene wasn't my girlfriend. That I was just using her in an underhanded way to crash my ex-girlfriend's wedding. But since my relationship with Tony only went so far as his selling me a suit and touching my legs a few times, I didn't feel comfortable explaining it all to him.

"She's a singer," I said, avoiding the question. "She's singing at the wedding."

"You gonna marry her?"

I knew Tony was just being chatty in response to my being chatty, but I found his questions increasingly stressful. Part of the problem was that I was dying from the heat. It was already near one hundred degrees outside. It must have been one hundred and six in the store. And inside the suit? One hundred ten, one hundred fifteen easy. I'd already expended all my energy dealing with Soren Sonderby. And now the activity of changing clothes already had me sticking to my underwear. And now it felt as though I was stuck in a sauna and someone had turned up and broken off the temperature control.

"No, I don't think I'll marry her," I said, drowning in my own perspiration. For a moment I thought I might faint. It was stupid to be trying on suits in this heat. There should have been a metal tag around my neck that said: SHOULD NOT TRY ON SUITS IN THE SUMMER and on the back: DON'T ASK HIM ANY PERSONAL QUESTIONS. I started to panic. I suddenly saw myself dying of heat exhaustion. Getting waked in the oversized brown suit. People walking up to my coffin, saying: "He was supposed to wear this for a wedding. Who knew it would be for his funeral?"

Just as I was about to go over the edge and tear and claw my way out of the suit, Tony suddenly stood up and patted me twice on the back.

"Okay, you can get out of there. Kind of hot, eh?"

I sighed a moist breath of relief and retreated to the dressing room. While I was changing from my perspiration-soaked suit back into my perspiration-soaked clothes, I heard Tony say something in Italian. I didn't speak much Italian. Certainly not enough to have understood him. I wondered if someone else, a paisan, had come in to talk to him. But when I came out of the dressing room there was no one else there. Maybe he's talking to the suits, I thought. It was a lonely job, after all. If he wanted to talk to the suits, it was okay by me. And if he wanted to talk to them in Italian, that was okay too. Maybe they were Italian suits.

"You speak a little Italian?" he asked when I handed him the suit.

"Very little," I said.

"You know what I said?"

"No."

He repeated it. *L'amare vappassare il tempo. Il tempo vapassare l'amare.*

I shrugged.

"Love makes time pass. Time makes love pass."

I nodded like I understood.

"Don't worry so much about getting married," he said. "Get

married, yeah. Have some bambinos. But don't worry about it, eh?"

It seemed like some further explanation of the quote, his own personal interpretation.

"Okay," I said. But I wondered: Did I look like I needed little gems of wisdom hurled my way?

My next stop, in what was becoming by far the busiest day of my adult life, was a liquor store to buy schnapps. I had no idea where to find schnapps in a liquor store and I anticipated another long ordeal as I scanned the dizzying array of bottles. Luckily, an eager employee showed me an entire aisle of colorful bottles and pointed directly to the schnapps. I felt like buying the employee a gift, just for making my life a little easier.

I looked for that other stuff, that colorless liquor that Sonderby pulled out of his luggage, the liquor that was still burning a hole in my stomach, but I couldn't find it. Just as well, I thought. I didn't think it was a good idea to supply him with any more of that poison during his stay. If they'd had a bottle, I might have bought one to give to him at the airport, as a going-away present.

Instead, I bought four bottles of schnapps, thinking that I'd probably need three at most and I'd make a present of the fourth to Sonderby. The gesture was probably comparable to buying a can of Budweiser for an American in Europe going back to the United States, but I couldn't think of anything more creative.

While still in the same neighborhood I found a gourmet deli shop and went in search of Swedish cheeses. The variety of choices was staggering, but I couldn't find any cheese that was specifically indigenous to Sweden or Denmark. And this time there was no helpful employee, just a busy Korean cashier who seemed confused by my questions.

She would say, "Danish cheese, yes," and smile and say "Swedish cheese, yes," and smile but when we got around to "Where?" she would simply smile and shake her head helplessly. By this point in the day I was about out of patience. Cheese is cheese, I thought. Just like Bergman is Bergman, cheese is cheese. So I bought a big wheel of Edam. And then I splurged and bought a fancy cheese knife. It looked kind of Nordic. It had a Viking ship carved on the little wooden handle. I think it was a Viking ship— it's hard to get a lot of detail on the handle of a cheese knife and for all I knew about ships it could have been the Exxon Valdez. Anyway, I thought the cheese knife would look nice next to the cheese wheel. And maybe I could make the cheese knife my going-away gift to Sonderby instead of the booze.

I put the big Edam wheel on the passenger seat of the VW and hoped it wouldn't spoil in the heat, or for that matter, melt into the leather interior. By alternately watching the road and the cheese wheel, I kept missing my exit back to my neighborhood. I finally caught it the third time around. It was like that game where you try to get the ball in the little hole and you keep missing it.

Back at my apartment, I noticed Missus Calabrone's shopping caddy was gone from the side of the building, which meant she'd walked to the grocery store. I ran the cheese wheel up to my apartment and shoved it in the refrigerator, rushing to keep it fresh, like a donor heart. Then, taking advantage of Missus Calabrone's absence, I took a long, cool shower uninterrupted by broom handle thumps on my floor. I leisurely washed away the grime of the long day—washed off the Quality Nook and Tony's Suits for Stylish Gents and the liquor store and the deli. Jesus, I thought. Too much for one day. A normal person would be wiped out running errands in this heat, and in my sleep-deprived condition, I certainly was no match for the elements. How much could a person like me endure? As I stepped out of the shower, I thought I felt the broom handle thumping, but it must have been something that just stuck in my brain, a Pavlovian auditory hallucination.

I dressed, donning a pair of khakis and a clean white shirt I'd been saving for this weekend. No stains around the collar or cuffs. I even splashed a little cologne on my body. I often had allergic reactions to scented body applications, but I wanted to smell good in case Anne showed up at the film festival.

I descended the staircase with the cold cheese wheel under my arm. Maybe I'd even keep it on my lap while I drove, I thought. It might stabilize my body temperature, keep me from overheating. As I rounded the bottom of the stairs, I nearly hit Missus Calabrone with the cheese wheel.

"I thought we had an understanding about the water situation," she said, brandishing a dangerous-looking, red-stained wooden spoon.

"Jesus, you scared me," I said. "I didn't know you were still here."

"Somebody stole my shopping caddy," she said. "Do you know anything about that?"

"No, I haven't seen it."

"What is that under your arm?"

"It's a cheese wheel."

"Where are you going with cheese so big like that?"

"I have to get it to the theater. I have to hurry. I don't want it to spoil or melt."

"They won't let you bring a cheese like that in the theater."

"It's my theater. I can bring in any size cheese I like."

"Your theater? I thought you told me you ran a movie theater."

"I do. It's a special night tonight. Film Festival. We've got Soren Sonderby coming in."

"Never heard of him. How'd you get a big cheese like that home? You didn't use my shopping caddy?"

"No, I swear. I bought this cheese downtown. I have the receipt upstairs but I don't have time to show you right now. Check with the neighbor kids, I think they like to play around with it."

"If I find out you've got my shopping caddy, you're out of here. You understand? You can't just use my shopping caddy whenever you want to cart cheese back and forth. Not without asking."

"I wouldn't," I said. "I've never used it. I would help you look for it, but I have to get my cheese to the theater."

Missus Calabrone eyed me suspiciously. "You're not fooling anyone with that cheese under your arm," she said, and ambled off to the neighbor's house in search of her shopping caddy.

I found a card table in the supply room of the Arcadia Filmhaus. I set it up in the lobby and dusted it off. At first, I set it up near the entrance to the screening room. Then I thought better of it, realizing I didn't want people to assume they could take cheese and schnapps into the theater with them while the movie was on. Nor did I want to put the table adjacent to the concession stand, which would suggest I was selling liquor and cheese along with popcorn and soda. I finally settled on a remote neutral location, against the wall separating the men's rest room from the lady's rest room.

I carefully pulled the individually wrapped bottles of schnapps out of their brown bags from the liquor store. Once again, I needed to make some quick decisions. I didn't want to leave all four bottles out, fearing it might promote excessive drinking. I was particularly worried about Sonderby. Anyone who packed some cheap Swedish hooch in his luggage was someone I needed to watch out for. A single bottle of schnapps, however, looked decidedly unfestive. Two bottles, I decided, suggested something of a party. And it looked a little better, too, when I put out the Edam wheel, the cheese knife, the crackers and some napkins.

Still, I think the card table was too big or the spread too small. Something about the display seemed uninviting and tragic. I augmented the display with a few decoratively placed boxes of candy from the candy counter, some Milk Duds, Jujubes and Snickers, hoping it would perk the whole thing up. Then I thought— strawberries. I should have gotten some wild strawberries or just plain old strawberries in a bowl. Too late, I thought. Maybe tomorrow night. If I don't go to Lena's wedding, I'll pick up some strawberries. But first, we'll see how tonight goes.

I took a moment to engage in a bit of role-playing, approaching the table objectively as if I were a filmgoer instead of a theater manager.

"Ah, schnapps," I said, as if I'd just seen the table, and I tried to elicit some joy in my discovery. I took a plastic cup and pretended to pour myself a shot. Then I wheeled around as if to address another member of a film society. "They have schnapps," I called across an empty room.

Ginny was entering the lobby at this moment and saw me engaged in a conversation with my display. She kept moving, saying nothing. I put the plastic glass down and called her over.

"Ginny, wait a moment. About tonight . . ."

Ginny stopped and approached reluctantly.

"Do you know what schnapps is?" I asked. "It's a liquor— favored by the people of Norway, I think."

Ginny's eyes darted around the lobby like those squirrels that make suicidal runs in and out of traffic. She alternately looked at the odd buffet table with the bottles of schnapps and the doors to the rest rooms.

"I'm going to be serving schnapps during our film festival," I said. "And I'm going to have a cheese wheel and some crackers. You won't have to do anything. It'll just be set up on a table in the lobby. The thing is, I want to keep two bottles behind the candy counter and I was thinking maybe you could just refresh the bottles if they get empty. By refresh, I mean, don't open them, just put new bottles out when the others get low. We won't actually be selling it, just serving it. I mean, you're still in high school, so I assume you're not old enough to sell liquor or serve it. It'll be free, like the crackers and the cheese wheel. I don't know if that makes a difference. I don't even know if it's legal for you to have the bottles behind the counter with you while you're working. You don't drink, do you? I mean, I know, you're in high school, you probably drink a bit, but I mean, you don't have one of those teenage drinking problems, do you?"

Ginny shook her head.

"I'm not accusing you, you understand. I just need to check

this out with you. I could check with an attorney about the liability involved, but I'd rather not know, because I think he'll probably say it isn't a good idea, that we aren't licensed to serve liquor, and that we shouldn't be allowing a minor to serve liquor. I'm not advertising the part about the schnapps. I only mentioned 'refreshments' in the ad. But I think it would be nice to have schnapps. You know, appropriate, because it's a cordial, favored by the Swedish people.

"I don't have a drinking problem," Ginny said.

"No, I know. Of course you don't. That's why I'm going to trust you with two bottles behind the candy counter. If you see that the bottles on the buffet table are getting low, just replace them with a new bottle. But just one bottle at a time. Keep the other bottles behind the counter until we use them."

"You want me to keep the bottles where no one can get at them."

"Exactly," I said, amazed at our coincidental meeting of the minds. "By the way, the film festival is a three-day span, Friday through Sunday, but possibly off on Saturday. Anyway, I think that's the way it's going to go. But I think Saturday we won't be open. It depends on how well it goes tonight."

"Why wouldn't we be open on Saturday?" Ginny asked, with a terrified look in her eyes. It occurred to me that Ginny might think I was involving her in something that might bring in an ATF swat team to shut us down. Some serious schnapps violation perhaps, that could put her in teen-age jail where she wouldn't have access to makeup or diet cola.

"The thing is," I said, working up a really good lie, "Victor Sjöström died on that date, and I think, out of respect, we should be closed on Saturday."

"When Cary Grant died, they showed his films all day on television," Ginny said.

"Victor Sjöström was Swedish," I said. "Different culture. Different customs."

The look of consternation remained on Ginny's face.

"You'll still be paid for Saturday, of course."

This seemed to satisfy her, and she went away to make popcorn.

The next person I saw was Bix. He arrived around six-thirty and poked his head into the projection booth.

"What's up, Mal?"

"Nothing, nothing," I said, nervously checking every gear tooth in the sprockets to the projector.

"The girl charged me to get in again."

"I'm sorry, Bix. I told Ginny you didn't have to pay. I thought she knew who you were by now."

"No, I think she does, I just think she likes to bust my balls a little bit."

"I guess it's good to know it's not just me."

"Where's . . . what's his name?"

"Soren Sonderby. He should be here soon. Was there anyone down there when you came in?"

"You mean hanging out in your new cocktail lounge? No, nobody."

"How bad does it look?"

"I think you need a few more Snickers Bars to flank out the cheese wheel."

"Okay, so it's a little tacky. Do you think it looks festive, at least?"

"Don't worry," Bix said. "I'm sure the smell from the rest rooms will draw them over there like magnets."

"Great," I said. "Just great. Listen, you didn't smell any alcohol on Ginny's breath, did you?"

"I don't get that close to Ginny. She makes me nervous."

"I'm just a little worried about her keeping bottles of alcohol behind the candy counter with her. I know she's not old enough to drink or sell liquor and it's making me a little nervous. I don't even know if she's allowed to look at a bottle of schnapps."

"Don't worry so much, Mal. She's making popcorn. I don't think she's doing any drinking. When did you say Sonderby's getting here?"

"Soon," I said. "What's the rush?"

"Everything that guy knows about film —I want to tap into that guy's brain."

"Tap is a good word to use."

"What does that mean?"

"His drinking concerns me. He might be an alcoholic. He had some weird liquor packed in his luggage."

"He's from Sweden, Mal. Those guys aren't alcoholics, they just drink a lot."

"I don't know about that."

"I'm telling you, it's a different culture. Drinking is a part of their everyday existence."

"Just as long as he can answer questions about Bergman, that's all I care about."

"Are you kidding, Mal? The guy's probably an encyclopedia of knowledge."

"Somewhat abridged, I think."

"You want me to go downstairs and keep an eye out for him?"

"Yes. Thanks."

As Bix headed for the lobby, I re-checked everything that could go wrong, technically. I turned the house lights up and down, made sure the curtain opened and closed. Bix came back up to the projection booth around six forty-five and told me there was a taxi in front of the Arcadia with its blinkers on.

"I think you better come down, Mal," Bix said. "I think he's just sitting in the cab."

"I gave him money for a taxi," I said and dashed downstairs with Bix.

Soren Sonderby was in the back of a yellow cab. He looked worse than when he'd gotten off the plane. He was in a suit, kind of a light blue leisure suit, but he looked ghoulish, like he'd just climbed out of a coffin at his own wake. He'd opted not to wear his fisherman's cap and his ragged toupee seemed precariously perched on his head.

"What's going on?" I asked him. "Where's your cab fare?"

"I had to have dinner," he said. Based on his breath, it seemed Sonderby had drunk his dinner. He may have also drunk his appetizer and drunk his dessert.

I paid the cab driver and Bix and I pulled him out of the cab. We didn't need to hold him up, thank God, but we did stand on either side of him, like spotters, just waiting for him to fall over. We led Sonderby into the theater, directly past the buffet table with the schnapps on it.

"Ah, schnapps," he said.

"Later," I said. "That's for later."

I put him in my office and closed the door behind us. Sonderby sat down at my desk. If it wasn't already painfully clear that he was wearing a hairpiece, he drew attention to it by fussing with it, moving it to different sites on the top of his head. By turns he had a large forehead, then no forehead at all.

"Just relax for a few minutes," I said. "Can I get you a glass of water?" Sonderby nodded. "I'll be right back," I said.

Bix was standing outside the door to my office.

"What do you think?" I asked Bix. "Is he drunk? I mean, should I close the doors to the theater right now and not let anyone in?"

"No," Bix said. "He's great. Sure, he's had a couple, but he'll be great. I can't wait until we get into some solid Q and A with him."

"Q and A? Have you looked in the lobby? There's no one here to ask any Qs and I don't think he has any As."

"Naw, he'll be fine, Mal. Did you see that face? The guy's a fucking road map of experience."

"Really? I don't know. I mean, if you'd seen him this afternoon. I swear he aged another ten years in the past six hours. I think he's either too drunk or too old or too tired for this. Maybe all of the above. I think I should call it off."

Bix pointed to a young couple who'd walked in and were now buying tickets from Ginny.

"Too late, Mal," Bix said.

I went back into my office with a glass of water for Sonderby and sat down opposite him.

"Do you have a bio?" I asked.

"Bio?" He sipped the water slowly and blinked his bleary, unfocused eyes.

"Something listing your credits, your stage and screen work . . . ?"

"I was just in the one film, *The Seventh Seal*."

"No other acting . . . okay, okay. No problem. We'll just skip over the bio. I'll introduce you and then . . . did you have anything you wanted to say?"

"Thank you for bringing me here."

"No, I don't mean to *me*, I meant did you have any kind of . . . prepared statement or speech or anything for the audience?"

"No."

"All right then. That's okay. That's fine. We'll just leave it at questions and answers after the film. The audience will want to ask you a few questions, I'm sure, and I'm sure you wouldn't mind answering a few questions. How does that sound?"

"Fine. And then we drink and we have a nice party, eh?"

"Yes, yes, of course. After the movie and after the questions. Did you want to watch the film?"

"Whatever you think is best."

"Well, maybe you should rest. It's been a long day. I'll come and get you after the film."

When seven o'clock rolled around, I took a deep breath and then looked down on the theater from the projection booth. I counted fifteen heads. Sixteen counting Bix. No more than my best, non-film festival nights. The people looked vaguely familiar. I'd never really paid attention, but I think they were the same fifteen or so people who always came to see foreign films at my theater. I reviewed the heads again, searching in vain for Anne's head. I waited until five after seven, hoping she might show up, but she did not appear. Oh, well, I thought. What was I thinking? I dimmed the house lights and fired up the projector.

Everyone stayed for the duration of the film, a good sign, I thought. I had to remain in the projection booth to monitor the film, so I couldn't check up on Sonderby until it was over. I didn't watch the movie much, preferring to pace and chew on my cuticles. When the last reel ended I went down to my office to retrieve Sonderby. He was slumped over my desk.

"My God," I said.

He picked his head up. "Is it time? I was just taking a little nap." He reached in the vest pocket of his jacket, pulled out a flask and took a hit off it. Damn, I thought. I should have frisked him. But instead of taking the flask away from him, an idea he resisted, I put it back into his vest pocket. Then, against my better judgment, I led him into the theater. I had two chairs set up behind the curtain for our post-film discussion and I sat him down in one of them.

"I'll introduce you," I said.

I parted the curtain and walked out onto the stage.

"Thanks for coming," I said. "I'd like to introduce Soren Sonderby at this time."

There was a resounding response of "Who?" Some people, however, who'd read the little mimeographed flyer about *Wild Strawberries* I'd left in the lobby were past "Who" and were concerned with "Why."

"Was he in *Wild Strawberries*?" someone asked. "His name isn't listed in the credits."

"No," I said. "He is probably best remembered as one of the villagers with the plague in the *Seventh Seal*."

"Are you showing the *Seventh Seal* tonight?"

"No," I said.

"He has the plague?" someone else shouted out.

Within the confused din, I overheard someone telling their neighbor that one of the Village People had died of the plague.

"When is this Seven Seas movie?" asked an old man in the first row.

"*The Seventh Seal*," I said.

"When are you showing *The Seventh Seal*?"

"We're not showing that," I said, keeping my cool. "We're showing *Wild Strawberries*. And Soren Sonderby does not have the plague, he's here tonight."

"Which one of the Village People?" someone shouted.

"No. He was a villager." I gave up and went behind the curtain.

Soren Sonderby looked like he'd aged another ten years. He certainly couldn't afford to keep aging at this rate. He'd be one hundred and twenty years old by the end of the night.

"It's time," I said, like an executioner to a doomed convict.

Sonderby got up wearily and ambled onstage. He walked into the light, holding his flask. He shielded his eyes and looked out into what might be called an audience.

"Hey, get off the stage," someone yelled.

I didn't expect anyone to recognize him, I certainly wouldn't have, but worse, they appeared to have mistaken him for some drunk who'd wandered onto the proscenium by mistake. I quickly ran out of the wings before they started throwing things at him.

"This is Soren Sonderby," I said.

The chorus of "Who?" started up again in earnest. Some people looked disappointed. I'm not sure why. Maybe they thought I was going to bring out one of the Village People. I realized now, to the fullest extent, that this whole thing had been a mistake, and I wanted it to be over as soon as possible.

"We'll have a *short* question and answer period," I said.

There seemed to be a lot of buzzing among the fifteen people in the audience about who this man was and what he was doing here. It didn't seem like an excited buzz, but more of a be-wildered or perhaps even disappointed buzz.

"Does anyone have a question for Mister Sonderby?" I asked. The buzz abated, but it was replaced by silence rather than questions.

"Anyone can start," I said. "Just jump right in. Any kind of question at all." I waited a moment.

"What do you think Bergman was saying in *Wild Strawber-ries?*" someone asked, at last.

Sonderby looked at me and I nodded at him to answer the question, as though I were his lawyer.

"I don't know," Sonderby said. "I haven't seen the film."

A few people chuckled, thinking it was a joke.

"You mean," I said, "that you haven't seen the film in a while."

"No," he said peevishly. "I never saw it. I didn't see it when it came out and they don't have a theater in Sweden that shows old Bergman movies. And I was in the office back there this evening, so I still haven't seen it."

"Mister Sonderby was resting in my office," I said, almost as an aside. "I think," I continued, "we should probably restrict our questions to more general matters. What it was like work-ing with Bergman, that sort of thing."

It got quiet again. People may have been trying to figure out exactly how to restrict themselves to generalities. Finally it was Bix who spoke up.

"What was it like, working with Bergman?"

Sonderby looked over at me again, this time with a smug look as if we both knew the answer to this one.

"Bergman is Bergman," he said, in that same brusque tone

he'd used with me the day before. He took another hit off his flask to punctuate his remark.

There was another embarrassing silence which was followed by an embarrassing spatter of applause. Bix stood up and clapped alone, like Orson Welles in *Citizen Kane*, adding an exclamation of "Damn right."

A few other people clapped, but even if everyone, all fifteen of them, had clapped, it would have sounded pathetic.

"I think the audience might be interested in the relationship between director and actor," I said.

"We got up very early every day of shooting," he said.

"Yes," I said, encouraging him, hoping his remark would pan out into an elaborate monologue about a typical workday with Bergman.

"Very . . . early," he said, and that was the end of that lively anecdote.

Bix chimed in again. It was a mixed blessing. No one else in the audience seemed inclined to ask any questions and, as such, they were quite content to turn the job over to Bix. Still, it lacked a certain spontaneity, as though the audience sensed Bix was a plant. "As an actor," Bix began, making sure everyone in the room knew he was an actor, "I'm interested in how you physicalize a disabling disease."

Sonderby looked at me helplessly and took a draw off his flask.

"I think, if I understand this man correctly," I said, "he wants to know how you act like you have the plague."

Sonderby stopped drinking and pocketed his flask. He stood up, wobbling a bit as he got out of his chair. He hunched his body over. His face went limp and he collapsed onto the edge of the proscenium. There were several gasps from the audience. Sonderby didn't get up. I rushed over and lifted his head. His eyes opened.

"Was that okay?" he breathed. He wasn't dead. Just drunk.

"That's fine," I said.

Bix clapped again and this time everyone clapped, I think out of sheer relief that they hadn't witnessed Sonderby's death.

"I think that'll do it for this evening," I said. "Thank you all for coming."

On these words, most of the audience were up out of their seats and heading up the aisle. In their haste to clear the theater, none of the audience remained to socialize around the cheese wheel and drink schnapps. They probably didn't wish to remain in the vicinity of anyone who could portray someone with the plague so realistically. Understandable, I thought.

After I put Sonderby in a cab and released Ginny from her duties, explaining to both of them that we'd be skipping the following night's film festival, I told Bix I wanted to be alone.

"Where's the cheese knife?" Bix asked. "I don't want you doing anything crazy."

"I appreciate your concern," I said. "But I'm not going to do anything crazy."

Bix agreed to leave me alone, but insisted on taking the cheese knife with him.

The prudent thing for Bix to have done, however, would have been to remove all the schnapps from the premises. As soon as he was gone and I'd locked up the theater, I found the bottle behind the candy counter. Ginny hadn't opened it, thank God. With the cheese wheel under my arm and the schnapps in my fist I retired to my office. I shoved the cheese into a small refrigerator next to the closet. Then I sat at my desk and cracked open the bottle. I wasn't much of a drinker, so my tolerance was low. After the first few shots, I barely felt it going down anymore. It only took a half a bottle for me to get good and schnappled and ready to make drunken phone calls.

I picked up the receiver and poised my finger over the dial. Being drunk, I thought, would make it that much easier to dial the first seven letters of Dialogue and omit that silent "e." But I didn't even get that far. I dialed the first four digits, then quickly hung up the phone. No, I thought. If I call and find out she didn't work tonight, I'll just be that much angrier that she's blown off my film festival. And what would I say to her if she was there? No. No point in raging against Anne. She was right to pass on a loser like me. And besides, there were easier ways to accelerate my downward spiral.

I picked up the phone again and dialed Darlene's number. I got an answering machine. When I heard the beep I cleared my throat.

"This is Malcolm," I said. "I have a suit."

chapter thirteen

I picked up the suit Saturday morning, the day of Lena's wedding to Doctor Andrew Buntrock.

"What happened to you?" Tony Riccarelli asked when I walked into Tony's Suits for Stylish Gents. "You look awful."

"I had a bad night last night."

"Let's get the suit," he said. "Maybe things will improve."

When I tried it on in front of the three-way mirror it looked a little better than it had the day before. But it still looked huge.

"It looks great, eh?" Tony said. He said this enthusiastically, while brushing off my shoulders, smoothing the brown material and patting me down like I was Rex, the Wonder Horse. I stepped away from the mirror as far as the walls of the store would allow, trying to make myself and the suit look smaller.

I rolled my shoulders. I suavely put my right hand in my pocket and turned my body sideways, leaning towards the mirror. They weren't the kinds of poses I'd ever struck in real life. But I tried them now because I'd seen other people do these kinds of moves in front of mirrors and seem pleased with themselves. But it still looked big.

It was the day of the wedding, however, and I couldn't afford to be picky. I could see my hands and feet poking out from the edges of the cuffs. That was something, anyway.

"It does look good, doesn't it," I said, trying to convince myself.

"You look sharp," Tony said.

"Okay, let's wrap it up."

I paid for the suit and Tony stuffed it into a large green garment bag. I hefted the suit over my shoulder and lugged it out of the store.

"She's gonna love it," Tony said, as I dragged the suit away.

The wedding was scheduled for five o'clock. At around three, I got in the shower, turned on the cold water and stayed in as long as I could without turning blue. I ignored the thump of Missus Calabrone's broom handle after my allotted three minutes and stayed in the shower a full five minutes. I was hoping to reduce my body temperature, preserve myself in some primitive, cryogenic way, so that I wouldn't be a sweaty mass by five. But a few minutes outside of my shower I was once again toweling beads of perspiration off my forehead, back and neck.

I stepped on my bathroom scale and noted that I'd dropped another five pounds that week. I'm wasting away, I thought. I donned the suit that was even bigger now that I was even smaller. *The Incredible Shrinking Man.* Maybe I'll just keep shrinking, like Scott Carey, I mused. Use the suit for a tent when my body shrinks to the size of a Ken doll. I looked at myself in the mirror on the bathroom door. I pushed my hair out of my face and tried to smile. I did this several times. But each time the smile looked about as genuine as on those dummies in the window of Tony's Suits for Stylish Gents. Oh, well, I thought. I grabbed my keys, comb, chewing gum, sunglasses and wallet, locked the apartment and went downstairs.

At the bottom of the stairs I ran into Missus Calabrone. She was standing in the driveway with a ceramic bowl and wooden spoon, stirring some ground beef, I think. She stopped stirring and pointed the greasy wooden spoon at me.

"Listen, Mister," she said. "That's too much water you're using."

"Did you find your shopping cart?"

"Neighbor kids," she said. "I'm gonna break their little necks."

"I'm sorry about the water," I said. "But it's really hot up there. I just wanted to cool off."

"A small guy like you shouldn't need a lot of water to get wet."

"It was all cold water," I said. "I didn't use any hot water."

"Water is water," she said. "It's all water."

"Yes, I'm sorry. You're right. It's all water."

"You going somewhere in that getup?"

"I'm going to a wedding," I said.

"Your suit is pretty big," she said.

"I know," I said. "It's supposed to be big."

"My husband had big suits. Not because he wanted to. He got sick. Lost a lot of weight."

"I just bought this suit," I said. "From a guy named Tony Riccarelli, in the city."

"Riccarelli? Not the east side Riccarellis, I hope?"

"I don't know."

"Material looks expensive," she said.

"I got a pretty good deal on it."

"You look like a gangster," she said. "God forbid anyone sees me renting the place to someone wearing a suit like this."

"I won't be wearing it all the time," I said. "Believe me."

Missus Calabrone shrugged.

"I don't tell my tenants what they can wear. That's up to them. I just hope you have enough common sense not to be seen by too many people in that getup."

"I have a train to catch," I said.

To keep from sweating too much, I'd decided to take public transportation as much as possible. The train was smelly but cool. Besides, I didn't want to risk a breakdown with the VW. I also didn't want to create another opportunity for Darlene to want to jump me in my vehicle. Not in this heat. Not in this suit.

I bought a ticket and boarded a westbound train. Darlene had told me over the phone that she lived in a large apartment complex just off the tracks. I knew the building she was talking about. I'd seen it several times on the train when I'd missed my regular stop. The sight of those large impersonal buildings never failed to depress me. People living over you, under you, on either side of you. How could you develop a sense of individuality when your doors, windows, kitchenettes and balconies were exactly like your neighbor's? I assumed the tenants liked being close to the train for commuting, but I worried about living too close to a moving vehicle like that. Derailments didn't discriminate between open fields and apartment blocks. Sure, I had yellow jackets in my wall. But I didn't have to worry about a cattle car roaring through my bedroom in the middle of the night. And I guess the idea of large compartmentalized living, so close to a train stop, was distressing in some way. It sort of reminded me of *Night and Fog*.

I'd failed to remember Darlene's exact address, so when I got to her apartment complex I worked methodically. I started from the far left building and worked my way to the right, checking each mailbox for her name. I finally found "Bleeker, D." on a scratched mailbox in building three. I pushed the grimy buzzer next to her name and wiped my finger on the back of my pants. Darlene buzzed me in without confirming my identity and I took the elevator up to the fifth floor. I followed the narrow hallway to her apartment and rapped on the door.

Darlene answered the door in a lacy black slip with cleavage you could have hidden things in. She was brushing her teeth and had foam around her lips like a rabid dog. Sexy, but something you might need to take shots for later, I thought. She nodded me inside and closed the door.

"Nice suit," she said, garbling her words as she pushed the toothbrush over to one side of her mouth. "Kinda big, though."

"It's supposed to be big," I said.

"Hang out for a bit," she said. "I still have to get dressed."

Darlene disappeared down the hallway of her apartment and left me alone in her living room. I sat down on the couch, pushing aside an enormous, overfed house cat sprawled belly-up across the cushions.

Darlene didn't have much in the way of possessions. She had some CDs and tapes strewn about the apartment. An old stereo on top of makeshift brick shelves was playing cello solos. She had those old speakers that lit up, reacting to the highs and lows of the music. It cheapened Bach, made him seem part of the glitter rock scene rather than baroque music. She had a few plants and books. That was about it. I couldn't tell if she was making a minimalist statement or just didn't have a lot of stuff.

It looked like most of what she owned was cluttered on her coffee table. Keys, loose change, sheet music, highball glasses and a half-empty dish of Peanut M&Ms. There was also an allotment of space for drug paraphernalia: rolling papers, a couple books of matches from the 3-D Club. An ashtray loaded with extinguished cigarettes of both varieties. And a zip lock bag that looked like it had lawn refuse in it.

"Help yourself," I heard Darlene call from down the hall. "And roll one for me."

"Oh. Okay," I said, dubiously. I didn't think it was such a good idea. Not from a moral or legal standpoint, necessarily. It was just that it didn't seem like a good idea for a singer to smoke. Particularly this kind of unfiltered, funny smoke. But I knew better than to argue with her about it. I certainly couldn't argue that she'd ever sounded raspy from smoking—quite the contrary. Maybe she'd stripped her lungs down to some purer level.

Anyway when all was said and done, I knew she'd end up rolling one herself and we'd get going that much later because I hadn't done it. Based on the butts I'd seen in the ashtray, I knew I'd have to roll a big one. I didn't want to have her complain that it was too small and have to do it again herself. I scooped some of the stuff out of the zip-lock bag and dumped it onto a piece of rolling paper. I dusted my fingers off into the bag and wrinkled my nose at it. It didn't make much sense, I thought. Partaking of something of which the source was so shadowy and unreliable. No one I knew ever knew where the stuff had come from, beyond the fact that it allegedly originated on a vine somewhere in Jamaica or Mexico. It invariably reached the user through a friend of a friend, without the benefit of

FDA approval. So who knew what you were ingesting? You might as well be eating something you found in your back yard.

But I'd also had a bad experience that had soured me on marijuana. Once, when I was in college, I'd gone with Lena to a party hosted by some friends of hers and they were all smoking a lot of dope. To be sociable, I did my part by taking a hit off whatever was passed my way. These friends of Lena's, Lennie and Cookie, lived a block away from a mile-deep stone quarry. I used to drive by it on the way to their house and slow down the car to marvel at its depth. But on this particular night, the higher I got, the more I became convinced that I would wander away from the party, stumble into the quarry and plummet to my death. I would lie unnoticed for several days, get covered by gravel and eventually become part of someone's new driveway. This scenario was unlikely, however. The quarry not only had a ten-foot high chain link fence around it, but it was also a block away from Lennie and Cookie's and I was having enough trouble navigating myself across the living room in my altered mental state. My fear became so intense, however, that I barricaded myself inside the bathroom, putting the clothes hamper against the door. I lashed my wrist to the bathtub faucet with my necktie to prevent myself from coming to any harm. I recalled the episode vividly as I rolled the fat joint I'd prepared for Darlene. I licked it closed, rolled it between my thumb and forefinger and carefully laid it in the ashtray. Evil weed. Stay away.

Darlene came into the room wearing a burgundy dress with black lace trim. The plunging neckline seemed more revealing than her slip. She had on dark hose and black high heels. Her shoes came to such a severe point that I couldn't imagine where one toe had nestled, let alone five. She looked as though she'd gained a little weight since the first time she'd worn the dress, but she looked good packed into it. I didn't mind an ample figure. It was probably all those European women I'd seen in films from the forties and fifties. Bergman's women weren't fat, but they also didn't worry about having an extra helping of kippers at breakfast. I was, in fact, envious of the way the dress hugged her. It defined her shape with such clarity while I felt formless and lost in my big suit.

"Does this look okay?" Darlene asked.

I nodded.

Darlene reached in front of me for the joint in the ashtray and a headful of perfumed hair filled my nostrils. I didn't move away, drinking in as much of it as I could. I snatched up a book of matches and lit the joint for her. The smell of her perfume was soon replaced by the pungent odor of a very special kind of smoke. Darlene took a voracious suck and handed it to me.

"Take a hit," she said, her offer spoken entirely as an inhale.

"No, thanks," I said, as politely as if I'd been offered one of those little cocktail wieners wrapped in bacon. I handed it back to her and she took another substantial hit off it, turning a quarter inch of it into ash.

"Kind of small," Darlene said, smiling and blinking.

"I think it has something to do with my suit," I said. "It makes everything around me appear smaller."

As Darlene took another enthusiastic pull on the joint, I was transfixed by the sight of her bright red lips around it. Like a freshly-painted hydrant gripping a gray fire hose. I imagined her lips on my lips. On my face. On my neck. On my chest. I suddenly thought I might want to experience one of her kisses again. But I kept thinking of the time. I didn't want to start something I couldn't finish. Maybe later, I thought. At the very least, however, I needed to feel something that those lips of hers had touched. If I'd been really enterprising, I suppose I could have excused myself, gone to her bathroom and rubbed her toothbrush all over my body. But I stared at the joint, glowing warmly in the ashtray with her red lipstick caked around the end of it. It was too tempting. I picked up the joint and held it near my mouth. The smell of the lipstick was intoxicating. Don't inhale, I told myself. Just touch it to your lips. I put the joint to my lips and inhaled deeply. What did I just tell you? I asked myself.

But it didn't seem so bad, so I took a few more puffs on it. I ignored what I knew, that it never seems so bad until it's too late. A few minutes later I started to feel buoyant. Like a balloon that slips from the grasp of a small child and sails heavenward. Suddenly it mattered very little to me whether or not it was getting late or whether or not there was a wedding at all. I didn't mind being right where I was. I did feel a little, however, like the room was getting smaller.

I got up off the couch and marched around, making sure I could still walk six or seven paces in whatever direction I chose. When I became self-conscious about doing this, I stopped in front of a framed photograph of a skyscraper. I studied it intently. Tall. Shiny. Hundreds of windows. I studied it so intently, in fact, that I suddenly felt my nose against the glass. I stepped back and rubbed away the smudge I'd made with my nose.

"This is nice," I said.

"How can you tell when you're on top of it?" Darlene asked.

"Sometimes you have to be on top of something before you can distance yourself from it," I said. I didn't know what I meant, but in my current mood it sounded wonderfully deep and philosophical. If only I'd been able to say it in Scandinavian. Then I sighed deeply and choked back a cry.

"What's wrong?" Darlene asked.

"Mmm. Nothing," I said, stoically. "We'd better get going."

What I couldn't tell her was that I'd been looking at all those windows on the skyscraper, wondering who was going to clean them. It seemed incredibly sad.

Darlene drove. I was familiar with the church where Lena was getting married, but I didn't let on by offering directions. I sat silently in the passenger seat and didn't say anything. Darlene pushed a tape into her cassette and a cacophony of loud funk-metal tore up the interior of the Pacer. The windows were open and my hair got tousled about. The rest of my body felt like it was underwater, the waves lapping gently at my ears.

When the Pacer arrived in the parking lot, I announced:

"I'm here."

When I realized how loud I'd said it, I slumped back down in the seat momentarily. Then I swung open my door, jumped out of the car and curled around to the driver's side to open Darlene's door for her. I was messed up, but I was a messed-up gentleman. I opened her door and a pair of legs slid out. Her black leather pumps shimmered in the late afternoon sun and her legs grew out of them, majestic and perfect. For a moment, the rest of her ceased to exist. I thought of a thousand and one things to do with her legs. I would caress them and kiss them and bathe them and wax them and write poems to them and then hump them. But later, I told myself. Not now. Not in the parking lot of Our Lady of the Immaculate Conception.

As Darlene walked up the steps of the church, I felt myself gliding behind her. Effortlessly and rapidly. Like a grocery store conveyor belt for ten items or less. As I entered the church, I looked furtively to my right and left, but didn't see Lena or anyone else I knew. The few who'd already gathered must be Andrew's family and friends, I thought. The Buntrock side. I shadowed Darlene closely as she moved up the aisle, crouching low behind her like Groucho Marx.

As Darlene and I neared the front of the church, I thought I recognized the person sitting behind the piano. He had blond hair tied back in a ponytail. I thought it might have been one of Lena's old high school friends, someone I'd met briefly at a party and forgotten, perhaps. I stayed close behind Darlene, prepared to pass myself off as her train, if necessary. But before I knew it, Darlene was introducing me to this person.

"Malcolm, you remember Kevin. The drummer? I told you he plays classical piano."

"Yes," I said, greatly relieved. I pumped his outstretched hand. "You're the drummer with the Circadian Rhythm Section. I've got all your albums."

"But we don't have a label yet," he said.

"So what are labels, anyway?" I said. "It's all very arbitrary."

Kevin frowned at me, then turned to Darlene.

"Who the fuck did you say this guy was?"

"It's Malcolm," she said. "The one in the men's room at the club."

His expression changed. He grinned and shook my hand more enthusiastically.

"The one who whimpers in his sleep? Too much, man! Too much!"

Warming to his sudden acceptance of me, I sidled up next to him at the piano.

"Outrageous threads," Kevin said. "Way big."

"Thanks," I said, suddenly confident in my big suit.

I spaced out my fingers on my left hand and played a C chord. It was all I could remember from a year of childhood lessons. In my current condition I thought it might come back to me in a sudden rush. I cracked my knuckles, placed my fingers over the piano again and waited for inspiration.

"What shall we start off with?" I said. "Something in a popular vein, I should think. Something up-tempo to put the crowd in a good mood. 'Girl From Ipanema'? 'Ventura Highway' perhaps? Keep in mind I can only play the one chord."

I spaced my fingers and played the C chord again.

"This guy's too much," Kevin said, slapping his knee and grinning from ear to ear.

"He's high," Darlene said. "Keep his hands off the piano."

Kevin gently lifted my hands off the keyboard and put them in my lap.

"There's a guy who's been looking for you," he said.

Dope paranoia kicked in, full gear.

"Looking for me? Who? Who would be looking for me?"

"Ricardo Pisces."

"Oh," I said, feeling the blood flow back into all the regular areas of my body.

"He said you're unsigned," Kevin said. "That you don't have a label yet."

"It's true," I said solemnly. "I'm unsigned. I have no label."

This is how I'll be remembered, I thought. The Man With No Label. He rode into town, played one chord on the piano, whimpered in his sleep and moved on.

Darlene pulled a stack of sheet music out of her feedbag purse and thumbed through the papers until she found the one she wanted. She set the music up on the piano and Kevin began pecking it out on the piano.

"What music are you doing?" I asked.

"Something from *Lakme* by Delibes," Darlene said. "Most people know it as the lesbian love scene music from *The Hunger* with that French actress . . ."

" . . . Catherine Deneuve," I said.

"That's the one."

"*Repulsion, Belle du Jour, Tristana, The Last Metro* . . ."

I was prepared to go on listing Catherine Deneuve films in an ever-louder voice when I suddenly spotted Lena's Uncle Don and Aunt Irene at the back of the church. I ducked my head down into my big suit and hid behind the sheet music. My stomach started jumping.

"I have to go now," I said.

"You can stick around," Darlene said. "You just have to shut up and keep your hands off the piano."

"I don't think I can trust myself here," I said.

I excused myself, got up and started moving down the far right aisle of the church, keeping my face pointed towards the windows. Jesus was everywhere. The stations of the cross were depicted in the stained glass and I pretended to study and admire them as I ambled along. Much to my surprise, my Catholic upbringing suddenly came to my assistance. I had a pretty good idea what the stations of the cross were and how they were laid out in a church. So I didn't have to turn around to check my bearings and I had a rough idea where the back of the church was. I was concentrating so hard on the stations, however, that I smacked my right shoulder against the side of the confessional.

The confessional was a maple structure with lots of lattice work. Three doors. One in the middle and two on either sides with vacancy lights above them like a cheap motel. The lights were off, meaning the rooms were unoccupied. But I didn't go in. With Catholic knowledge comes Catholic guilt and it just didn't seem right to hide out in a confessional.

There was a caneback chair stuck in the corner to the right of the confessional. It was a place for you to wait while the person ahead of you was confessing. Or a place to pause and consider if you wanted to confess everything now, or hold off for some greater, more cathartic confession later on. I eased myself into this chair and tried to bury my head in my suit so that just the eyes would show, like the guy in Bazooka comics. I was partially hidden from the eyes of the churchgoers by the confessional, but this didn't seem as great a sin as actually hiding in the confessional. So I sat there, unnoticed, and watched the wedding unfold.

It wasn't a big wedding. Lena's mother came up the aisle in a frilly peach dress and stiff, sprayed hair you could have hung pictures from. An usher escorted her to the first pew. She took out a tissue and began to daub at her mascara-heavy eyes. Most of the others who sat on Lena's side of the church were strangers. Could she have acquired a whole new set of friends since our breakup? Maybe they were Buntrocks who'd been lent to the other side of the church to even things out.

Another stranger appeared as the maid of honor. She was wearing a burgundy dress, not unlike the one Darlene had on, except it was worn off the shoulder. The maid of honor was far too skinny to look attractive in any kind of formal wear, but this dress made her clavicle look like a tuning fork was being pulled out the front of her body. So who was this? Maybe a Buntrock sister. Maybe Lena had cut herself off entirely from her old life and embraced the Buntrock clan. Considered them her new family. Like the Mansons.

The maid of honor was met at the altar by the best man. A slick, blond gentleman. A Buntrock brother, I assumed. Then Andrew Buntrock appeared. He wasn't the little, bespectacled heart surgeon I'd sort of hoped for. Shoulders broad, teeth gleaming, he was a tan, fair-haired Trojan nightmare of a man. He looked like someone you could use as the central support beam in your basement. I could see him in the operating room throwing aside his scalpel and manually ripping out his patient's heart with one swift clean jerk.

Finally Lena was escorted up the aisle by yet another stranger. A Buntrock uncle, perhaps. Lena was a small woman and her flowing alabaster dress made her look a bit like a midget at Carnival in Rio. She had on a lot of makeup. Or was pale with fear, I'm not sure which. Anyway, she looked nervous and chalky. She wasn't smiling. Why are you marrying this support beam, I wondered.

Kevin was noodling something on the piano as a processional piece. Not "Here Comes the Bride" exactly, but something similar. Subtly different, like "My Sweet Lord" compared to "She's So Fine." I remembered what Darlene had told me about Kevin writing "Cry Me a River" and I wondered if he'd plagiarized this song and called it his own as well.

Lena was deposited at the altar and stood at Andrew's side. When he put his hand in hers I felt as though I was watching someone put the key into the ignition of a car I once owned. It wasn't a car I wanted any more, but I'd had some good times with it and it frequently got me where I needed to go. It just looked funny watching someone else in the driver's seat, driving away. I felt a little lightheaded. I breathed in and exhaled hard enough to wheeze. But it only left me dizzier. More stoned and zephyrlike.

I felt confident I wasn't going to do anything rash. I'd seen *The Graduate* plenty of times and I wasn't suppressing any impulse to scream Lena's name, steal her away from the altar or block the doors of the church with a cross. I was just sort of . . . there. Anonymous and invisible. And when it was all over, I'd leave. No trouble. All in all, I thought I was comporting myself admirably. I shouldn't have gotten high, but I was doing okay. As long as I didn't have to interact with anyone, I figured I'd make it through the whole thing without a problem.

As Lena and Andrew exchanged rings, however, and Kevin started playing the lesbian love scene music from *The Hunger* and Darlene began to sing, I started feeling not at all well. I felt my stomach moving up, crawling towards my throat. I hadn't given any consideration to the effect of Darlene's singing on my nervous system. The muscles in my throat began to constrict as great brimming buckets from my well of tears began being hauled to the surface.

There wasn't anything wrong with crying at a wedding. It was expected and encouraged. But I knew this was different. The type of sobbing and moaning I could produce would undoubtedly draw attention to my clandestine location in the rear of the church. I bit hard on the sleeve of my big suit and tasted the bitter tang of freshly pressed cotton. I thought about making a break for it. A quick dash out the back door before anyone noticed. But in my altered state I was determined to beat this thing. I'd either weep softly like everyone else or learn to compose myself. So I held the caneback chair in a knuckle-whitening grip and endured it. One agonizing chorus after the next. I felt as if I was going to explode or perhaps implode. Something felt as though it was bound to burst, anyway.

Then, just as I thought I was reaching my breaking point, the song ended. Darlene stopped singing and sat down. Kevin ended the piece, stopped playing the piano and closed the sheet music. It was over. I'd done it. I'd weathered the storm. My face cooled and the lump in my throat moved into the more manageable region of my stomach. I felt renewed. Strong. Confident. More than that, however, I had an overwhelming desire to *share* these feelings with everyone there.

So when I heard the priest say, " . . . and now a few inspirational words from a dear friend of the bride and groom," I was certain the priest was referring to me. Maybe even that the whole thing had been a masquerade and everyone knew I was sitting in the back of the church all along and had just been waiting for me to rise up and speak to them. So I rose up and headed up the center aisle to the front of the church.

I saw a man in the third row start to get up, apparently the dear friend who'd been scheduled to speak at that time. But when he saw me striding confidently to the lectern, he sat down again. He'd probably just flown in that afternoon, missed the rehearsal and wasn't sure exactly when he was supposed to do his thing. So he didn't make a fuss and smiled apologetically at me as I went by.

The moment I found myself behind the lectern, facing the crowd, I knew I'd made a big mistake. There were a few faces that seemed eager to hear what I had to say. But for the most part there were a lot of blank, bewildered expressions. Darlene's and Kevin's were among them. Lena was pale. More pale than I thought was possible under all her white makeup. But inside her dead person's pallor were a pair of gleaming eyes. Huge, disgusted and indicting.

Andrew was whispering questions into Lena's ear, but she stared unflinchingly at me with those accusing eyes. There was only one way, I thought, to save the moment. Say something. Make it look like the whole thing had been planned. I cleared my throat and opened my mouth.

"What can I possibly say at a time like this?" I began, wistfully. It's a wedding, I reminded myself. Warm, loving, happy, brief comments would be in order.

"This is certainly a warm, loving, happy, brief occasion," I said.

A few people smiled. This is good, I thought. Say some nice things and get off.

"I've known the lovely bride for many years," I continued. "She's an excellent driver and very organized. And although our hearts are now strangers, I just want to say one thing. I've seen this woman naked on my desk in the sunlight and I know now that all things are possible."

As it spilled out of my mouth it seemed like a nice affirmation of life and a wonderful capper to my speech. But it was, of course, a dreadful thing to say. Just the kind of inappropriate remark you'd expect from a stoned guy in a big suit. I voiced it in such a heartfelt way, however, that I thought the congregation might rise up as one and burst into enthusiastic applause. But it didn't work out that way.

Andrew was up and moving on the word "naked." By now he knew who I was and, more importantly, that I didn't belong.

So he took it upon himself to remove me. For the good of all, I guess. I had my arms outstretched on either side of me, prepared to be crucified. I had no intention of putting up a struggle against a tuxedoed Terminator like Doctor Andrew Buntrock. But when he grabbed me, his shirt cuff rode up on his massive arm and there, strapped to his thick, smooth wrist, was a watch that looked mighty familiar. A Timex watch with a black leather band.

Andrew pulled me off the podium. As we descended from the altar he apologized to the people we passed, as though I was a bad dog who'd gotten into a neighbor's garden. Meanwhile, I grabbed his wrist and tried to undo the clasp on the watch. I guess he thought I was trying to get free, which I wasn't, and he pushed my head down, put me in a headlock and started dragging me up the aisle. My eyes became buried somewhere in the forearm of a rented tuxedo. But since he wasn't protecting his wrist, I was able to scratch and claw at the watch even though I couldn't see it. Somehow I managed to wrangle it off his arm. I didn't have to find a place to conceal the watch. When it slipped off his wrist I felt it fall somewhere inside my big suit. I'd look for it later.

One of the advantages of being high was that it didn't really hurt being dragged out of the church in a headlock. Tomorrow, yes, I wouldn't be able to turn my neck half an inch. But for now it wasn't unpleasant at all. Andrew pushed open the doors of the church with my head and roughly deposited me on the front steps of the church.

"I'm sorry," I mumbled weakly.

"Sorry!" Andrew's face filled with blood. "I should destroy you!"

I wasn't sure what he meant exactly by "destroy." Whether he meant he wanted to literally crush me underfoot like Godzilla destroying Tokyo or whether he meant he'd destroy my public speaking career—make sure I never spoke at a wedding again as long as I lived. I sat on the stairs and waited for him to dish out whatever he intended to dish out.

"Lena says you don't know what you're doing," he said. "That you have some kind of sleep disorder."

"She's being far too kind," I said. I wondered what kind of a doctor would buy into such a simplistic explanation of what I'd just done. Not the kind of guy I'd ever want poking around in my chest. But I didn't say anything about it. Lena probably told him not to kill me. Maybe she wanted to do that later, herself, when I wasn't expecting it.

"You'd better just get out of here," he said. "There's a lot of people in there who'd like a piece of you. And they're not going to show you the same kindness I have."

I knew I'd be rubbing Ben Gay on my neck the next day with that word "kindness" still ringing in my ears, but I let that pass, too. He was probably right about the people inside the church. Once they got in the parking lot and no longer had God's eyes directly upon them, they'd happily tear me apart. I couldn't imagine Darlene was too happy with me at this point either. By now she must have figured out I'd had more than a casual interest in Lena and Lena's wedding and that I'd bamboozled my way into the wedding by using her. I got up and started walking down the steps of the church.

Andrew stood at the top of the stairs as I walked away. I felt his eyes on my back, making sure I was properly banishing myself from the area.

"I'm sorry," I said again. I think Andrew had been hoping I'd say something else. Something provocative. Something that would justify his being able to go ahead and pummel me. Or something he could respond to by verbally releasing some of the unexpressed anger he'd built up by not being able to pummel me. Anyway, I knew he was frustrated and I actually felt a little sorry for him.

I wasn't walking too well and the cuffs of my pants kept getting caught under my heels. I began to feel smaller as I walked away. Like I was still sitting on the steps of the church watching myself fade into the horizon.

"Hey," I heard Andrew call before I was completely out of earshot. "Your suit's too big."

I hoped it made him feel a little better.

chapter fourteen

With my jacket tied around my waist and a dull throb developing in the base of my neck, I slowly made my way back home. There weren't many transportational choices in the area around the church. You couldn't exactly wait around for a taxi or a bus. So I shuffled down the hot pavement, following streets I knew until I got to the train station.

It was Saturday and I didn't know the weekend train schedule, so I just stood next to the tracks and waited. The station was deserted, which wasn't a good sign. While I was standing there, looking at the tracks, I thought of that Stones song, "Love In Vain."

I got to the line about how the train had two lights on behind, *the blue light was my baby and the red light was my mind*, and the words sort of made sense to me for the first time. And I figured if they did, I must still be high. I wondered if anything short of a blood transfusion would make me feel different.

I reached inside my jacket and found the watch I'd pulled off Andrew's wrist. This day hasn't been completely wasted, I thought, clutching the prize tightly in my fist. But then I looked at the watch more closely. It wasn't my watch. It looked a little like the one I remembered, but it wasn't mine. It wasn't even the same brand.

I made sure it wasn't inscribed or anything and then I laid it on a steel rail. I waited a few minutes and finally a slow-moving westbound freight train lumbered into the station and rolled over it, smashing it into hundreds of tiny pieces.

I briefly entertained the notion of hopping on the freight train and letting it take me wherever it was going. I'd drift from one hobo junction to the next, forage for food and at night, pitch my suit like a tent. But something told me instinctively that it was a bad idea. I was hungry and fatigued and I couldn't imagine trying to forage for dinner.

I just wasn't the foraging type. So I waited around for a regular old eastbound commuter train, which took me back home.

Missus Calabrone was still sweeping the sidewalk when I got back. I smelled linguini in calamari sauce simmering just the other side of her kitchen door. My stomach made a pitiful, yerping sound. I thought, in my current state, I might be able to work up the courage to beg for a plateful of the stuff. But I was equally paranoid that I'd attempt to speak and make some unintelligible sound. I stood in front of Missus Calabrone for a moment and stared at her. I felt saliva flowing freely on the roof of my mouth and my jaw dropped open. For a moment I thought I might drool on her.

"What's wrong with you?" she asked. She gripped her broom tighter and held it close to her body.

"I have to take this suit off," I finally said. "I'm never wearing this suit again."

"Well, good," she said, eyeing me suspiciously. "Don't tell me about it. Just do it."

I nodded and moved away from her.

Once inside my apartment, I slid out of my suit and peeled off my underwear. I put the sticky garments in a pile on the coffee table. I sat naked on the sofa for a few minutes and stared at the pile. I should do something symbolic, I thought. Burn the suit, perhaps. But I couldn't figure out exactly what it would symbolize and I knew I was in no shape to tend to a small apartment fire.

The seductive aroma of the linguini in calamari sauce was wafting impudently through the vents. I must eat, I told myself. If I don't eat soon, I'll end up storming Missus Calabrone's apartment with a gun in one hand and a jar of grated parmesan in the other. I opened my freezer door and stared inside. The closest thing I could find to Italian cuisine was a frozen pizza, wedged between a couple of chicken pot pies. I pulled the frozen disc out of the freezer and swiped at the frost on the cellophane so I could read the directions. It seemed a bit complicated. So I simply tore off the wrapper and headed for the oven, spilling slivers of frozen cheese onto the linoleum along the way. I shoved the pizza onto the middle rack of the oven and slammed the heavy metal door shut.

I retired to the living room, sat on the sofa, stared into space and waited.

An hour must have passed. I was still sitting naked on the sofa, blinking in the dark, trying not to think. Trying not to drool. There was a knock at the door. My palate dried up so fast it felt like I'd sucked the moisture out of my mouth with one of those little dental hoses. This is it, I thought. The angry mob has found me. And now they will kill me. They would show no mercy. I'd be convicted in some kind of kangaroo court like Peter Lorre in *M*.

" . . . and he was sitting naked in the dark waiting for a pizza to satisfy his drug-crazed hunger."

"For shame! For shame!"

The door wasn't locked and Darlene walked in. I casually took a copy of *Film Quarterly* off the coffee table and placed it over my lap.

"Hello," I said.

"What are you doing in the dark?" she asked.

"I'm making a pizza," I said.

Darlene clicked on the kitchen light and I squinted against the harsh sudden glare. Darlene opened the oven door, looked inside and closed it again.

"You forgot to turn the oven on," she said, twisting one of the dials on the oven. "Not that you couldn't cook a pizza up here without it. Jesus, it's hot up here!"

She kicked her shoes off, threw her feedbag-sized purse in a corner and walked into the living room.

"I'm not dressed," I said.

"Don't worry about it," she said.

"The thing is," I said, "I don't think I can get up and get dressed right now."

"No problem," she said.

Darlene reached behind her, unzipped the burgundy dress and slithered out of it. She hooked her thumbs under the straps of her slip and let it fall to the ground. Her breasts stared at me, full and round, and I stared back. Those wonderful legs of hers that I'd watched getting out of the car were soon shed of stockings and now fully exposed, attached to milky thighs and hips. She was now blissfully nude, stretching her body and massaging her breasts as if they ached from being confined all day.

"How do you stand it up here?" she asked, wiping perspiration from under her breasts and behind her neck.

"I'm expecting a cross breeze," I said.

My conversational voice had returned, a good sign that my high might be wearing off. But as my head gradually got clearer, the pain in my neck from being dragged up the aisle in church gradually got worse. It felt like weasels with ankle weights were wrapping themselves tightly around my neck and biting into my nape. I tried to concentrate on something else. I looked anew upon Darlene's nude body. It looked ripe and supple and glowed white with the kitchen light behind her. Something in my lap was trying to turn the pages of *Film Quarterly*. Darlene came up to me and carefully peeled up one edge of the magazine.

"May I?" she asked.

"Certainly," I said. "But I need it back. I haven't read the article on Wim Wenders yet."

Darlene pulled the magazine off my lap and placed it on the coffee table next to my big suit. I was now fully exposed and shining pinkly. She sat down next to me on the couch, leaned down and started caressing and nibbling.

"I . . . I thought you might be angry at me," I stammered, swallowing hard.

"No," she said. "What was that all about back there, anyway?"

"I'm not sure I know," I said. "I dated Lena for a long time."

"I figured out that much," she said.

I shrugged and shook my head sadly.

"I wanted to get some kind of closure, I guess. And I couldn't find my watch and I thought maybe her fiancé had it."

"Did he?"

"No."

Darlene seemed satisfied with this explanation of my afternoon shenanigans and returned to her caressing and nibbling.

"What happened . . . what happened after I left?"

"It came off okay," she said. "They still got married. People were pretty shook, at first, yeah. And Lena looked pretty upset. But Kevin starting playing 'Girl From Ipanema' and that calmed everyone down a little. Kevin loved what you did. He thought it was brilliant. He can't wait to talk to you about it."

"Kevin?"

I suddenly pictured Kevin arriving at my apartment, followed by all sorts of post-punk musicians and groupies. They'd get naked, destroy my apartment and eat all my pizza.

"He isn't on the way here, is he?"

"No," Darlene said.

It was odd making chit-chat with her while she caressed and nibbled me. She seemed to have it under control, however, and neither activity suffered. All I could see was the back of Darlene's head, her black hair flowing onto my lap. I couldn't tell exactly what she was doing, but she was creating some truly extraordinary sensations. All sorts of things came to mind as she worked her magic: someone writing on a balloon with a magic marker. Boars rooting for truffles. People getting in line for a bus. Going into the attic for Christmas ornaments.

I was trying to enjoy it, but the pain in my neck was getting worse. I could have asked Darlene to rub my neck, I suppose. But I thought I ought to give this other thing she was doing a chance to work first. But then I wondered: What if I come down from my high and discover my neck is broken? Things like that could happen. I remembered reading in a film magazine how

Buster Keaton did a stunt where he got dumped out of a water tower and splashed onto a railroad track. He didn't know he'd broken his neck until a doctor discovered it years later.

I suddenly realized the gravity of the situation. If I let this event proceed to its physically intense conclusion, I could wind up with a serious problem. I was already wiped out. It was hot, I was hungry and tired and I had weasels tightening themselves around my neck. What if I had, indeed, broken something and I required immediate medical attention? What if this post-punk fellatio brought on post-ejaculatory exhaustion and I couldn't move or put my pants on to go to the hospital? And even if Darlene called 911 and they came and carted my naked, soiled body away on a stretcher, what would happen to my pizza? Surely in all the confusion it would be forgotten and left behind.

"I wonder how the pizza's doing," I said.

Darlene took my remark as an indication to hurry along the matter at hand and she kicked it into high gear. I suddenly felt as though I was being pulled through the car wash of love and I'd reached the part with the high-speed, chrome-cleaning brushes. A thousand tongues, each of them speaking a different language, now spoke directly to my groin. Her sudden intensified assault caught me by surprise and I nearly lost it. I grabbed her pumpkin head and plucked her out of my patch.

"Wait," I said. "Whew! Please wait. I have to eat. Honestly. If I don't eat something soon, I think I'll die."

Darlene sat up and smiled slyly at me. Like the cat who'd come very close to swallowing the canary. I looked down into my lap to make sure my canary was still there. It was. Darlene's eyes were moist and her nose was red, slightly swollen and runny. It looked as though she had a bad case of hay fever.

"You want me to get the pizza out of the oven?" she asked, sniffing and blinking her watery eyes.

"No. I can do it. Go blow your nose."

I watched her naked body disappear down the hallway. I slowly eased off the couch and shuffled into the kitchen, my affected member leading the way like a drunken gate at a railroad crossing. Watch yourself when you open the oven, I reminded myself. Keeping the lower part of my body a safe distance away, I pulled open the heavy door and pulled the pizza out of the oven with a pair of white oven mitts my Grandma Cicchio had crocheted for me. I set the pizza on top of the stove. I found a pair of scissors buried in a kitchen drawer and clipped the pizza into eight slices. I threw the scissors, now thick with cheese and sauce, into the sink.

The smell was overpowering. I allowed myself to drool freely now. I made a quick survey, decided which was the largest, messiest piece of pizza and shoved that one into my mouth. Gooey mozzarella stuck to the roof of my mouth in a great coagulated mass. I ignored it and chomped down on the crust, which at the moment was absolutely the best thing I'd ever tasted in my life. Then pain shot home and I realized the melted cheese was searing a hole in my palate.

I dashed to the sink and opened the faucet for cold water full blast. Water splashed on the counter, all over my chest, and onto the floor. Everywhere but my mouth. I ducked my head down and let the cold water gush into my mouth. When I felt extinguished, I pulled my head up out of the sink and felt a sharp spasm in my neck. I winced. Please God don't let it be broken, I prayed. I straightened up slowly and tried to hold my neck and shoulders rigid. I carefully transported the pizza to the kitchen and dropped it on the table.

I didn't bother putting out plates, utensils or napkins, but I got two cans of orange Crush out of the refrigerator and dropped them on the table next to the pizza. There, I thought, standing stiff as a rail. I've done all I can in the way of entertaining. I lowered myself into a chair at the kitchen table and took another whack at eating. I blew on my food and nibbled it cautiously, like a cat. Unlike a cat, however, I had my orange Crush gripped in my other hand, in case of another oral emergency. The up and down motion of my jaw, essential to chewing, caused further discomfort in my neck. I didn't care now, as long as I was eating. But what would I do when I finished eating? I shouldn't be naked, I thought. I wasn't prepared to do anything I would normally do when I was naked.

"Could you bring me the Ben Gay from the medicine chest?" I yelled.

Yelling across the room was painful too.

I heard Darlene open the medicine chest and let out a startled scream. I resisted the impulse to turn my head suddenly or scream back.

"What is it?" I asked in a calm but concerned voice.

"Bugs," she said. "You've got bugs in here!"

"What kind of bugs?" I asked.

"How should I know. Some kind of flying things. Wasps."

"Probably yellow jackets," I said. "There's a nest in the wall, behind the wallpaper."

I heard Darlene make several disapproving grunts, like someone was poking her with a stick.

"God," she said. "They're all over the place. There's one in the medicine chest."

"Is it alive?"

"I don't know."

"Is it moving?"

"No."

"Then it's probably dead," I said. "Or resting."

Darlene made several more noises to express her disgust, then I heard her slam the medicine chest shut. She came out, blowing her nose in a clump of balled-up toilet paper. She tossed the Ben Gay on the coffee table.

"I hope you don't have anything weird planned with that stuff," she said.

"It's for my neck," I said.

Darlene plopped herself down on the couch and fished through her feedbag purse for a cigarette. She shivered. "I hate bugs."

For some reason I felt I should have come to the yellow jacket's defense. I didn't like them either. But her remark struck me as annoyingly flippant. Where did she get off slamming an entire subspecies of insect just because of a run-in with a couple of sluggish yellow jackets? Sure, they were a bother, but I *lived* with them. I *knew* them.

They were my soul mates. I paused to consider this last assessment. If yellow jackets were my soul mates, it was no wonder I had so few friends.

Darlene extinguished a half-smoked cigarette in the sink and joined me at the kitchen table. We sat there and dined on pizza and Orange Crush. Two people without clothes, having dinner. A nudist picnic. I ate voraciously, like a puma on a fresh gazelle. And the more the pizza cooled, the more savagely I ate it. Darlene seemed to eat as much as I did, in about the same amount of time. But there wasn't the same manic desperation to her eating as there was to mine. Occasionally, a bit of pizza sauce would grace her lips and I'd watch her collect it efficiently with the talented, indefatigable tip of her tongue.

Most of the time, however, I was too busy gorging myself to notice her. Or to appreciate the rare occurrence of dining with a pair of naked breasts across from me. As the hot pizza passed through my system, I found myself sweating more profusely. I had to struggle to keep my buttocks on the slippery vinyl seat of the kitchen chair. I wondered if Darlene was having the same problem. But I didn't ask. In fact, I didn't say anything while we ate. It might have been the heat, or my neck. Or it might have been that I just didn't have anything to say to her. It was Darlene who finally broke the silence.

"How can you live like this?" she asked, licking her lips and wiping them with the back of her hand. I sensed some irritation in her remark.

"Like what?" I asked.

She sighed. "The bugs and the heat and everything. How can you stand it?"

I wondered what she'd meant by "*and everything*." What else was there besides the bugs and the heat? Sure there *were* other things. The plumbing, the cracks in the wall and a fascist landlady, to name a few. But Darlene didn't know about any of those things. Maybe she was still perturbed about seeing the yellow jackets.

Part of me wanted to apologize for my surroundings. But I was also feeling a little defensive. She'd arrived unannounced.

If I'd known she was coming, maybe I'd have swept up some of the dead bugs. And anyway, it wasn't like I lived in squalor. And suppose I did? What kind of non-bohemian post-punk dirge singer was she, anyway?

"A better question might be, what are *you* doing up here?" Now there was irritation in my voice. I got up from the table and walked into the living room. I hoped my statement wouldn't lose any of its sting followed by the sight of my buttocks swaying back and forth. I sat down on the couch, crossed my arms and closed my eyes.

"I thought we were going to party," she said, flatly.

"Sure," I said, yawning and holding the back of my neck. "Let's party."

"You think you could manage to stay awake? You drop off to sleep every time I see you."

She seemed peevish. More peevish than I was. It probably was the heat. The heat made everything more unbearable. Particularly when you're penned up inside, upstairs in an apartment with no air conditioning. So why *was* I living there?

"I just want to put some cream on my neck," I said. "Then we can do whatever you want."

I didn't know what I might be committing myself to. She couldn't expect much from me. Drinking, dancing and getting high again were out. We'd already eaten. What did that leave? Maybe if she went back to that caressing and nibbling she was doing in my lap, and could do it in such a way that I didn't have to move much, that might be partying. It didn't sound much like partying. And there was an unspoken, mutually understood, reciprocal nature to sex that would demand I return the favor. It doesn't matter if you want to or not, or if you're good at it or not. The key is to equal out the giving and receiving, like Christmas or a good swap meet. Could I possibly do the same thing for her with my neck the way it was? I thought maybe I could outfit myself with a brace of some kind. Take one of those cardboard collar stays they put inside new shirts and line it inside a turtleneck to keep my head stable. And then she could kind of . . . lean into me. But would that really be partying? It sounded pitiful. And dangerous.

I squeezed a large globule of white paste from the tube into my palm and applied it to the sore and tender areas of my neck. It was difficult to reach. Reaching meant pain, and I couldn't seem to get the places that needed it the most. I squirted out another handful and tried again. If my neck was broken, however, a whole zeppelin full of Ben Gay wasn't going to do the trick. The strong, medicinal odor reached my eyes and made them begin to water.

Darlene watched me from the kitchen but didn't offer any help. I finally gave up. I got up from the couch, took the cushions off and, with a great heave, opened the couch into a bed. It was, by far, the most challenging and painful thing I'd done that day. I stretched my exhausted body out on the bed, face down.

"Okay," I mumbled into the mattress. "Let's party."

chapter fifteen

Darlene got up from the kitchen table, turned all the lights off and came into the living room. She sat down on the edge of the bed.

"Look at you," she said. "You're a wreck."

I didn't argue. She squeezed some Ben Gay out of the tube and rubbed it between her palms. Then she began to rub my neck and shoulders. She worked in smooth, even circles, like someone re-paving a driveway with hot tar. My body started to loosen up.

"That feels good," I mumbled into the mattress.

It did feel good. But I wondered if she had some ulterior motive. Was she simply being gracious or was she lubricating me as a preparatory act of foreplay? Greasing me up for some grander, carnal plan? I grew more suspicious as she moved down from my neck and shoulders to the small of my back. Then lower. To my buttocks and thighs. It was supposed to be erotic, I guess. And under normal circumstances this kind of comprehensive rubdown would have lit a pilot light under my genitals. But it was quite the contrary. It was putting me to sleep. I was pretty sure that wasn't what Darlene had in mind, so I struggled to keep my eyes open. It wasn't easy. I felt like kneaded bread dough ready to lie in the oven for an hour.

The way I figured it, there were only two ways to stay awake. Turn over and let her massage my other side, the fun side, or start up a conversation. I didn't feel ready for another of Darlene's supercharged sexual assaults. So I stayed on my stomach.

"That Kevin's quite a piano player," I said, apropos of nothing. I couldn't think of anything else to talk about.

"He's going to give it up," Darlene said.

"Really?"

"Yep. Drums too," she said, pushing the heels of her hands under my shoulder blades. "He's not going to play any more. He wants to manage, full-time."

"Manage? That doesn't sound like such a good idea. He's got some talent as a drummer and piano player."

"He thinks he can make more money managing."

"Really?"

"Yeah. He'd like to manage you. I'm not supposed to tell you that, but don't be surprised if he mentions it next time you come to the club."

I buried my head back into the mattress. I sighed heavily and emerged again.

"That's about the stupidest thing I've ever heard. Why would he want to manage me?"

"He likes your work."

"Work? What work? You mean that stuff at the church? Is that what he's referring to as 'work'?"

"Yeah. Well, that and the thing you did at the club. He thinks you have a unique way of expressing yourself. A really original style."

"That's not style," I insisted. "It's the desperate act of someone who's not getting enough sleep. Someone who lives with yellow jackets."

She shook her head sadly, as if she didn't understand.

"I don't know. You're pretty strange, that's for sure. But Kevin said it took real balls to do what you did."

Real balls? It wasn't a character trait I'd ever associated with myself. I wasn't sure how to react to it. It suggested authority, initiative, courage—all qualities that had never shown up on any of the personality profile tests I'd ever taken in the back of *GQ* while at the barber waiting for a haircut. I always assumed real balls were reserved for men who saved dogs from burning buildings. Or men who pulled drowners out of the deep end of the pool at the Y. The things I'd done recently hadn't taken real balls. Had they?

"Do you think it took real balls?" I asked her.

"I don't know," she said. "Like I said, I think you're pretty strange. But there was something exciting about seeing you out of control in the church like that. Kind of sexy." Darlene gripped my buttocks tightly and then released them.

I guess she was being complimentary. But I couldn't sit comfortably with it. Was Darlene only spending time with me because she believed there was something attractive in my anti-social behavior? Would she expect more acts of anti-social behavior in exchange for staying up late with me? Suddenly Darlene's hands felt rough on my body.

"It isn't as though I were performing," I said slowly, the aggravation rippling down my neck, back and legs. "You know better. You knew my circadian rhythms were out of sync when you met me."

"True art is born out of crisis, isn't it?"

"I don't think you understand. I don't feel very good about what happened today. I feel pretty crummy, in fact. I ruined what should have been the happiest day in Lena's life. I nearly got my head pulled off, and for what? To get my hands on a watch that wasn't even mine."

"That's what I'm talking about. That's crisis."

I sighed, beaten.

"Well that may be. But I don't want to be the one who creates the crisis. I'm happy enough letting crises happen on their own."

"Wow," she said. "You're in a funk. You need to chill."

Darlene got up and collected her purse. Good, I thought. Maybe she's leaving. My temples were throbbing and I wanted to face this recurrence of pain alone. Darlene returned to the bed with her purse and tumbled the contents out onto the mattress. She scooped up the various pieces of her mini-marijuana travel kit from among the combs, brushes and other things in her bag.

"You'll feel better after a little smoke," she said.

I didn't doubt it. I could probably lose the pain in my neck again after a few puffs. Maybe I could even find Darlene attractive again. But I just couldn't work up any enthusiasm for it. Pain or no pain, I didn't feel right about getting high again after everything that had happened and everything I'd screwed up. Right now I just wanted Darlene to go away. But even though I had the alleged persona of a man with real balls, I couldn't come right out and tell her to leave. So, just to spite her, I fell asleep on her again while she was rolling a joint.

When I woke up again it was still dark. The only light in the room came from the television. It was one of those old black and white films from the 1950s about teenagers, soda shops and hygiene. I lifted my head slowly and looked at the clock. It was three-ten in the morning.

I noticed that the red digital numbers on the clock and the light from the television were both bathed in a milky, gauze-like haze. I wondered if I was dreaming. Then I felt a tickle in my nose and throat and I realized I was enveloped in smoke. I sat up quickly and the pain pierced my neck again. Like several fondue forks all stabbing for the same piece of meat.

"Darlene," I whispered.

For a moment I thought she'd skipped out on me. Maybe this is how she got even with men who failed to party with her. Torch the place and split.

"What?" I finally heard from behind my bathroom door.

She sounded zonked, but she was still around.

"I think my apartment may be on fire," I said. I got up, held my neck and ran to the oven to see if perhaps I'd left it on. Maybe a stray piece of mozzarella had flared up and started the kitchen on fire. I was relieved when I found the oven was cold. Then I realized the cloud of smoke was concentrated in the living room. Maybe a cigarette smoldering inside my mattress? Then it hit me. In the stupor that comes after a deep sleep, I'd failed to recognize the distinctive odor of the smoke. Reefer.

I wrinkled my nose and waved at the air around me. I was thankful that smoke rose, rather than descended, otherwise Missus Calabrone would have called the narco squad by now.

When Darlene came back into the living room, she was still naked. She sauntered over to the bed and plopped herself down on it. Her breasts looked larger in the light of the television and they glowed like they were radioactive.

"Jesus. I didn't think you'd ever wake up," she said. "I shoved you and yelled at you, but you didn't move. I thought you might be dead."

"What convinced you otherwise?"

"I put a mirror up to your mouth. From my compact. I saw someone do it in a movie once."

There must have been a little leftover coke on her mirror because my lips felt kind of numb. At first I thought I'd slept on them funny, like when you sleep on your arm. But the feeling remained. I didn't think I could whistle if I needed to. I licked my lips, then dabbed at my tongue and lips with my finger.

"You talk a lot in your sleep," Darlene said.

I pursed my lips and stretched my mouth open to try to get some feeling back.

"What did I say?"

"You mumbled. You apologized a lot."

"Who'd I apologize to?"

"I don't know."

"Probably everyone," I said.

I eased my body up carefully and sat on the edge of the bed. I didn't feel like I could stand up. Sitting would have to be enough for now.

"What did you do while I was sleeping?" I asked.

"Smoked," she said. "And watched television. But there's nothing on."

She reached over me and turned up the sound on the teenage hygiene movie as if to demonstrate what she'd had to put up with.

"You've got a bunch of videotapes lying around your bookshelves but none of them are in English."

"They're subtitled," I said.

"I hope you don't expect me to sit here and read at three in the morning," she said, grunting.

"Maybe you should leave," I suggested. "It's very late. Or early. I don't know what you'd call it any more."

But she knew better. I was awake now and Darlene sensed there was little chance of me dozing off in the next few minutes. It was her opportunity and she seized it. She pushed my body back on the bed and rolled on top of me. I was about to tell her that my neck was still bothering me and that something like this could really aggravate it. But before I could get the words out of my mouth, she pressed her dry, smoky lips against mine. The kiss felt kind of numb. My lips were still a bit high, apparently. But I could feel her nose boring into my cheek. And I could feel her pubic bone rubbing against mine in hard, upward strokes, like she was planing the edge of a wooden table. As she rubbed and bored and planed, I lay there as still as I could. Trying not to move my neck.

"You can take an active part in this any time now," she breathed into my mouth.

I moved my left hand to areas of her body that I thought might make her happy. My movements were clumsy, however. As if I was four years old again, working with modeling clay for the first time. And in the background, the 1950s hygiene movie was distracting me.

"You kids have a good time," Dad was saying. "But make sure you're in by ten."

"Gee, Dad," said the perky young girl. "Wayne is the captain of the debating squad. He's one of the most responsible boys I know."

And while the responsible captain of the debating team drove off in a Buick station wagon with the perky young girl, I continued to paw roughly at Darlene. I tried to maintain a rhythmic motion. I recalled a Miles Davis record from memory and plucked out a walking bass line between her legs. "So Near, So Far," I think it was. Darlene started to moan. The moans seemed to occur in agreement with the movement of my hand, so I figured I was doing okay. Good, I thought. Maybe I can satisfy her with these apparently talented and underrated fingers of mine. Maybe I can get her off and out of here before the sun comes up. I increased the speed of my hand movement from grind to frappé. But then I began to hear a different kind of moan. And some mumbling about it getting sore and "rubbing the skin off." So I don't imagine I was closing in on bliss.

Darlene moved off me. I thought maybe she'd had enough. Maybe my ineptness had won me a reprieve. Suddenly I felt something foreign being forced down over my penis. It felt a bit like when I was eight and had donned my sister's bathing cap and pretended I was the Eggman. The same pulling of little hairs, the same sudden loss of circulation. But on this area of my body, the injurious consequences seemed far graver.

Once she'd sheathed me in plastic, Darlene mounted me, throwing her leg over my body like she was saddling a Palomino. I thought about that phrase: beating a dead horse. What good would it do? But one part of the horse was still up and rearing. I was surprised. Even though I now found the idea of having sex with Darlene distasteful, some biological memory function had kicked in and was going through the motions. Like those missiles at Norad you can't recall once you've fired them. There was no use thinking about something awful to make my erection go away. This was about as awful as it got.

In spite of my feeble attempts at foreplay, Darlene was ready, in a womanly kind of way, and she slid the old Palomino in. She rode high in the saddle at first, then plunged down hard, smothering my body with hers. Her chest pressed heavily against mine, blocking the flow of air to my lungs, while my mouth was smothered with her lips, teeth and tongue. A good way to kill a man, I thought.

As Darlene became more excited she started to slap her body against mine. It made an extraordinary suction sound. Like a rubber plunger trying to unclog a drain full of bacon grease. Thwock-thwock-thwock. The sound of two sweaty people, with a tad too much fat around their respective midriffs, trying to copulate. The thwocking sound was soon joined by a thumping sound, produced by one of the metal legs of the hide-a-bed banging against the hardwood floor. It was soft at first. No louder than the creaking of the bedsprings. But it began to thunder as Darlene worked herself into a frenzy.

There was nothing I could do to stop it. I was pinned under a horny, post-punk dirge singer, whose gelatinous brain was cruising somewhere beyond Saturn's rings. Amid the thwocking, thumping, creaking and the sound of "No, Wayne, no!" from the teen-age hygiene film, I thought I detected a rapping sound. A rapping that was echoing the thumping. It was hard to discern at first. But it sounded like Missus Calabrone's broom handle.

"My landlady," I whispered.

"My landlord," Darlene hissed in response. She kissed me hard, pushing my teeth in, nearly correcting a slight overbite. She shuddered violently and her body became rigid, as if she were all cartilage, devoid of soft flesh. Then she let out a high-pitched squeal. Something you might hear if you slammed into a deer on the highway. Then Darlene crumbled onto me. A pile of broken bones. A dead deer.

I reached over with my left hand, the only part of me that wasn't pinned beneath her, and clicked off the television. The room was dark again. Although the turbulent motion had ceased it continued to churn inside me. Like when you first step off the boat after a long cruise.

I brought my left hand to my face and tried to look at it in the dark. It was the only part of me that still coursed with blood. That still felt like it belonged to me. I used this hand to push Darlene off my body. She rolled over on her back and was out like a light. Once she'd satisfied herself, it apparently didn't matter to her any more whether or not I'd done the same. In truth, it was probably a good thing I hadn't. It would have sapped the last of my already waning strength. I wouldn't have been able to push Darlene off my body and I would have slowly asphyxiated beneath her. So, in that respect, I'd been lucky.

But how long before my luck ran out? It occurred to me that if I continued on this course, it was only a matter of time before Darlene killed me. Not that she would do it intentionally. She might not even be around when it happened. But, in time, simply being with Darlene would do me in. It would wear me down. Impair my senses. Slow my ability to react. And then some day, when I needed a clear head and a sharp mind, neither would be there and I'd end up the victim of a boating accident, or be electrocuted by some common household appliance. Some occurrence that would later be described as "something that didn't have to happen."

The light from the street lamp outside streamed into the living room and rolled across Darlene's legs, breasts and face. How uncomplicated she seemed when she was sleeping. Darlene wasn't really a bad person, I thought. She sure knew how to stay up late. But having shared circadian rhythms wasn't the bedrock of a really solid relationship, was it? And if that was true, then what *was* the bedrock of a really solid relationship? Lena and I had had very little in common. But we'd stayed together for seven years. Watched a lot of the same television shows at the same time together in the same places. It didn't seem like anything significant. Nothing to pine for into eternity, certainly. And if I let go of Darlene, what then? Would I find myself, some day, pining for her? Pining for some amber-colored recollection of our time together? Would I some day find myself at Darlene's post-punk wedding, not as a participant, but once again as some renegade party crasher in a big suit?

There was a hum in my brain. Irritating and relentless. I leaned my head back against the mattress and stared at the ceiling. I tried to block out the noise, push it between the cracks in the white stucco. But the hum persisted. And then the events of the past few weeks unfolded in my head. Frame by frame, they rolled by in dull gray monochrome. Like a long documentary film with no ending. Subtitles flashed on and off the screen. Stupid. Stupid. Stupid. Formerly benign tears that had caught in the far corners of my eyes during sex now loosened and ran down my cheeks.

The hum in my brain intensified to a buzz. It was only after considerable concentration that I was able to determine that its source was not within my head, but somewhere in the apartment. Specifically, the hallway. It was the yellow jackets. They were revving up. Swarming. They were going to prey upon me now. Now, when I was physically and emotionally bankrupt. Morally depleted. My worst-case-scenario self. Their short, tiny lives had been leading up to this moment.

I considered waking Darlene but thought better of it. Why alarm her? I thought. The yellow jackets wouldn't bother her, after all. It was me they were after. It was me they wanted. But I wouldn't go down without a fight.

I used the last bit of energy from some internal reserve tank and sprang from the bed. I ignored the stabbing pain in my neck and charged down the hall. In the murky darkness I found their home and scratched at the wallpaper with my fingernails, ripping and tearing off long strips with great abandon. I closed my eyes and shouted into the uncovered lair.

"All right! This is it! I can't stand it anymore! Just get the hell out of here! I mean it! Get out! GET OUT! GET OUT! GET OUT!"

I fully expected to be swarmed upon, en masse, by the winged horde. From the moment I started screaming at the wall I began to think what a horrible death I'd suffer. No one, not even my parents or family physician, would be able to identify my swollen, stinger-ridden corpse. I'd had a fleeting thought that maybe I should have used the last of my energy for something more constructive. Like making a dash for it out of the apartment, down the stairs and into the next county. But it actually felt good to yell at the yellow jackets. And once I'd begun it was hard to stop. So I kept screaming at them. Vicious remarks. Angry epithets. Unkind insect slurs.

What finally ended my spewing exorcism was the sobering sound of Missus Calabrone's broom handle thumping beneath my feet again. I backed away from the wall, my naked body trembling in the steamy hallway. The thumping of the broom handle stopped shortly after I stopped yelling and once again it was quiet. I stood absolutely still and listened. It was unusually quiet. More quiet than I ever remembered it being in that apartment.

I slowly raised my hand and extended it into the darkness towards the wall. I felt around cautiously, prepared to jerk my hand back at the first sensation of anything with six legs and a retaliatory nature. But I felt neither an angry insect's nest nor a gaping hole leading to an angry insect's nest. I felt a smooth wall.

I clicked on the light in the bathroom. In the harsh illumination my eyes confirmed what my fingers had felt. I turned off the bathroom light, put my ear to the wall and listened. I heard only the faintest buzz. Something that couldn't have been made by any more than one or two yellow jackets. I thumped at the wall softly like a doctor examining a torso, then listened again. The buzzing sound grew ever more faint. Then it stopped altogether.

I stood in the hallway for a while and waited. I don't know what I was waiting for. When I finally walked back into the living room, my bed was empty. All of Darlene's belongings and her clothes were gone. I went back into the kitchen for another piece of pizza. But she'd taken that, too.

chapter sixteen

On Sunday morning I crawled into the kitchen to make myself a pot of coffee. If my head hadn't been dragging on the linoleum, I might not have noticed the folded piece of paper near the door. I thought it might be a letter from Darlene, explaining her sudden departure earlier that morning. I unfolded the note and read it. It wasn't from Darlene.

> I don't know what went on up there last
> night and I don't want to know. I mind
> my own business. But I think you should
> get out. If my husband was alive I think
> he'd say the same thing. I'm sorry.
> I always thought you were a nice young man,
> but I don't want any trouble.
> Please be out by the first of the month.

The note was unsigned, but it was easy to guess its authorship. I put on a shirt and a pair of pants and went downstairs.

I knocked on Missus Calabrone's door but no one answered. Sunday morning—she was probably at church and had slipped this little offering of Christian charity under my door on her way out. I'm not sure what I would have said to her anyway. I felt like yelling—it had worked with the yellow jackets. Maybe if I just yelled, everyone would go away.

I went back upstairs and took a shower. A very long shower. I even thought about leaving the water running when I got out, but thought better of it. As I dried off and started sweating again, I noticed the unusually calm surroundings, the distinct lack of insect noise. Interesting, I thought. Just when I manage to get rid of my noisy neighbors, I get myself evicted.

My suit was still lying in a heap on the living room floor. I picked it up, dusted it off and put it on. Then I went downstairs, got into my VW bus and drove to Quality Nook.

I parked in front of the motel and went inside. I was headed for Sonderby's room when the man behind the front desk called out to me.

"Sir? Are you the man who brought in Mister Sonderby?"

My heart had already begun to race when the man approached me. I recognized him as the manager who'd checked Sonderby in on Friday. He was wearing the same white short-sleeved shirt and green and blue checked tie. He shook my hand, then put his left hand over our clasped hands, as though in a conciliatory manner.

"I'm Dave Zenk," he said. "The manager here at Quality Nook."

"What's going on?"

"Mister Sonderby is gone, I'm afraid."

"Gone? What do you mean gone. He's dead?"

"I'm afraid so, sir."

"No. Are you sure? I mean, sometimes he can appear to be dead and he's not. It's very hard to tell with him."

"No, he's definitely dead. They've already shipped his body back to Sweden."

"My God."

"I'm very sorry. I thought since you were wearing a suit that maybe you already knew."

"No, I didn't. What happened?"

Dave Zenk sighed and folded his hands together in front of him.

"Well, your Mister Sonderby called the front desk Saturday afternoon. He complained about not being able to sleep and asked if someone would bring him something to drink. You know, some liquor. But, as I explained to him, there's no room service and no cocktail lounge.

"Next thing I know he's in the lobby here asking where he can find a liquor store. I told him there's no place within miles, but he goes out anyway. Well, darned if he didn't turn up some two hours later with a liquor store bottle under his arm. Must have walked the whole time. He didn't look so good when he got back, but then he didn't look all that good when he left, you know? He sat down in the lobby—in one of those red chairs over there and he closed his eyes. And then he didn't get up again. I thought maybe he was asleep. I couldn't tell, you know? So I checked on him. I put a mirror under his nose. I saw in a movie once where they did that. And he wasn't breathing."

"Good Lord."

"I figured, you know, must have been a heart attack. A man his age, in his condition, walking around in this heat for two hours. Well, anybody really, in this heat. You're taking your chances."

I stood in the lobby for a moment, my stomach fluttering. "You'll have to excuse me. I'm kind of . . . stunned. Is there anything I need to do? Papers I need to sign?"

"No, no. Police took care of everything. The police are out here at Quality Nook quite a bit, actually, so they responded pretty quickly."

"Did he have a family back home? Friends?"

"I don't know. I don't believe so. Actually, I think they contacted the Veteran's Administration."

"Veteran's Administration."

"Yes, I believe your Mister Sonderby was a veteran according to the identification they found in his luggage."

"A veteran? Are you sure? I thought Sweden was neutral during World War II."

"I don't know about that. Anyway, that's what I was told."

I looked around the lobby. There were two red vinyl chairs near a table with some magazines on it.

"There?"

"Yes," he said. "Right there in that red chair. Like I said, hard to tell whether he was alive or not."

"That was his specialty," I said, a bit wistfully. "He was an actor."

"An actor? No kidding. I don't know that we've ever had any actors come through here. Not that I knew about. Celebrities usually stay at the more expensive hotels in town."

"With room service and a full bar," I said sadly.

Dave Zenk lowered his head. "He, uh . . . he died with sort of a smile on his face. I thought maybe you'd want to know that. Maybe it'd make you feel a little better."

"It doesn't," I said.

"Well, from what you told me, he could have been acting, anyway."

I nodded. "Did Mister Sonderby leave anything behind, his cap or anything like that?"

"I don't have his cap, no. I think we may still have his toupee. It may have been thrown out, but I can check with housekeeping."

"No, that's all right," I said.

I left Quality Nook and got back in my VW bus, counting up the ways I'd contributed to Soren Sonderby's death. I thought about the four bottles of schnapps I'd kept at the theater. I'd made sure Sonderby left without any of the schnapps, thinking that I was protecting him. But maybe if I'd just given him a bottle or two he wouldn't have gone out. Maybe if I'd put him up in a place with room service or a cocktail lounge. Maybe if I'd had my film festival instead of crashing Lena's wedding, I'd have been able to look after him.

I drove around aimlessly for a while. I didn't want to go back to my apartment, which was now a tentative dwelling at best. Nor did I look forward to another row with Missus Calabrone. I had my suit on, but I didn't feel like hosting a film festival. How was I supposed to host a film festival without Soren Sonderby? Indeed, I was never quite sure how I was supposed to have a film festival *with* him, but without him the idea seemed completely ludicrous.

Still, I ended up back at the Arcadia Filmhaus that afternoon. I threaded up the film and put the cheese wheel back on the buffet table, going through the motions automatically. Some kind of denial, I guess. When I'd done all the things I could do without thinking too much, I called Bix.

"Soren Sonderby's gone," I said.

"Where'd he go, Mal?"

"Back to Sweden. He died in the lobby of a Quality Nook Saturday afternoon."

"He's dead? Are you sure?"

"Yes. This is the real thing."

"You're kidding, Mal. What happened?"

"I don't know. The heat, I guess. He was having trouble sleeping and he went out walking for a couple of hours looking for a liquor store."

"In this heat? Oh, man."

"Heart attack. The manager of Quality Nook told me he died with sort of a smile on his face."

"Wow. What do you make of that?"

"He was probably dreaming he was back in Sweden. Tell me something, Bix. Wasn't Sweden neutral during World War II?"

"Yes, I think so. Are you okay, Mal?"

"I'm not sure. I'm thinking, you know, I'm the one who brought him here. He wasn't really used to this hot weather and then I put him up in a really crummy motel. I don't think coming here was good for him."

"You're not blaming yourself, are you?"

"I think I'm headed in that direction, yes."

"You can't think like that, Mal. If he hadn't died here, he would have died two weeks from now in Sweden. The guy had one foot in the grave when he got here."

"Is that your best shot at making me feel better?"

"The thing is, Mal, his last days were really special."

"Special? He died in the lobby of a Quality Nook."

"Yeah, but you don't know how things were over in Sweden. Maybe he was miserable there."

"It was Sweden. How bad could that be?"

"Things aren't always perfect in Sweden, Mal. You know that. If they were, Bergman wouldn't have had so many unhappy people in his movies. You know, Sweden has a high suicide rate and it's dark over there a lot. Don't glamorize Sweden too much."

"He told me he was in love once. But I think he was pretty lonely."

"And you put a little spice back in his life. Just in time, too, I'd say. He got to see America. And he had a real nice moment there on the stage of the Arcadia Friday night."

"Falling over."

"Not just falling over. He got to be a somebody for a day or two."

"I don't know."

"You know what we should do, Mal? There's a John Cassavetes film festival in the city. Let's go check it out. Don't sit there and brood on this."

"Where's it at?"

"Downtown. We could see the movie, go get a few drinks. You know, drink a toast to Soren Sonderby, right? I'd like to get back to that club, you know, the 3-D Club? We could knock a few back and you could see that girl again."

I saw myself back in the 3-D Club in my big suit. Seeing Darlene again. Crying in the men's room. Back in that old circadian cycle. With this sobering possibility before me, I decided to tell Bix everything that had happened to me the previous weekend.

Actually, I didn't tell Bix everything. I left out quite a bit. I didn't mention getting high, crashing Lena's wedding, hiding behind the confessional, telling the masses about Lena naked on my desk and getting yanked by my neck down the aisle of the church. All I really told Bix was that I'd had Darlene over to my apartment on Saturday, but that I think I might have scared her away when I'd yelled at my yellow jackets.

Then I read Bix the note that had been surreptitiously slipped under my door some time Sunday morning.

"Apparently, I'm being evicted," I said.

"Well, that's got to be a good thing, Mal. From what you told me, you've got to be better off living somewhere else."

"Maybe I should move to Sweden."

"You know, Mal, I know from your perspective it may be hard for you to see it, but this is all good stuff."

"Which part was the good stuff?"

"All of it. It's all good stuff."

"Is it? How do you figure that?"

"Experientially. Experientially it's all good stuff."

"Oh."

"Well, I mean, in one sense, no. It isn't good. Sonderby dying, that's not good. And that girl running out on you and getting kicked out of your apartment. No, that's not good, either. But in another sense, yes. It's all good. I mean, for an actor, stuff like this is invaluable. It's the experience that counts. Experience. Very good. Very useful for an actor."

"But I'm not an actor, Bix."

"But you know about acting, Mal. You can appreciate good acting. You love characters whose lives are screwed up. You can relate to this, I'm sure."

"But I'm not an actor now. And I don't want to relate to characters whose lives are screwed up. I'm saying, how do these experiences benefit me, Bix? Personally. Now. In a non-acting context."

"Well, it's hard to say within that narrow a context, Mal. These things aren't immediately apparent. I'll tell you what, let's go to the Cassavetes festival and we won't go to a bar, we'll just get some coffee and maybe by then we'll be able to make some sense out of it."

"No, thanks. I don't think so. Besides, I don't want to go to someone else's film festival. I've got my own film festival."

"You're not having the film festival tonight, are you?"

"Well, you know, I've got the cheese wheel out and I've got a suit on."

"You've got a suit on?"

"Yes. It's kind of big, but it is a suit."

"Well, think about what I said, okay, buddy? About experience. In a way, I envy you. I can only imagine the experience. You're lucky enough to have had it."

Bix was right. I'd had it. I made some excuses to Bix about my needing to thread the film and how, if anyone showed up, I'd be stuck at the theater anyway, so there was no point in making definite plans, so forth and so on, blah-blah-blah. Finally we made tentative plans to do the Cassavetes festival some other night. I'd call him.

When the receiver was safely back in its cradle, I took a deep breath and let it out slowly. While I appreciated his concern, Bix could be exhaustingly optimistic. Still, I couldn't deny that Bix drank fully from the cup of life while I only sipped. Swished a little bit of life around in my mouth and often spat it out.

So a few minutes after I'd gotten off the phone with Bix, I began to consider what he'd said. I thought about the conversation near the end of *Scenes From a Marriage* where Liv Ullman is looking back over her life and her marriage and wondering if she's missed something somewhere. Something of value that's slipped by somehow. Was there something I'd missed? Something of value I could take from my recent experiences? I didn't think so. But I took a moment to consider it.

I couldn't say for sure whether I'd actually scared away the yellow jackets with my screaming. Maybe. I'm sure it shook up Missus Calabrone. But the yellow jackets?

It's more likely they had just died off on their own. Summer would soon wind down. And they don't live very long, yellow jackets. Once they're done mating, that's pretty much the end of their little wing-ding. The whole bunch of them pack it up and curl up like Cheetos.

It occurred to me that the same thing had happened with Darlene. Not that she curled up and died, no. But I don't think I really scared her away, either. She wasn't the type to scare easily. But she may have sensed, like the yellow jackets, that the summer of love was coming to an end. At least my participation in it, anyway. I suspect she was in it for the short term all along. So she mated with me and moved on. All for the best, I'd told myself the next day. I'd woken up around seven the next morning, pulled the dry, crusty condom off myself and discarded it. Like a used cicada shell. And that was that.

It's true that my neck started to feel better on Sunday, but I don't know if it had anything to do with releasing all that pent-up anger or getting rid of Darlene. It probably had more to do with the stuff I'd smoked. It had screwed up my sense of perception. Made me unable to distinguish major sensations from minor ones. Sort of like being physically tone deaf for a while. Anyway, I figure my neck would have gotten better eventually. In time.

As for sleep, I wasn't sure exactly where I stood. I'd stopped counting the hours. My sleep schedule had gotten so screwed up, who knew how many hours I was getting any more? Maybe

I was going to die in sixteen months from a heart attack, maybe I'd live to be as old as Sonderby. But who knew?

I thought about the watch again, the one Lena had given me. I'd spent a lot of energy trying to get it back. But now it seemed like watching the time had been part of my problem. I think I was a person who was better off without a watch. Or maybe I needed a watch without hands, like the clock in *Wild Strawberries*.

I guess there'd been a hope somewhere in my brain that once I'd gotten all that business about Lena and her wedding and the wristwatch and everything out of my system, it might improve my sleep. But that seemed like a lot to hope for. And now I'd never be able to face Lena again. Not in a year or twenty years. Not ever. Not that I wanted to, or even felt like I needed to see her again. It's just that I felt sorry and stupid about the whole thing. By now Lena was probably honeymooning on an island somewhere with Doctor Andrew Buntrock, trying to push the whole disgusting event from her mind. Then again, maybe not. She'd looked pretty angry. Maybe she'd rented an apartment across the street, loaded a rifle with one bullet, one with my initials on it, and was waiting at her window for me to take two steps outside the theater. I'd seen Lena pick off ducks in a shooting gallery at an outdoor carnival one summer. Like a marksman. Take aim . . . bang.

A knock at my office door made me bolt up in my chair.

"Come in," I said, pushing the little hairs on the back of my neck back down where they belonged.

Ginny poked her head in the door. She saw my flustered expression, the sort of thin glaze over my eyes, and decided to keep the rest of her body out in the hall.

I knew she wouldn't fail to come to my office to let me know if the theater was empty. Once she did this, she knew she'd be free to leave. It would afford her a few hours to do whatever a teenager does while her parents think she's working behind a candy counter. It was an adolescent opportunity too great to pass up.

"There's pretty much no one here," Ginny said.

"Pretty much?"

"Well, there's one person."

I had my pen in my hand and absently wrote the single number "one" in the margin of the newspaper on my desk.

"One. Okay."

Ginny still had her head in the door.

"Oh," I said. "Yes, you can go home. Or whatever. You're free to leave. I don't think we're going to have the film festival tonight."

"Why not?"

"Soren Sonderby died Saturday night."

"The old actor?"

"Yes," I said.

"Boy," Ginny said. "Everyone from Sweden dies."

"Eventually," I said.

Ginny still had her head in the door. She was beginning to look like a Ginny finger puppet. But now she edged her whole body inside my office. Tentatively. She still looked furtively around the room as if she expected something to jump out of one of the corners and climb up her leg. But she seemed to regard me differently in my brown suit. Maybe it made her feel safer somehow.

"If Swedish actors keep dying, won't we always have to be closed?"

"That's an interesting point," I said. "Would that bother you? Do you . . . do you like this job?"

"It's okay," she said. "I like to be able to buy my own things."

"Well," I said, "don't worry about it. I think there are still enough . . . living actors that we can show films of."

"Okay," she said. But she still didn't leave my office.

"Something else?" I asked.

Ginny produced a folded piece of paper from behind her back. It was folded much like the eviction note I'd received from Missus Calabrone and I thought: Ginny has been kicked out of her home. She's going to ask me if she can live here for a while and sleep in the leg room aisle of the theater. Or worse, it's a note from her boyfriend, ending their relationship. And now she's bitterly determined to have nothing more to do with immature high school boys. She's made up her mind she's ready for the kind of men who can allow her to release the woman inside her. Older, more sophisticated men. Projectionists.

"It's from my teacher," Ginny said. She came forward, put the note on my desk and then backed away. Back closer to the door.

I read it. It was from her cinema studies teacher. It was a letter asking for confirmation that Ginny had watched a number of films I'd shown over the summer. And furthermore, that she could be considered "knowledgeable" about these films. The films, twelve in all, were listed in the order I'd screened them. Under the list was a place for my signature.

"You have to sign it," Ginny reminded me from her remote corner of the room.

"Yes, I see," I said.

I poised my pen at the signature line and paused. I looked

over the list, fondly, for they were all films I had great affection for. Then I tapped my pen on the form a few times.

"Did you actually watch any of these films?" I asked.

She wrinkled her brow. Gave it some good thought.

"I saw the one . . . which one was it? The Japanese one . . ."

"I showed a lot of Japanese films," I said.

She pointed to the list from afar. "The one where the little boy gets kidnapped."

"*High and Low*?"

"Yeah. I watched that one."

"You watched the whole thing?" I asked, encouraged by her response.

"No. Just the part you made me watch. That time you were in your office. Remember? For at least twenty minutes."

"Oh," I said. "Yes, I remember." I looked over the list again. "Didn't you tell me you watched *Wild Strawberries* in your cinema class?"

"Sort of. They made us sit through it for two periods."

"Oh," I said glumly. "So you haven't watched any of these films . . . voluntarily."

She wrinkled her brow again and shrugged. "You mean because I *wanted* to?" She made it sound like the stupidest question anyone had ever asked her. "I don't think so."

I pressed my pen to the paper and signed the form. What else was I going to do? I knew it must have been hard for Ginny to bring it to me. Besides, she had me feeling guilty about those twenty minutes worth of *High and Low* I'd made her watch. Also, I'd had *Wild Strawberries* for three days and I hadn't even watched it myself. I held out the form to Ginny and she reached out and took it.

"So I guess apart from the money, you don't really need this job any more."

"I can get three credits for doing it again," Ginny said. "For a different class. Humanities, I think."

"Oh," I said. "Okay."

Ginny stood in the doorway, looking around the office.

"Oh, yes. You can go," I said.

After Ginny was gone, I went upstairs to the projection booth and hauled *Wild Strawberries* out of the can. As I threaded the film through the projector I wondered, Why am I doing this? For one person? I was reminded of another Bergman film.

Winter Light. At the end of the film Gunnar Björnstrand, who's in the middle of a theological midlife crisis, holds afternoon church services, even though the only person sitting in the pews is Ingrid Thulin. And he does this even though he wanted God to speak to him and God remained silent. Well, what's God going to say, anyway? My Grandma Cicchio used to tell me about a woman who claimed she had a talking dog. "Crazy woman," Grandma Cicchio used to say. "What's a dog gonna say? Give me a hamburger?"

I didn't imagine I was winning any points in heaven equating God's silence with a dog's silence. But I figured God's either got to talk all the time or hold His almighty tongue. So why did Gunnar Björnstrand hold the service, anyway? Devotion? Is that why I ran my films to nearly empty theaters? Some pious devotion to film? I doubted it. Was it such a bad thing to want to show these films because I loved them? Run my projector and bring these people to life again and again on screen? And because I couldn't think of anything better to do?

The other person who had nothing better to do was my audience of one, seated down below. I peered down out of the projection booth to see what kind of person I'd snared. But the theater was empty. Oh, well, I thought. That happens. People find themselves alone in a movie theater and get spooked. Think they're in the wrong place or there at the wrong time and make a quick exit before the opening titles.

Well, I'll run the film anyway, I thought. Maybe I'll watch it myself this time. I kept an eye on the clock and at seven I lowered the house lights and started up the projector. I watched the beginning of the film to make sure it was in focus, properly framed and not jumping. While I was doing this, I saw someone enter the theater from the right side door and take a seat. Eighteen rows back, center. It was a woman.

I guess I was still paranoid about Lena because it seemed the dark hair that fell across the back of the green velvet seat could have been hers. Moreover, the long brown package that she'd carried in and placed in the seat next to her could have contained a rifle. Suddenly I wished Ginny was still on duty. Not that she'd prevent me from getting shot. But maybe she'd be willing to call an ambulance for me rather than risk losing three credits in Humanities.

I went downstairs, making as little noise as I could manage, and went into my office. I looked around for anything I might be able to defend myself with. There was nothing. Even my stapler was empty. I cursed myself again for not having acquired one of those big Zen master sticks or something like it.

I grabbed an empty cardboard tube used for mailing film posters. It wasn't much of a weapon. But maybe, in the dark, it might look like it was. It looked a little like the package the woman in the theater had. So maybe she'd think mine was a rifle, too. And if I could get the jump on her with my brown package before she got to her brown package, maybe she'd just give up. It was a long shot. But I'd found that paranoia produced the very finest in long shot ideas.

I turned off the lights in the lobby so she wouldn't see the light coming in when I entered the theater. I opened the door. It squeaked a little but she didn't turn around. I sat down eight rows behind her, unnoticed. My cardboard tube at my side. In the semi-darkness I could make out a pair of wire rim glasses, frames anyway, around the corner of her head. Lena wore contacts. She never wore glasses in public. Unless it was a disguise.

Feeling a bit braver, or perhaps more curious, I got up out of my seat. I walked down the right aisle, pretending to be looking for a seat, which must have looked kind of lame in an empty theater. I still had my cardboard tube at my side in case there was trouble. I walked past her aisle, trying to inconspicuously catch a glimpse of her out of the corner of my eyes. Then the woman in the theater said hello to me. It wasn't Lena. It was Anne.

"Hello," I said.

"Hello," Anne said. "That's a nice suit."

I hadn't thought about Anne recently. She just didn't fit into the whole negative configuration I'd structured around myself. I sat down in her aisle, separated by the seat that held her brown package. It was a cardboard tube, much like mine.

"What's in there?" I asked.

"Posters," Anne said. "New ones, with the new fall hours for the hotline."

"Oh," I said. I put my cardboard tube down in the empty seat to the right of me.

"I thought maybe you were coming to see *Wild Strawberries*."

"I am," she said. "I bought a ticket. But when I went back out to the lobby for popcorn, the girl was gone."

"Ginny. I sent her home. Not much business."

"Is Soren Sonderby going to be here tonight?" Anne asked.

"No, he's gone back to Sweden."

"I'm sorry I missed him. Was he interesting?"

"Yes," I said, "he was quite interesting."

Anne nodded and returned her attention to the film.

"I'll get you whatever you want from the concession stand," I said. "What would you like?"

"Popcorn. With butter. And a large diet cola. If it isn't any trouble . . ."

"No trouble. There's still an entire cheese wheel and a lot of schnapps left . . ."

She shook her head.

"Are you sure?"

"I just like popcorn and soda with my movies, thanks."

I went back out into the lobby and turned the lights back on. I filled a box with popcorn and topped it off with butter. Extra butter. Then I filled a large cup with ice and diet cola. I grabbed a handful of napkins. Then I carried it all back into the theater and handed it over to Anne. She was still involved in the film but acknowledged the armful of refreshments.

"Thanks," she said. "What do I owe you?"

"Forget it," I said.

"Thanks." Anne settled back into her seat, munched on popcorn, licked butter from her fingers and watched the film. While

I'd been in the lobby, Anne had removed the cardboard tube from the seat between us. But when I sat back down, I left a space all the same.

"Great film, isn't it?"

She nodded and munched.

"It's a good print," I said. "I've been lucky in that respect. Getting good prints from the distributors. Very little in the way of scratches or splices. I could tell you stories about badly spliced films . . ."

Anne nodded.

I settled into my seat a little more comfortably.

"You know, all the time I've worked here, I've never sat down here in the theater and watched a film."

Anne nodded. In her glasses I saw the reflected twin images of Victor Sjöström watching Bibi Andersson pick strawberries.

"I'm sorry," I said. "You probably don't want to talk right now. You probably want to watch the film."

Anne nodded. I nodded too. She seemed to really be absorbed in the film, so I tried to keep quiet. I even tried to enjoy the film. I had to go up to the projection booth once to change the reel. When I came back downstairs, I went ahead and sat next to her.

"Maybe after the film . . ."

"Hmmm?" she said, her eyes still glued to the screen.

"I'm sorry. I was just saying, maybe after the film we could go get some pie and coffee. Or maybe a little cheese and schnapps."

Anne's lips moved as she finished reading a subtitle. Then she nodded again. I'm not sure she'd heard or understood my offer. But her nod was good enough for me. I sat back and watched the film and didn't say anything else.

It was a good film. I'd forgotten how much I liked it. At the end of the film Victor Sjöström is lying in bed. He has this warm, wonderful dream about his childhood, a dream far removed from the threatening nightmares he's been suffering from lately. Then he wakes up and you see his face and it looks very tranquil. But also very old. You think maybe he's going to die. But actually, he just sighs, settles his head back into the pillow and peacefully drifts back to his happy dreams.

Now there's a guy who knows how to get a good night's sleep, I thought. Even after all he'd been through. Re-evaluating his life and all. I don't know. Maybe he knew the worst of it was behind him.

Oh.